DEADPOOL

& WOLVERINE

MARVEL UNIVERSE DEADPOOL & WOLVERINE. Contains material originally published in magazine form as MARVEL ADVENTURES SUPER HEROES #4, MARVEL UNIVERSE ULTIMATE SPIDER-MAN: WEB WARRIORS #8, FREE COMIC BOOK DAY 2009 (WOLVERINE: ORIGIN OF AN X-MAN) #1 and MARVEL ADVENTURES SPIDER-MAN #3. First printing 2016. ISBN# 978-1-302-90024-3. Published by MARVEL WORLDWIDE, INC., a subsidiary of MARVEL ENTERTAINMENT, LLC. OFFICE OF PUBLICATION: 135 West 50th Street, New York, NY 10020. Copyright © 2016 MARVEL No similarity between any of the names, characters, persons, and/or institutions in this magazine with those of any living or dead person or institution is intended, and any such similarity which may exist is purely coincidental. **Printed in the U.S.A.** ALAN FINE, President, Marvel Entertainment; DAN BUCKLEY, President, TV, Publishing and Brand Management; JOE QUESADA, Chief Creative Officer; TOM BREVOORT, SVP of Publishing; DAVID BOGART, SVP of Operations & Procurement, Publishing; C.B. CEBULSKI, VP of International Development & Brand Management; DAVID GABRIEL, SVP Print, Sales & Marketing; JIM O'KEEFE, VP of Operations & Logistics; DAN CARR, Executive Director of Publishing Technology; SUSAN CRESPI, Editorial Operations Manager; ALEX MORALES, Publishing Operations Manager; STAN LEE, Chairman Emeritus. For information regarding advertising in Marvel Comics or on Marvel.com, please contact Jonathan Rheingold, VP of Custom Solutions & Ad Sales, at jrheingold@marvel.com. For Marvel subscription inquiries, please call 800-217-9158. **Manufactured between 12/4/2015 and 1/11/2016 by SHERIDAN BOOKS, INC., CHELSEA, MI, USA.**

10 9 8 7 6 5 4 3 2 1

MARVEL ADVENTURES SUPER HEROES #4

WRITER: *PAUL TOBIN*

PENCILER: *RONAN CLIQUET*

INKER: *AMILTON SANTOS*

COLORIST: *SOTOCOLOR*

LETTERER: *DAVE SHARPE*

COVER ART: *CLAYTON HENRY* & *BRAD ANDERSON*

MARVEL UNIVERSE ULTIMATE SPIDER-MAN: WEB WARRIORS #8

BASED ON THE TV SERIES WRITTEN BY *MAN OF ACTION* & *ED VALENTINE*

DIRECTED BY *ROY BURDINE*

ADAPTED BY *JOE CARAMAGNA*

WOLVERINE: ORIGIN OF AN X-MAN

WRITER: *FRED VAN LENTE*

ART: *GURIHIRU*

LETTERER: *DAVE SHARPE*

COVER ART: *ED MCGUINNESS*, *MARK FARMER* & *JUSTIN PONSOR*

MARVEL ADVENTURES SPIDER-MAN #3

WRITER: *PAUL TOBIN*

PENCILER: *MATTEO LOLLI*

INKERS: *TERRY PALLOT* & *DREW HENNESSY*

COLORIST: *SOTOCOLOR*

LETTERER: *DAVE SHARPE*

COVER ART: *KARL KERSCHL*, *SERGE LAPOINTE* & *NADINE THOMAS*

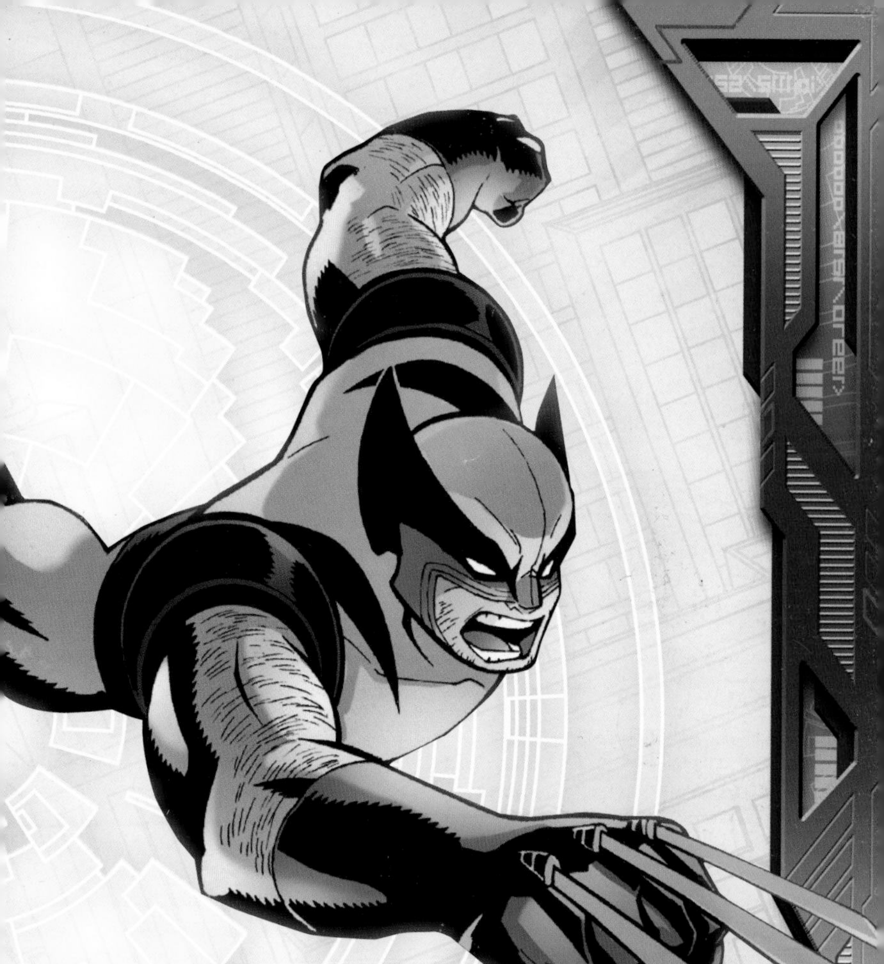

Collection Editor: **Alex Starbuck**
Assistant Editor: **Sarah Brunstad**
Editors, Special Projects: **Jennifer Grünwald & Mark D. Beazley**
Senior Editor, Special Projects: **Jeff Youngquist**
SVP Print, Sales & Marketing: **David Gabriel**
Book Designer: **Adam Del Re**

Editor In Chief: **Axel Alonso**
Chief Creative Officer: **Joe Quesada**
Publisher: **Dan Buckley**
Executive Producer: **Alan Fine**

Deadpool created by Rob Liefeld & Fabian Nicieza

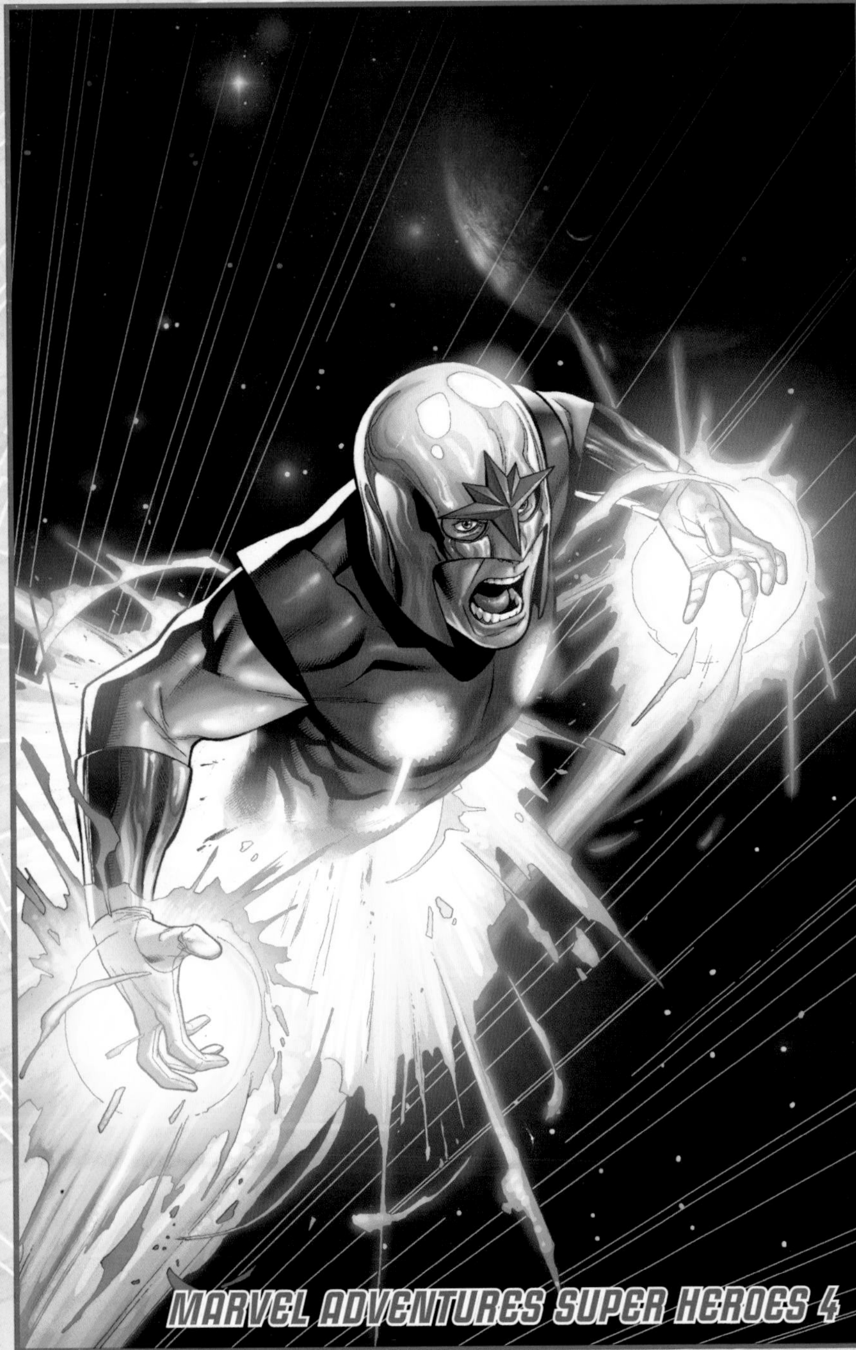
MARVEL ADVENTURES SUPER HEROES 4

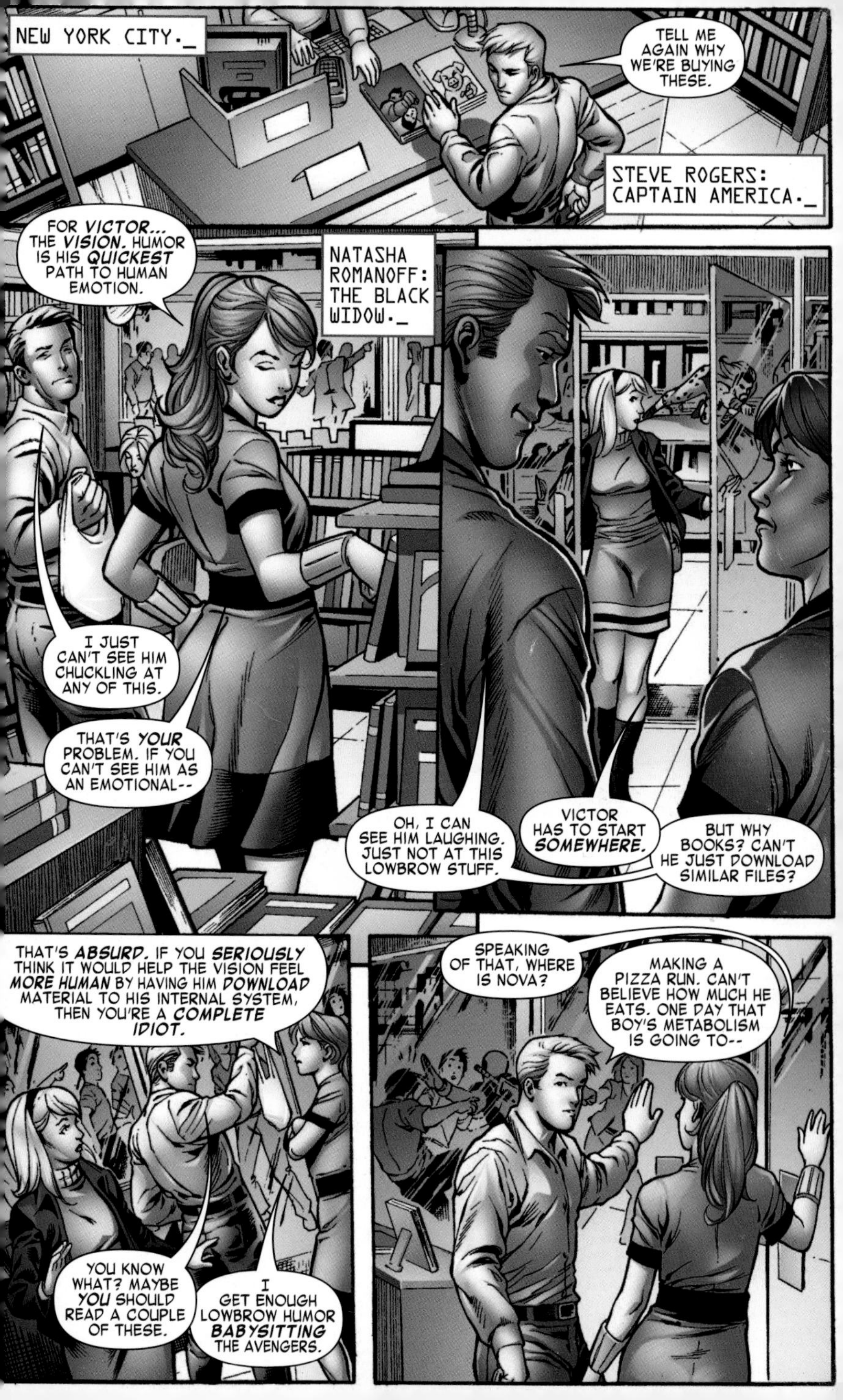
NEW YORK CITY.
TELL ME AGAIN WHY WE'RE BUYING THESE.
STEVE ROGERS: CAPTAIN AMERICA.
FOR VICTOR... THE VISION. HUMOR IS HIS QUICKEST PATH TO HUMAN EMOTION.
NATASHA ROMANOFF: THE BLACK WIDOW.
I JUST CAN'T SEE HIM CHUCKLING AT ANY OF THIS.
THAT'S YOUR PROBLEM. IF YOU CAN'T SEE HIM AS AN EMOTIONAL--
OH, I CAN SEE HIM LAUGHING. JUST NOT AT THIS LOWBROW STUFF.
VICTOR HAS TO START SOMEWHERE.
BUT WHY BOOKS? CAN'T HE JUST DOWNLOAD SIMILAR FILES?
THAT'S ABSURD. IF YOU SERIOUSLY THINK IT WOULD HELP THE VISION FEEL MORE HUMAN BY HAVING HIM DOWNLOAD MATERIAL TO HIS INTERNAL SYSTEM, THEN YOU'RE A COMPLETE IDIOT.
YOU KNOW WHAT? MAYBE YOU SHOULD READ A COUPLE OF THESE.
I GET ENOUGH LOWBROW HUMOR BABYSITTING THE AVENGERS.
SPEAKING OF THAT, WHERE IS NOVA?
MAKING A PIZZA RUN. CAN'T BELIEVE HOW MUCH HE EATS. ONE DAY THAT BOY'S METABOLISM IS GOING TO--

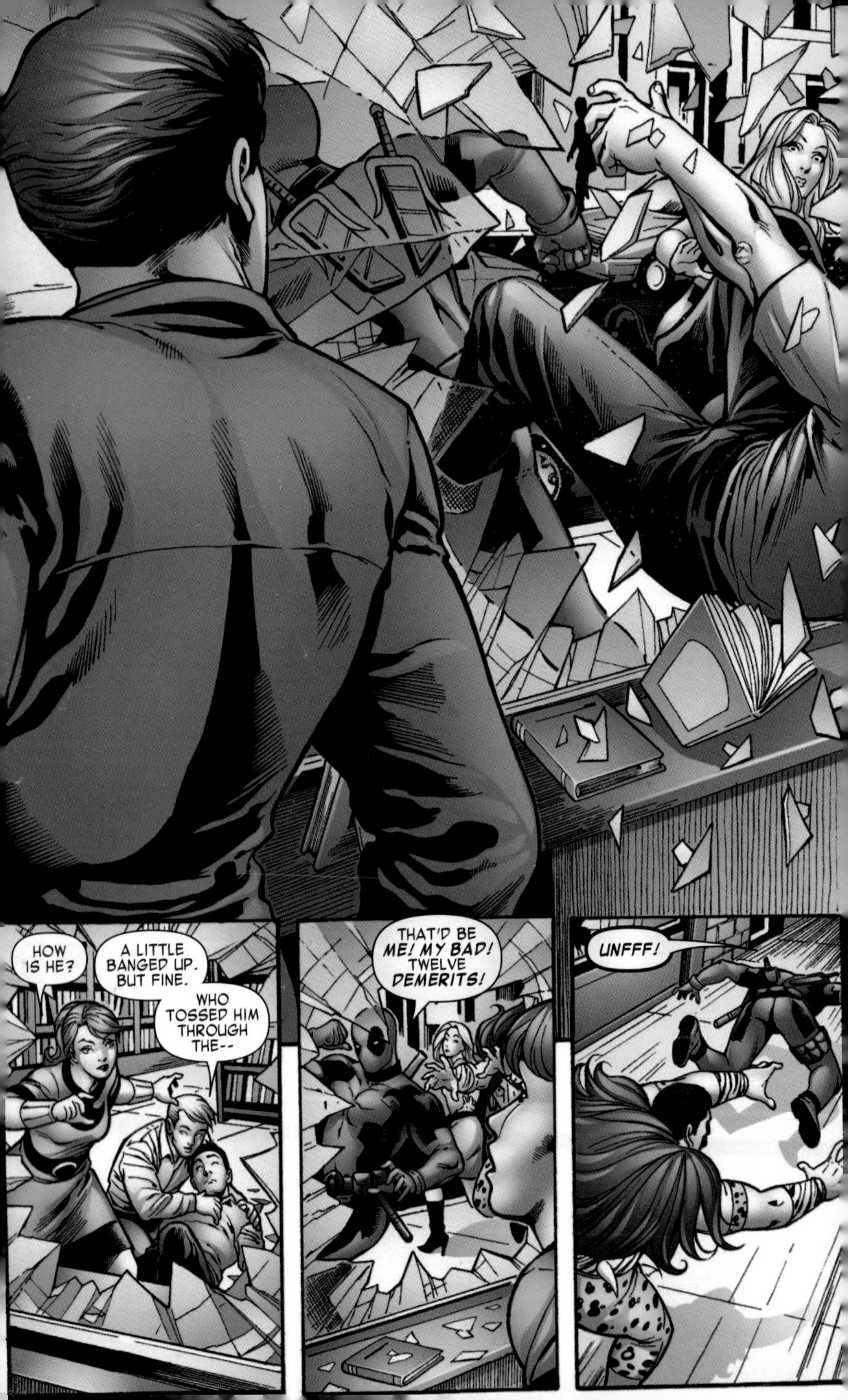
HOW IS HE?
A LITTLE BANGED UP. BUT FINE.
WHO TOSSED HIM THROUGH THE--
THAT'D BE ME! MY BAD! TWELVE DEMERITS!
UNFFF!

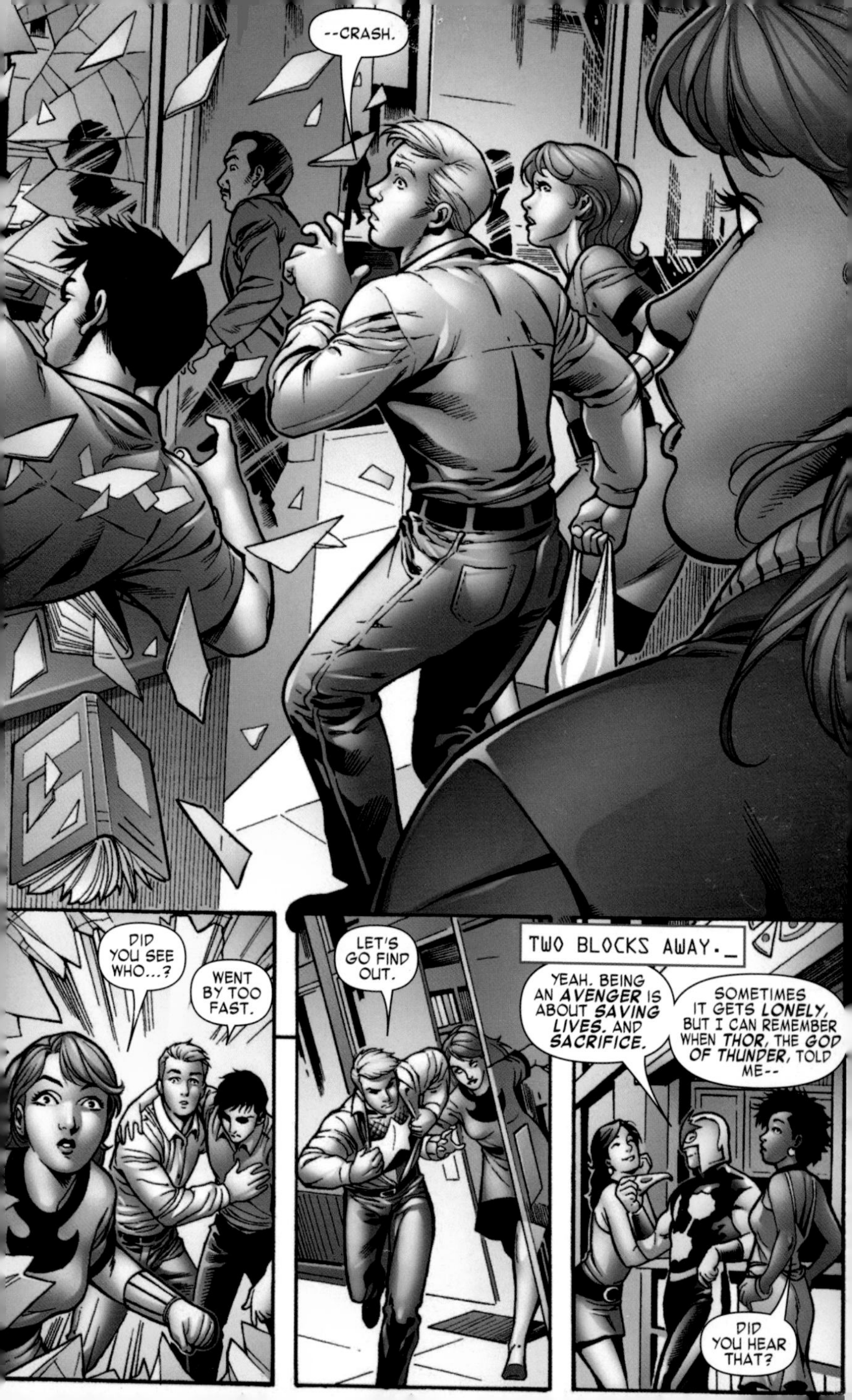
--CRASH.
DID YOU SEE WHO...?
WENT BY TOO FAST.
LET'S GO FIND OUT.
TWO BLOCKS AWAY.
YEAH. BEING AN AVENGER IS ABOUT SAVING LIVES. AND SACRIFICE.
SOMETIMES IT GETS LONELY, BUT I CAN REMEMBER WHEN THOR, THE GOD OF THUNDER, TOLD ME--
DID YOU HEAR THAT?

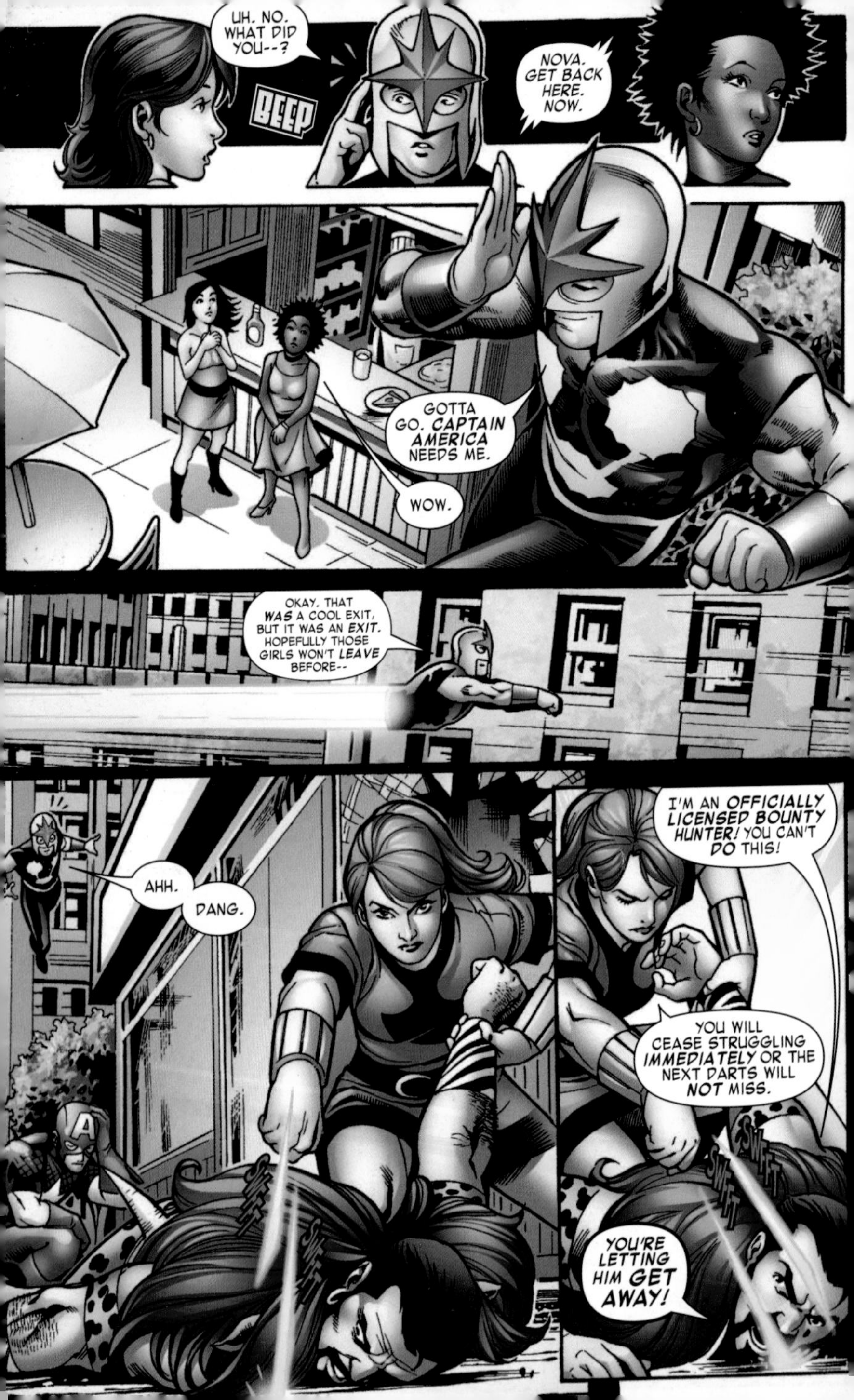
UH. NO. WHAT DID YOU--?
BEEP
NOVA. GET BACK HERE. NOW.
GOTTA GO. CAPTAIN AMERICA NEEDS ME.
WOW.
OKAY. THAT WAS A COOL EXIT, BUT IT WAS AN EXIT. HOPEFULLY THOSE GIRLS WON'T LEAVE BEFORE--
AHH.
DANG.
I'M AN OFFICIALLY LICENSED BOUNTY HUNTER! YOU CAN'T DO THIS!
YOU WILL CEASE STRUGGLING IMMEDIATELY OR THE NEXT DARTS WILL NOT MISS.
SWFFT
YOU'RE LETTING HIM GET AWAY!

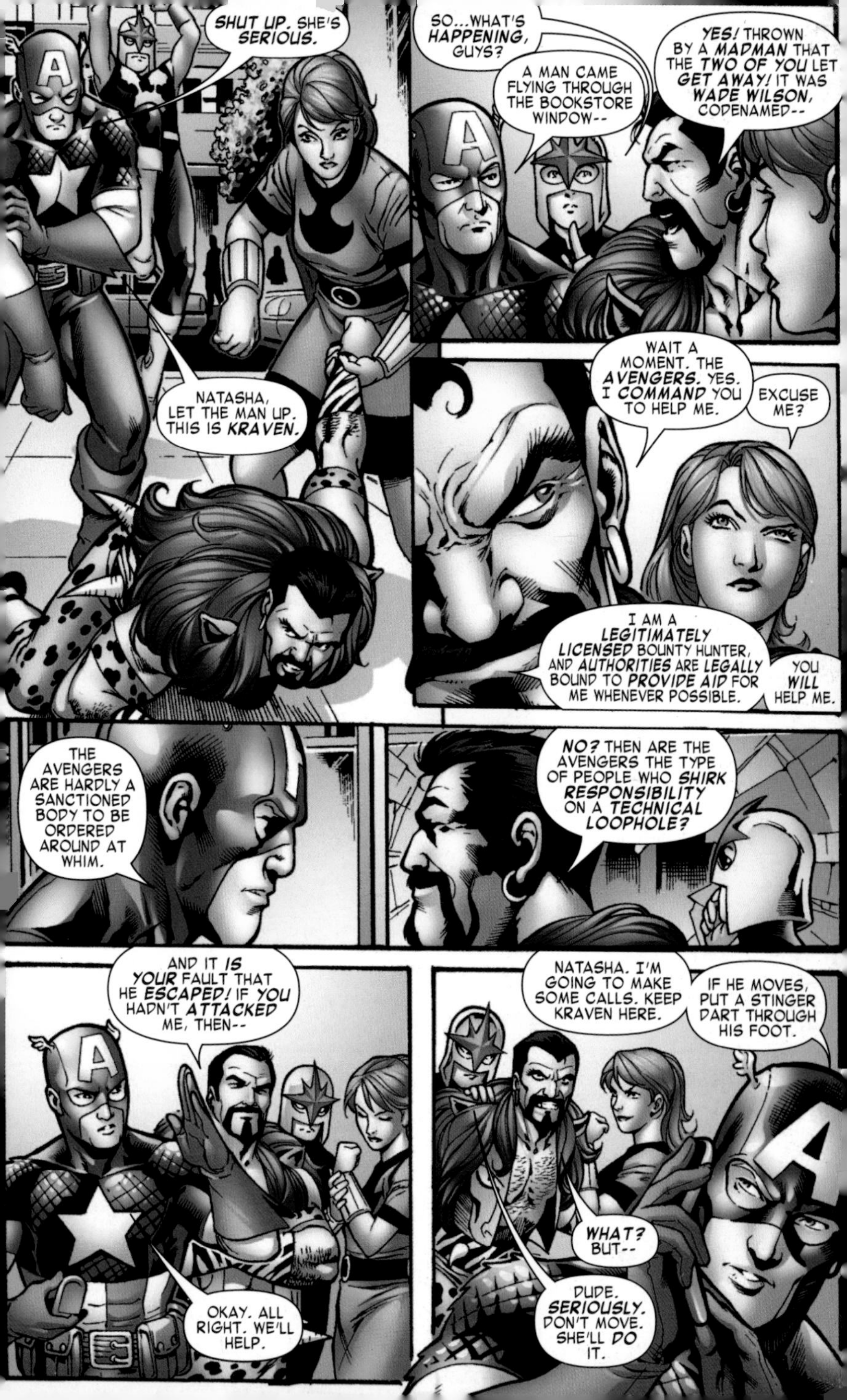
SHUT UP. SHE'S SERIOUS.
NATASHA, LET THE MAN UP. THIS IS KRAVEN.
SO...WHAT'S HAPPENING, GUYS?
A MAN CAME FLYING THROUGH THE BOOKSTORE WINDOW--
YES! THROWN BY A MADMAN THAT THE TWO OF YOU LET GET AWAY! IT WAS WADE WILSON, CODENAMED--
WAIT A MOMENT. THE AVENGERS. YES. I COMMAND YOU TO HELP ME.
EXCUSE ME?
I AM A LEGITIMATELY LICENSED BOUNTY HUNTER, AND AUTHORITIES ARE LEGALLY BOUND TO PROVIDE AID FOR ME WHENEVER POSSIBLE.
YOU WILL HELP ME.
THE AVENGERS ARE HARDLY A SANCTIONED BODY TO BE ORDERED AROUND AT WHIM.
NO? THEN ARE THE AVENGERS THE TYPE OF PEOPLE WHO SHIRK RESPONSIBILITY ON A TECHNICAL LOOPHOLE?
AND IT IS YOUR FAULT THAT HE ESCAPED! IF YOU HADN'T ATTACKED ME, THEN--
OKAY. ALL RIGHT. WE'LL HELP.
NATASHA. I'M GOING TO MAKE SOME CALLS. KEEP KRAVEN HERE.
IF HE MOVES, PUT A STINGER DART THROUGH HIS FOOT.
WHAT? BUT--
DUDE. SERIOUSLY. DON'T MOVE. SHE'LL DO IT.

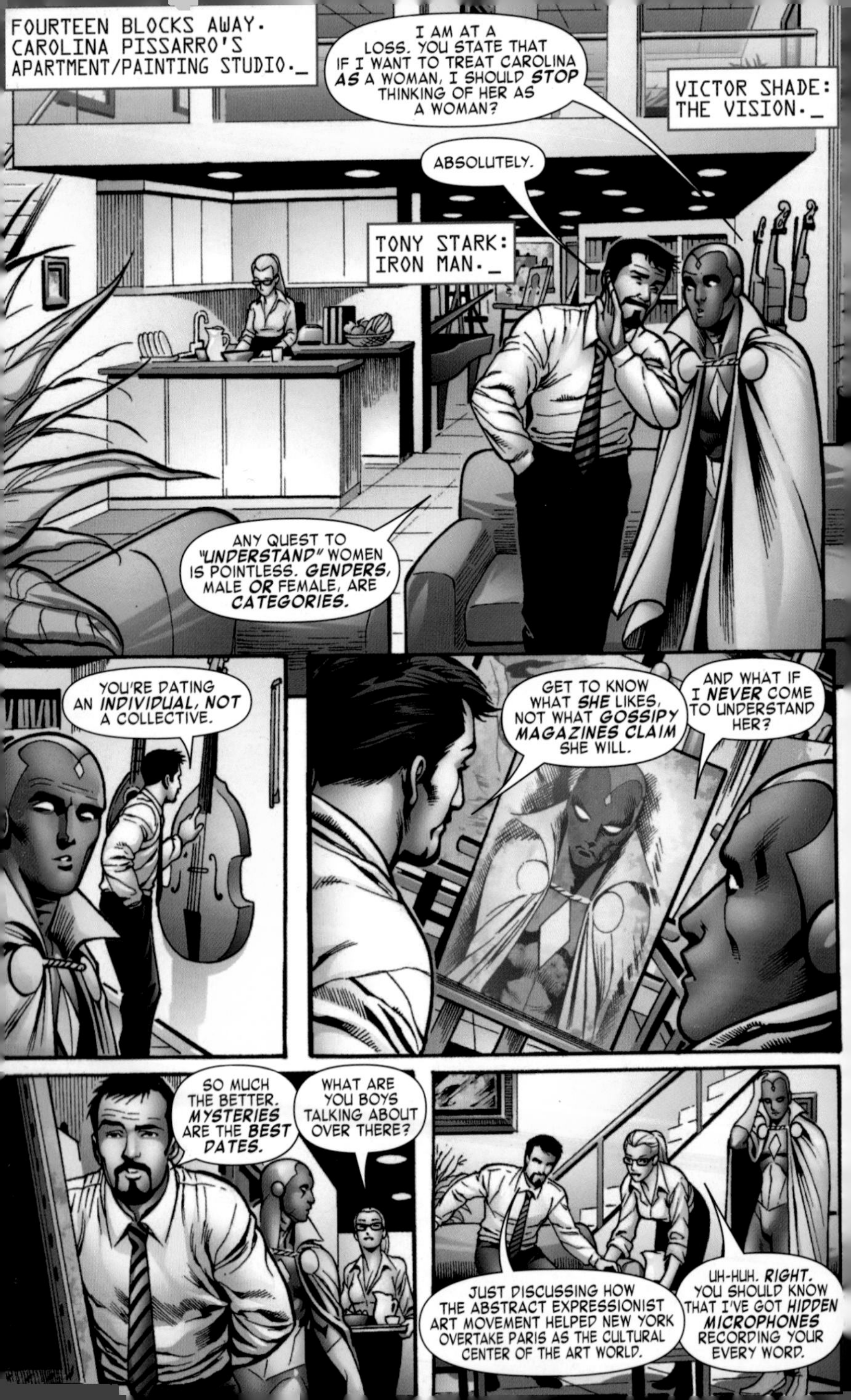
FOURTEEN BLOCKS AWAY. CAROLINA PISSARRO'S APARTMENT/PAINTING STUDIO._
I AM AT A LOSS. YOU STATE THAT IF I WANT TO TREAT CAROLINA AS A WOMAN, I SHOULD STOP THINKING OF HER AS A WOMAN?
VICTOR SHADE: THE VISION._
ABSOLUTELY.
TONY STARK: IRON MAN._
ANY QUEST TO "UNDERSTAND" WOMEN IS POINTLESS. GENDERS, MALE OR FEMALE, ARE CATEGORIES.
YOU'RE DATING AN INDIVIDUAL, NOT A COLLECTIVE.
GET TO KNOW WHAT SHE LIKES, NOT WHAT GOSSIPY MAGAZINES CLAIM SHE WILL.
AND WHAT IF I NEVER COME TO UNDERSTAND HER?
SO MUCH THE BETTER. MYSTERIES ARE THE BEST DATES.
WHAT ARE YOU BOYS TALKING ABOUT OVER THERE?
JUST DISCUSSING HOW THE ABSTRACT EXPRESSIONIST ART MOVEMENT HELPED NEW YORK OVERTAKE PARIS AS THE CULTURAL CENTER OF THE ART WORLD.
UH-HUH. RIGHT. YOU SHOULD KNOW THAT I'VE GOT HIDDEN MICROPHONES RECORDING YOUR EVERY WORD.

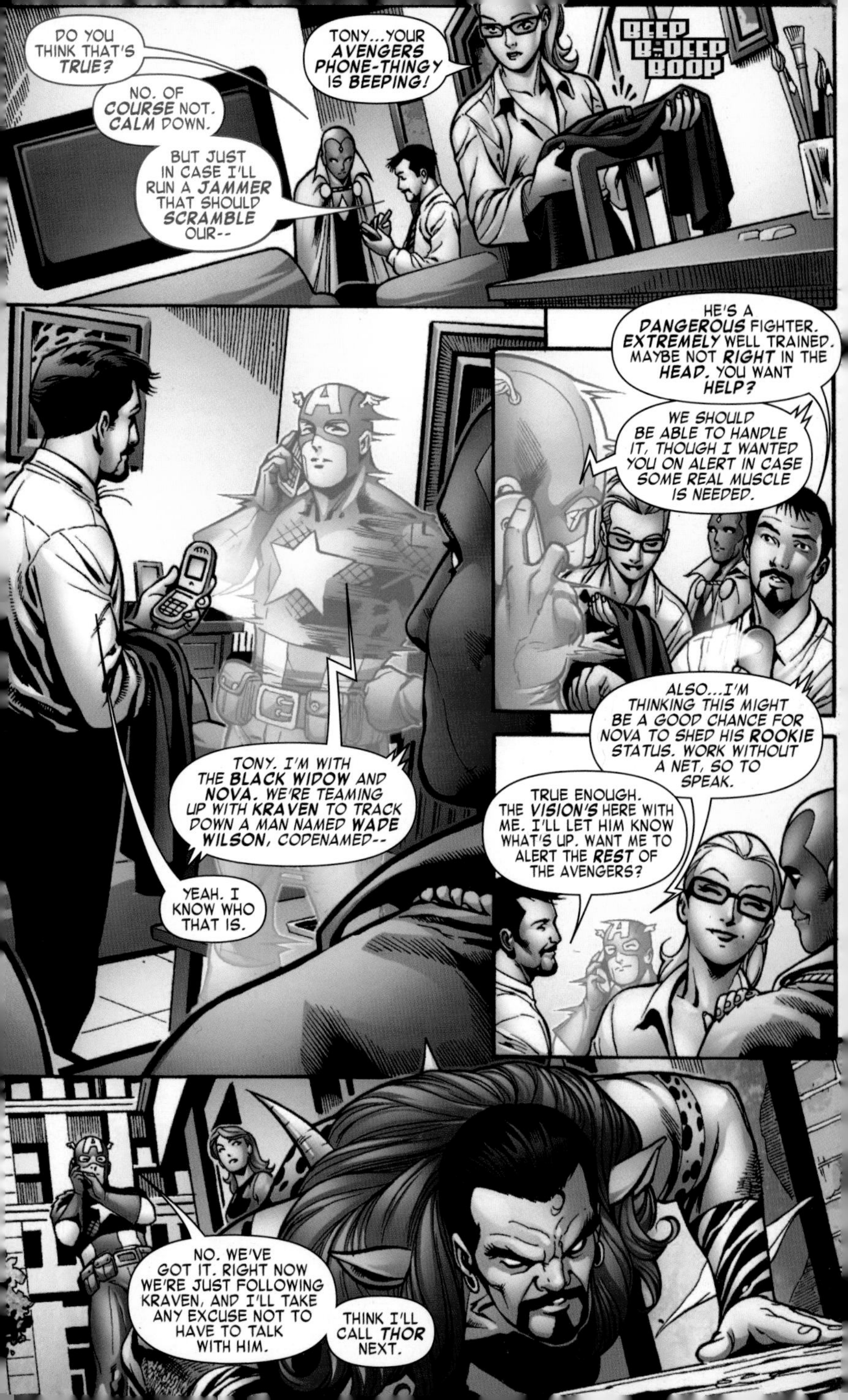
DO YOU THINK THAT'S TRUE?
TONY...YOUR AVENGERS PHONE-THINGY IS BEEPING!
BEEP B-DEEP BOOP
NO. OF COURSE NOT. CALM DOWN.
BUT JUST IN CASE I'LL RUN A JAMMER THAT SHOULD SCRAMBLE OUR--
TONY. I'M WITH THE BLACK WIDOW AND NOVA. WE'RE TEAMING UP WITH KRAVEN TO TRACK DOWN A MAN NAMED WADE WILSON, CODENAMED--
YEAH. I KNOW WHO THAT IS.
HE'S A DANGEROUS FIGHTER. EXTREMELY WELL TRAINED. MAYBE NOT RIGHT IN THE HEAD. YOU WANT HELP?
WE SHOULD BE ABLE TO HANDLE IT, THOUGH I WANTED YOU ON ALERT IN CASE SOME REAL MUSCLE IS NEEDED.
ALSO...I'M THINKING THIS MIGHT BE A GOOD CHANCE FOR NOVA TO SHED HIS ROOKIE STATUS. WORK WITHOUT A NET, SO TO SPEAK.
TRUE ENOUGH. THE VISION'S HERE WITH ME. I'LL LET HIM KNOW WHAT'S UP. WANT ME TO ALERT THE REST OF THE AVENGERS?
NO. WE'VE GOT IT. RIGHT NOW WE'RE JUST FOLLOWING KRAVEN, AND I'LL TAKE ANY EXCUSE NOT TO HAVE TO TALK WITH HIM.
THINK I'LL CALL THOR NEXT.

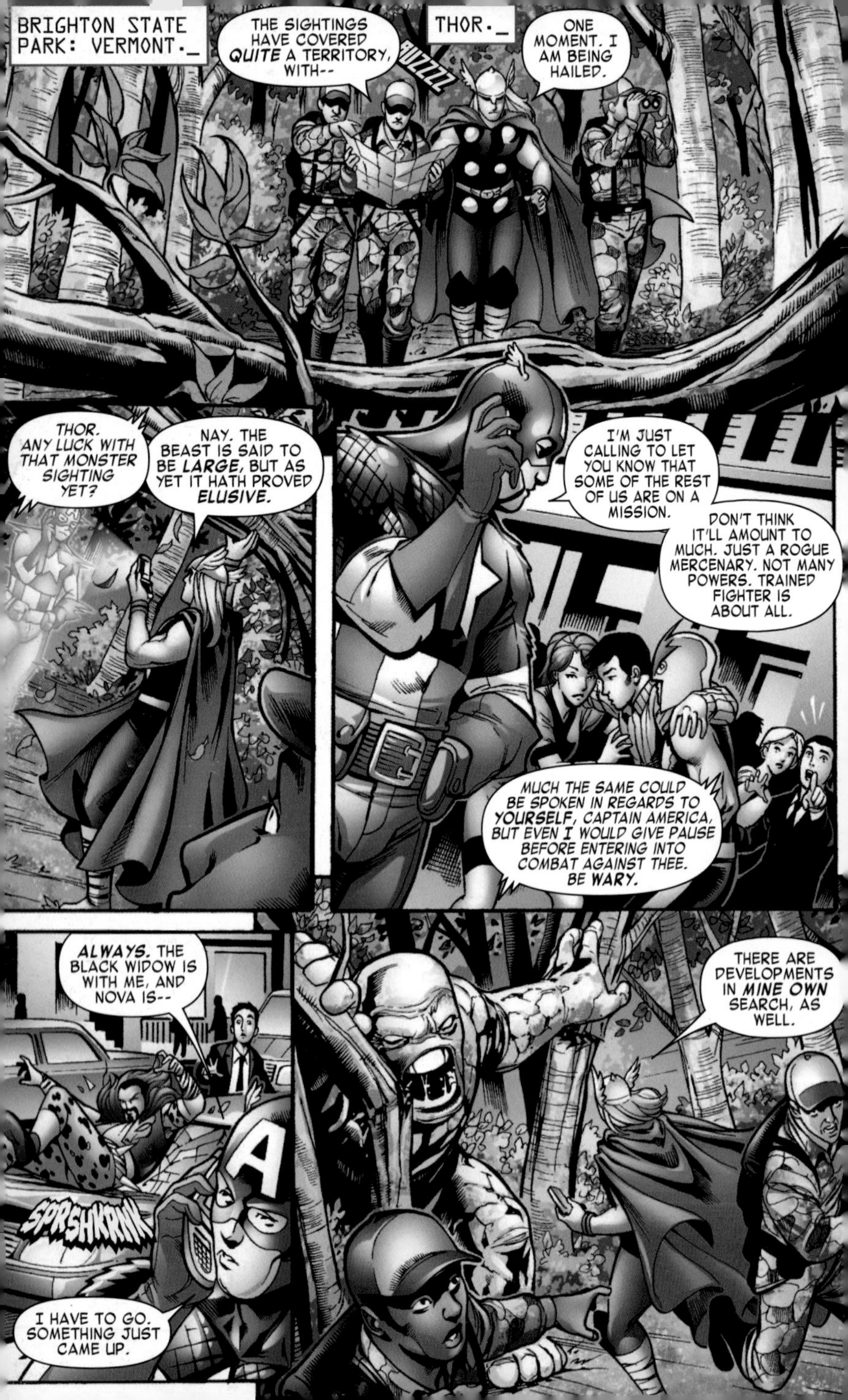
BRIGHTON STATE PARK: VERMONT._
THE SIGHTINGS HAVE COVERED QUITE A TERRITORY, WITH--
BUZZZZ
THOR._
ONE MOMENT. I AM BEING HAILED.
THOR. ANY LUCK WITH THAT MONSTER SIGHTING YET?
NAY. THE BEAST IS SAID TO BE LARGE, BUT AS YET IT HATH PROVED ELUSIVE.
I'M JUST CALLING TO LET YOU KNOW THAT SOME OF THE REST OF US ARE ON A MISSION.
DON'T THINK IT'LL AMOUNT TO MUCH. JUST A ROGUE MERCENARY. NOT MANY POWERS. TRAINED FIGHTER IS ABOUT ALL.
MUCH THE SAME COULD BE SPOKEN IN REGARDS TO YOURSELF, CAPTAIN AMERICA, BUT EVEN I WOULD GIVE PAUSE BEFORE ENTERING INTO COMBAT AGAINST THEE. BE WARY.
ALWAYS. THE BLACK WIDOW IS WITH ME, AND NOVA IS--
SPRSHKRNK
I HAVE TO GO. SOMETHING JUST CAME UP.
THERE ARE DEVELOPMENTS IN MINE OWN SEARCH, AS WELL.

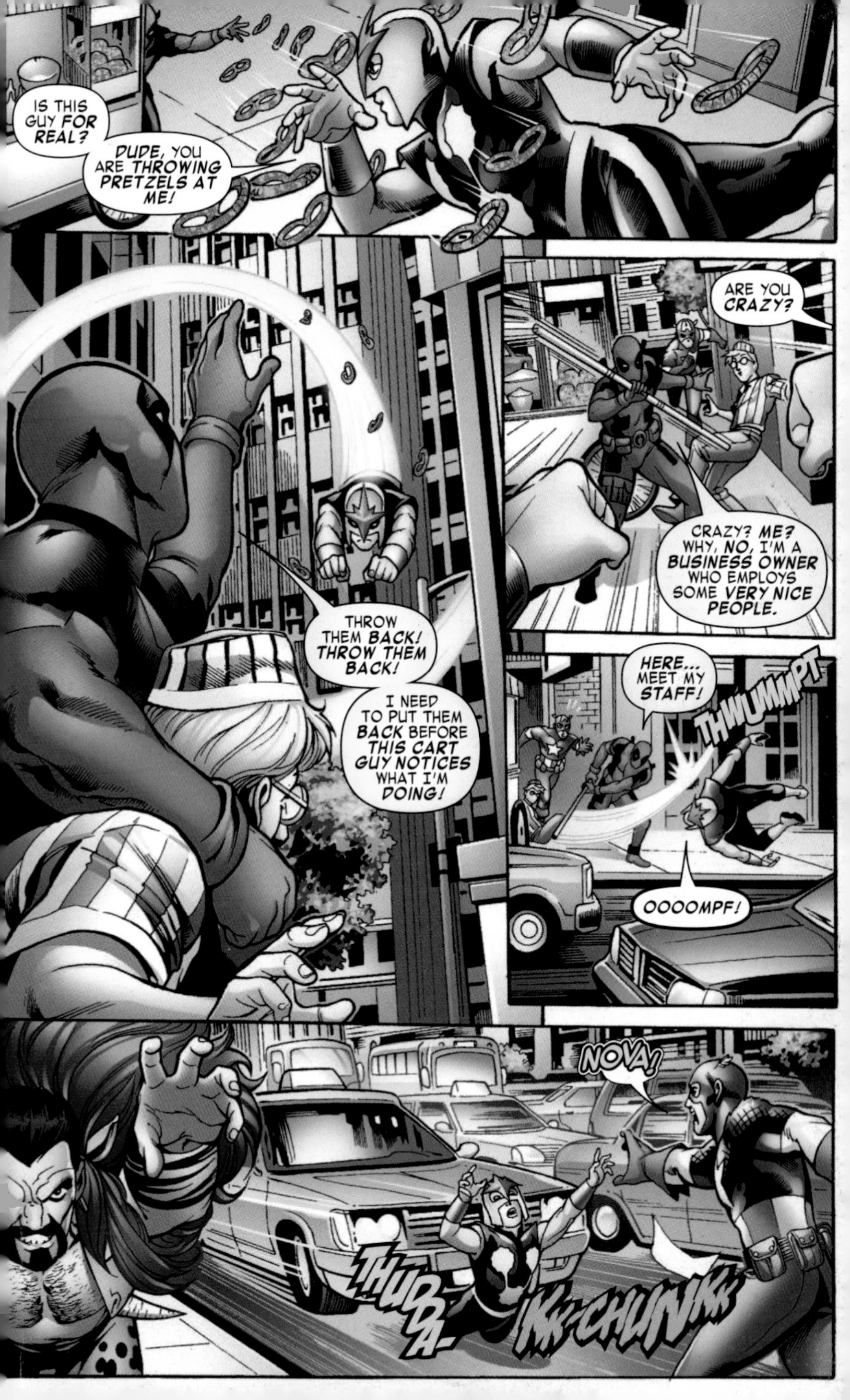

IS THIS GUY FOR REAL?
DUDE, YOU ARE THROWING PRETZELS AT ME!
THROW THEM BACK! THROW THEM BACK!
I NEED TO PUT THEM BACK BEFORE THIS CART GUY NOTICES WHAT I'M DOING!
ARE YOU CRAZY?
CRAZY? ME? WHY, NO, I'M A BUSINESS OWNER WHO EMPLOYS SOME VERY NICE PEOPLE.
HERE... MEET MY STAFF!
THWUMMPT
OOOOMPF!
NOVA!
THUDDA-
KA-CHUNKK

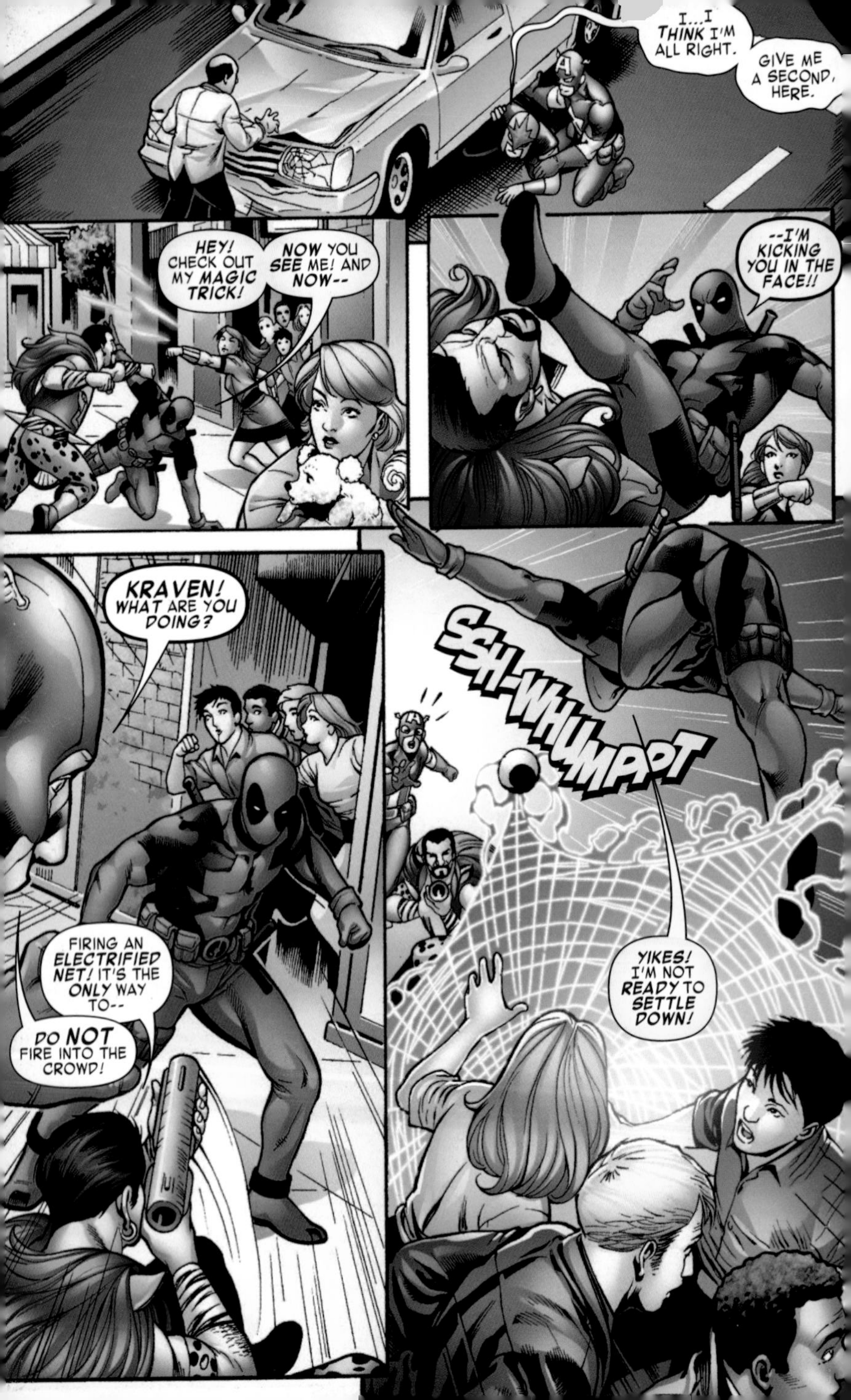
I...I THINK I'M ALL RIGHT.
GIVE ME A SECOND, HERE.
HEY! CHECK OUT MY MAGIC TRICK!
NOW YOU SEE ME! AND NOW--
--I'M KICKING YOU IN THE FACE!!
KRAVEN! WHAT ARE YOU DOING?
SSH-WHUMPPT
FIRING AN ELECTRIFIED NET! IT'S THE ONLY WAY TO--
DO NOT FIRE INTO THE CROWD!
YIKES! I'M NOT READY TO SETTLE DOWN!

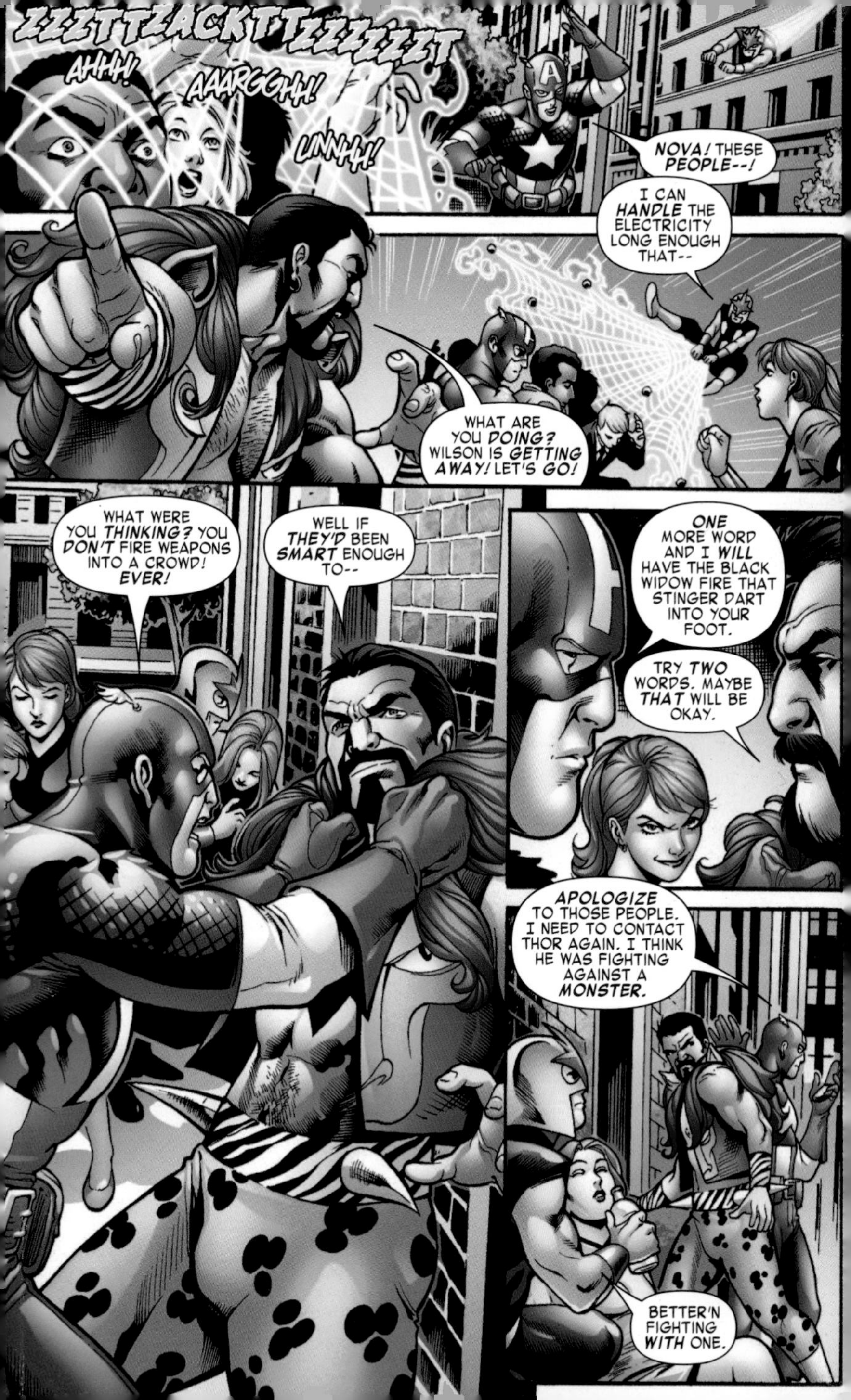
ZZZTTTZACKTTZZZZZZZT
AHHH!
AAARGGHH!
UNNHH!
NOVA! THESE PEOPLE--!
I CAN HANDLE THE ELECTRICITY LONG ENOUGH THAT--
WHAT ARE YOU DOING? WILSON IS GETTING AWAY! LET'S GO!
WHAT WERE YOU THINKING? YOU DON'T FIRE WEAPONS INTO A CROWD! EVER!
WELL IF THEY'D BEEN SMART ENOUGH TO--
ONE MORE WORD AND I WILL HAVE THE BLACK WIDOW FIRE THAT STINGER DART INTO YOUR FOOT.
TRY TWO WORDS. MAYBE THAT WILL BE OKAY.
APOLOGIZE TO THOSE PEOPLE. I NEED TO CONTACT THOR AGAIN. I THINK HE WAS FIGHTING AGAINST A MONSTER.
BETTER'N FIGHTING WITH ONE.

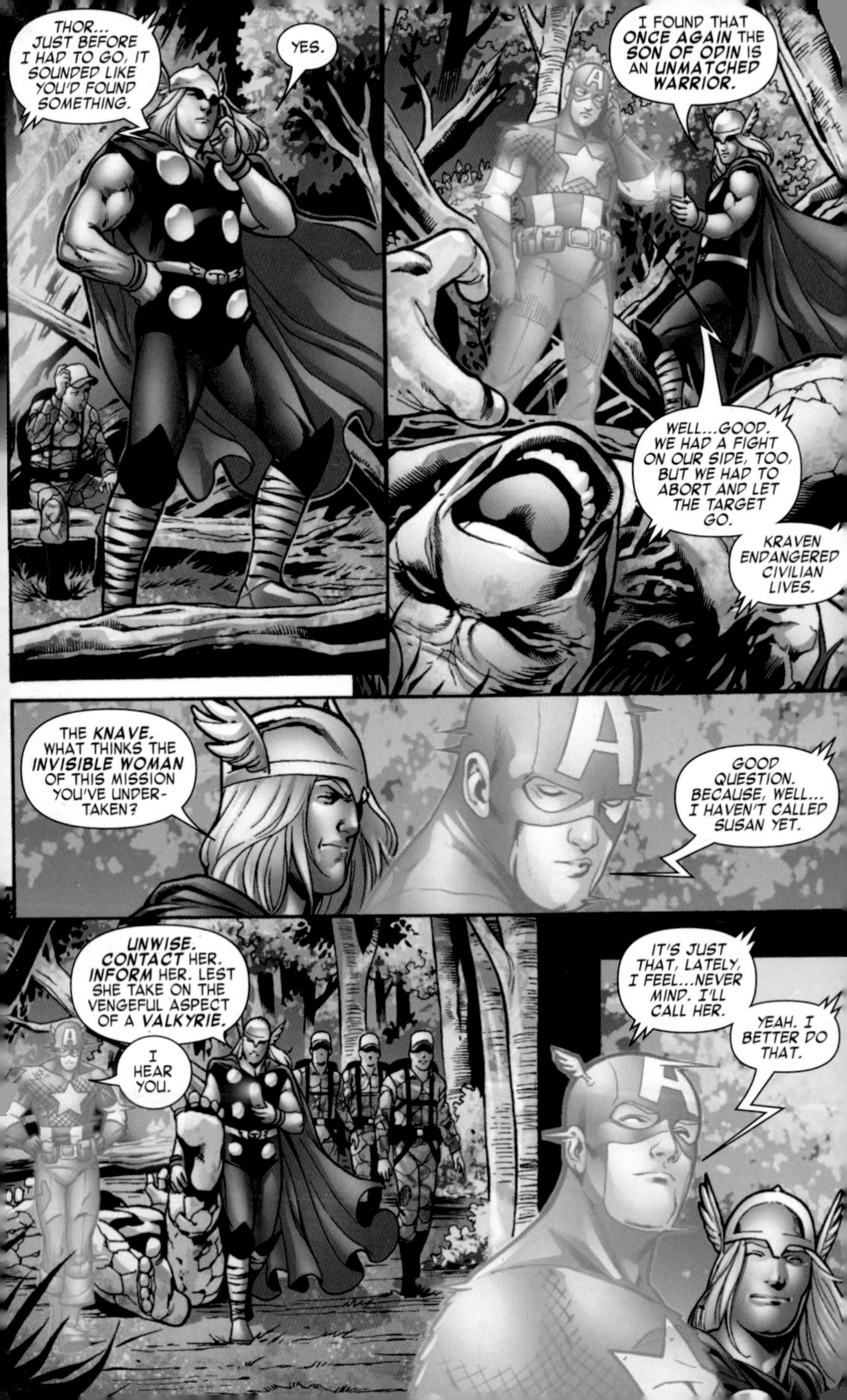
THOR... JUST BEFORE I HAD TO GO, IT SOUNDED LIKE YOU'D FOUND SOMETHING.
YES.
I FOUND THAT ONCE AGAIN THE SON OF ODIN IS AN UNMATCHED WARRIOR.
WELL...GOOD. WE HAD A FIGHT ON OUR SIDE, TOO, BUT WE HAD TO ABORT AND LET THE TARGET GO.
KRAVEN ENDANGERED CIVILIAN LIVES.
THE KNAVE. WHAT THINKS THE INVISIBLE WOMAN OF THIS MISSION YOU'VE UNDER-TAKEN?
GOOD QUESTION. BECAUSE, WELL... I HAVEN'T CALLED SUSAN YET.
UNWISE. CONTACT HER. INFORM HER. LEST SHE TAKE ON THE VENGEFUL ASPECT OF A VALKYRIE.
I HEAR YOU.
IT'S JUST THAT, LATELY, I FEEL...NEVER MIND. I'LL CALL HER.
YEAH. I BETTER DO THAT.

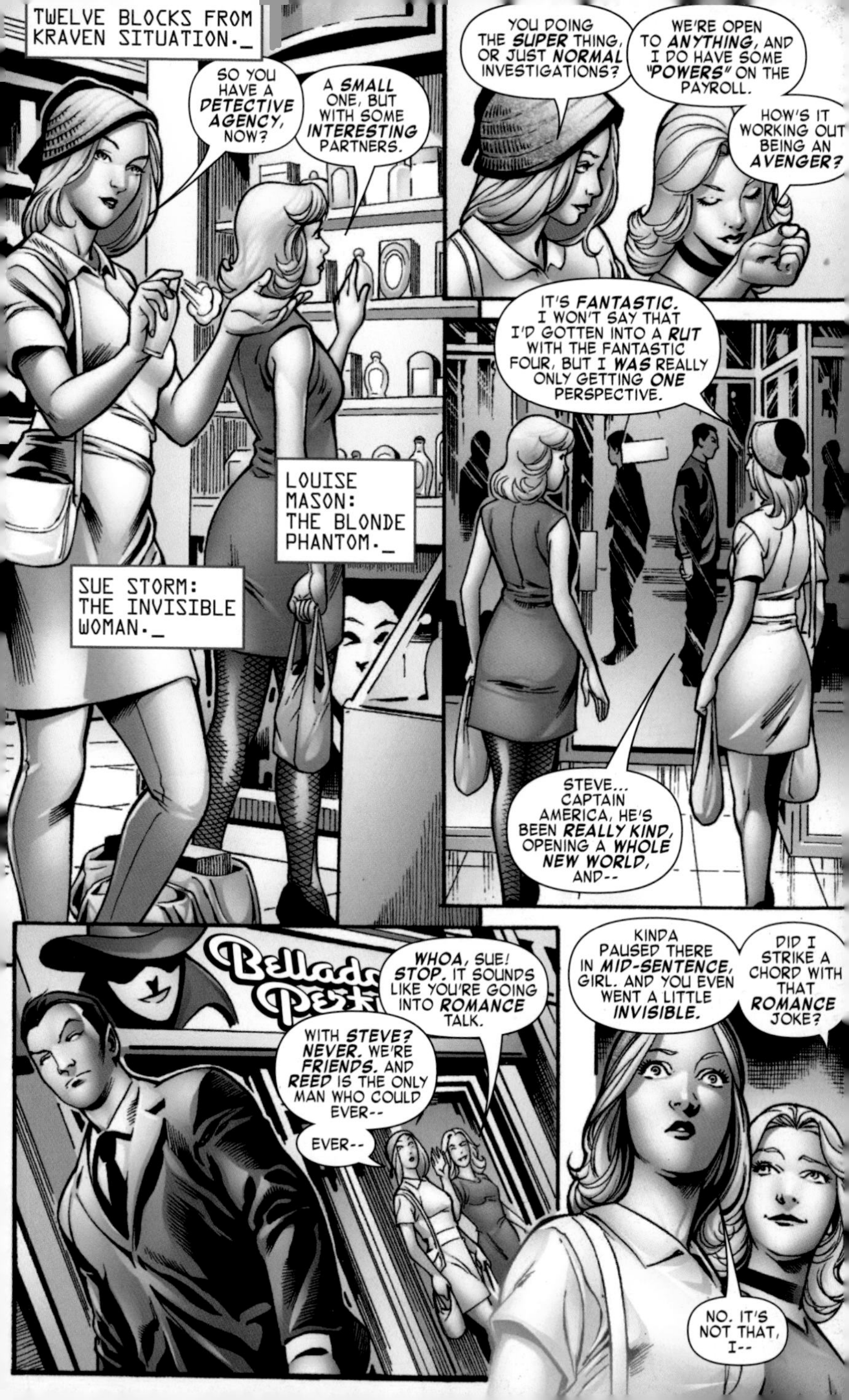
TWELVE BLOCKS FROM KRAVEN SITUATION._
SO YOU HAVE A DETECTIVE AGENCY, NOW?
A SMALL ONE, BUT WITH SOME INTERESTING PARTNERS.
LOUISE MASON: THE BLONDE PHANTOM._
SUE STORM: THE INVISIBLE WOMAN._
YOU DOING THE SUPER THING, OR JUST NORMAL INVESTIGATIONS?
WE'RE OPEN TO ANYTHING, AND I DO HAVE SOME "POWERS" ON THE PAYROLL.
HOW'S IT WORKING OUT BEING AN AVENGER?
IT'S FANTASTIC. I WON'T SAY THAT I'D GOTTEN INTO A RUT WITH THE FANTASTIC FOUR, BUT I WAS REALLY ONLY GETTING ONE PERSPECTIVE.
STEVE... CAPTAIN AMERICA, HE'S BEEN REALLY KIND, OPENING A WHOLE NEW WORLD, AND--
WHOA, SUE! STOP. IT SOUNDS LIKE YOU'RE GOING INTO ROMANCE TALK.
WITH STEVE? NEVER. WE'RE FRIENDS. AND REED IS THE ONLY MAN WHO COULD EVER--
EVER--
KINDA PAUSED THERE IN MID-SENTENCE, GIRL. AND YOU EVEN WENT A LITTLE INVISIBLE.
DID I STRIKE A CHORD WITH THAT ROMANCE JOKE?
NO. IT'S NOT THAT, I--

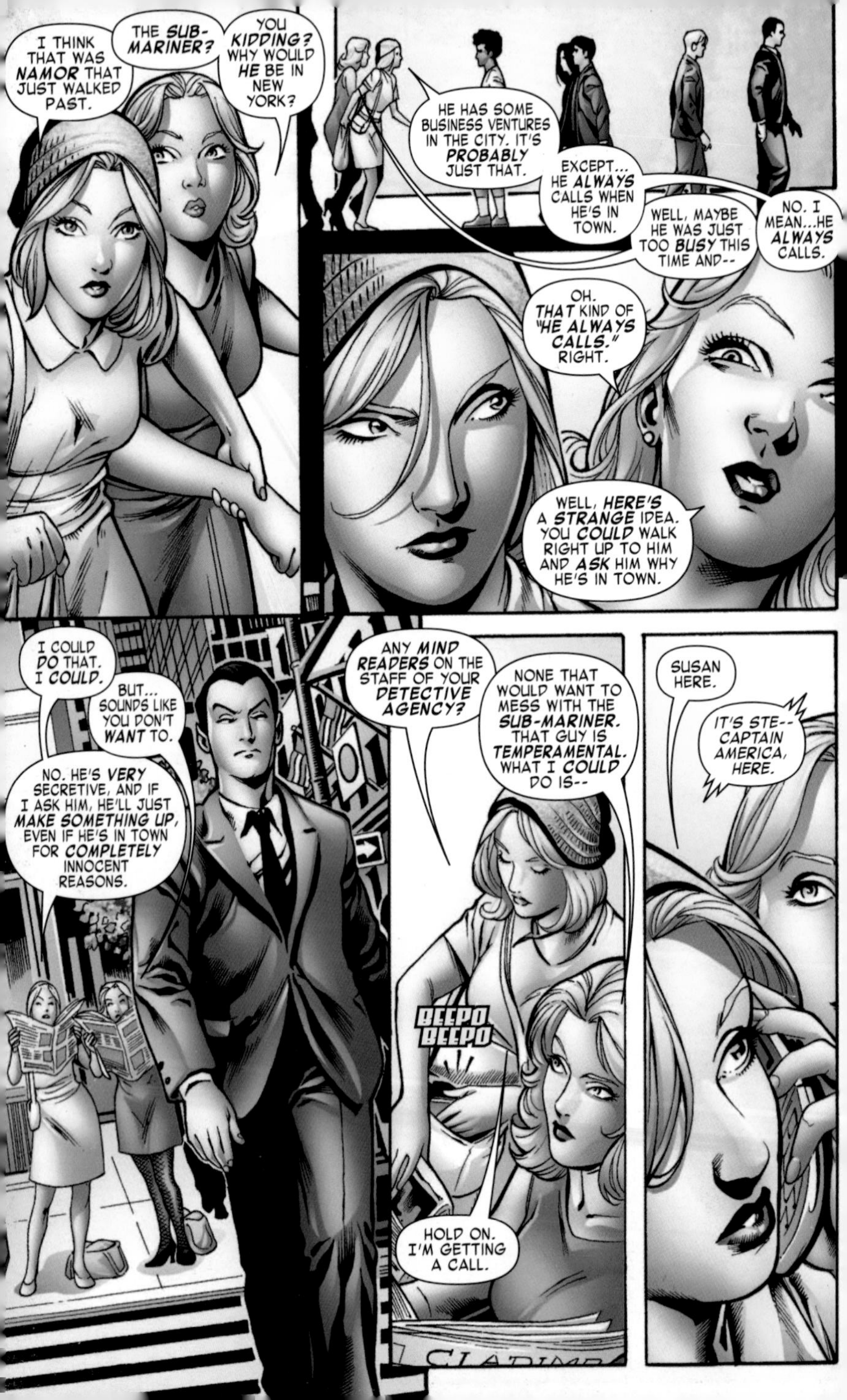
I THINK THAT WAS NAMOR THAT JUST WALKED PAST.
THE SUB-MARINER?
YOU KIDDING? WHY WOULD HE BE IN NEW YORK?
HE HAS SOME BUSINESS VENTURES IN THE CITY. IT'S PROBABLY JUST THAT.
EXCEPT... HE ALWAYS CALLS WHEN HE'S IN TOWN.
WELL, MAYBE HE WAS JUST TOO BUSY THIS TIME AND--
NO. I MEAN...HE ALWAYS CALLS.
OH. THAT KIND OF "HE ALWAYS CALLS." RIGHT.
WELL, HERE'S A STRANGE IDEA. YOU COULD WALK RIGHT UP TO HIM AND ASK HIM WHY HE'S IN TOWN.
I COULD DO THAT. I COULD.
BUT... SOUNDS LIKE YOU DON'T WANT TO.
NO. HE'S VERY SECRETIVE, AND IF I ASK HIM, HE'LL JUST MAKE SOMETHING UP, EVEN IF HE'S IN TOWN FOR COMPLETELY INNOCENT REASONS.
ANY MIND READERS ON THE STAFF OF YOUR DETECTIVE AGENCY?
NONE THAT WOULD WANT TO MESS WITH THE SUB-MARINER. THAT GUY IS TEMPERAMENTAL. WHAT I COULD DO IS--
BEEPO BEEPO
HOLD ON. I'M GETTING A CALL.
SUSAN HERE.
IT'S STE-- CAPTAIN AMERICA, HERE.

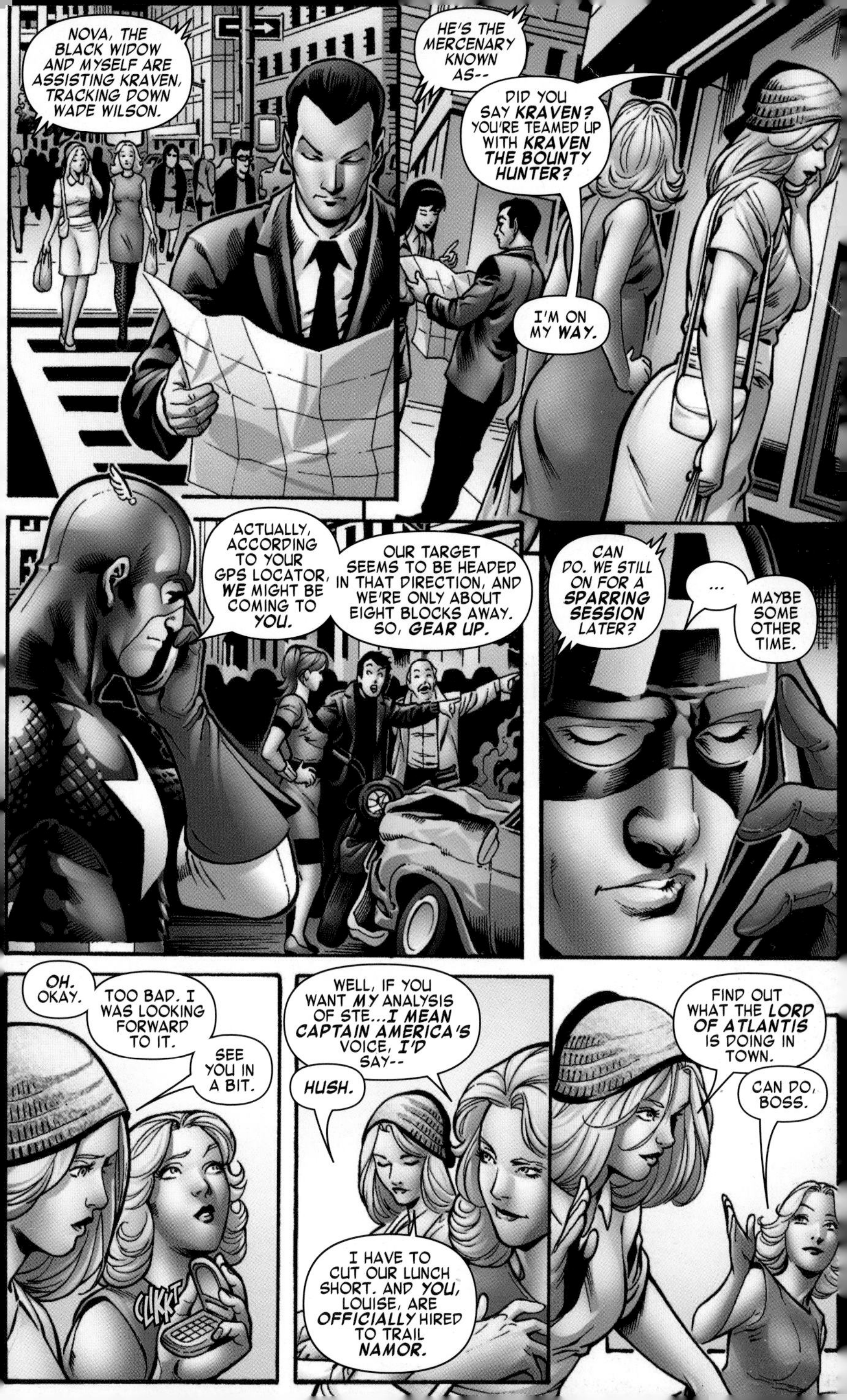
NOVA, THE BLACK WIDOW AND MYSELF ARE ASSISTING KRAVEN, TRACKING DOWN WADE WILSON.
HE'S THE MERCENARY KNOWN AS--
DID YOU SAY KRAVEN? YOU'RE TEAMED UP WITH KRAVEN THE BOUNTY HUNTER?
I'M ON MY WAY.
ACTUALLY, ACCORDING TO YOUR GPS LOCATOR, WE MIGHT BE COMING TO YOU.
OUR TARGET SEEMS TO BE HEADED IN THAT DIRECTION, AND WE'RE ONLY ABOUT EIGHT BLOCKS AWAY. SO, GEAR UP.
CAN DO. WE STILL ON FOR A SPARRING SESSION LATER?
...
MAYBE SOME OTHER TIME.
OH. OKAY.
TOO BAD. I WAS LOOKING FORWARD TO IT.
SEE YOU IN A BIT.
CLIKK
WELL, IF YOU WANT MY ANALYSIS OF STE...I MEAN CAPTAIN AMERICA'S VOICE, I'D SAY--
HUSH.
I HAVE TO CUT OUR LUNCH SHORT. AND YOU, LOUISE, ARE OFFICIALLY HIRED TO TRAIL NAMOR.
FIND OUT WHAT THE LORD OF ATLANTIS IS DOING IN TOWN.
CAN DO, BOSS.

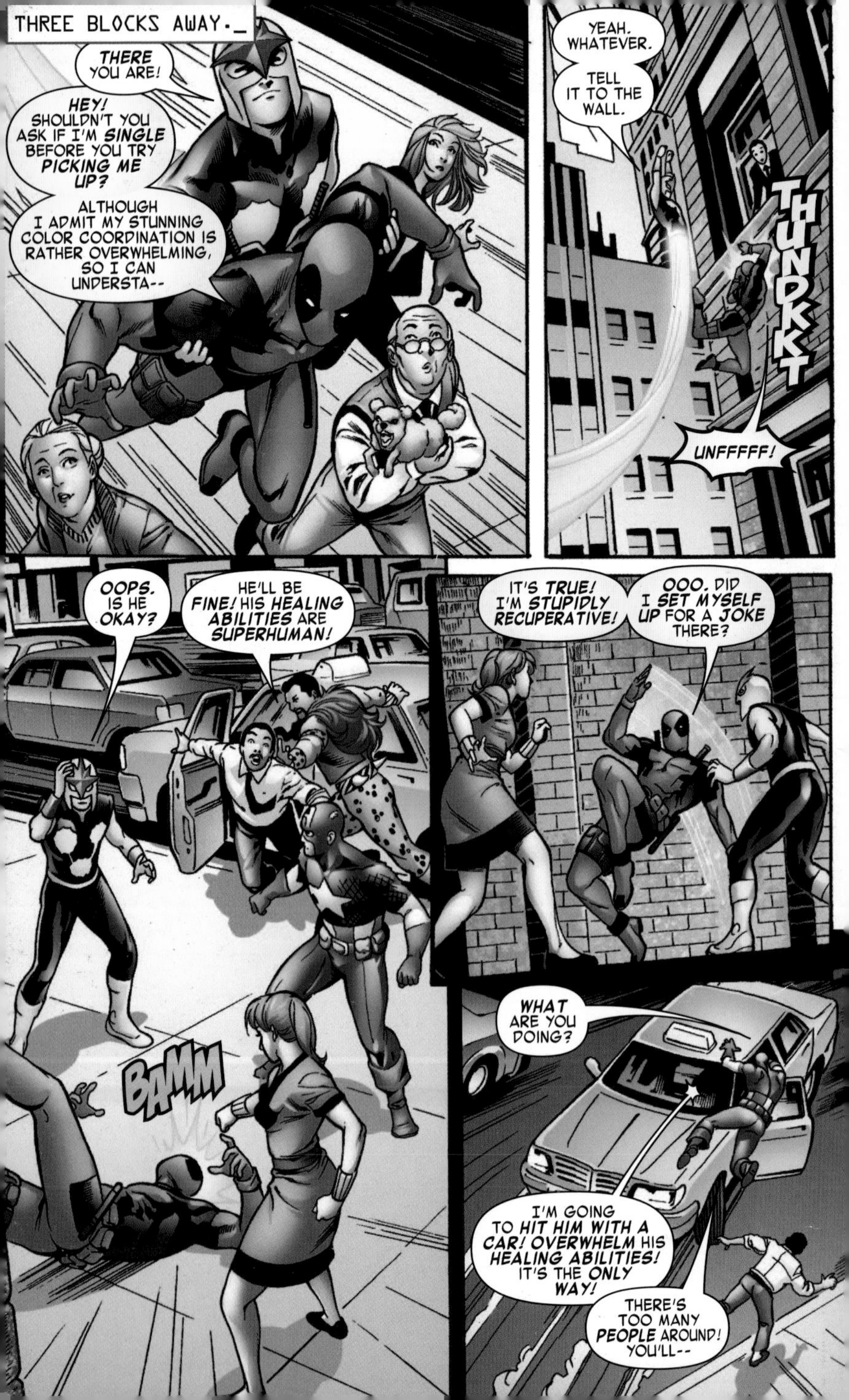
THREE BLOCKS AWAY._
THERE YOU ARE!
HEY! SHOULDN'T YOU ASK IF I'M SINGLE BEFORE YOU TRY PICKING ME UP?
ALTHOUGH I ADMIT MY STUNNING COLOR COORDINATION IS RATHER OVERWHELMING, SO I CAN UNDERSTA--
YEAH. WHATEVER.
TELL IT TO THE WALL.
THUNDKT
UNFFFFF!
OOPS. IS HE OKAY?
HE'LL BE FINE! HIS HEALING ABILITIES ARE SUPERHUMAN!
BAMM
IT'S TRUE! I'M STUPIDLY RECUPERATIVE!
OOO. DID I SET MYSELF UP FOR A JOKE THERE?
WHAT ARE YOU DOING?
I'M GOING TO HIT HIM WITH A CAR! OVERWHELM HIS HEALING ABILITIES! IT'S THE ONLY WAY!
THERE'S TOO MANY PEOPLE AROUND! YOU'LL--

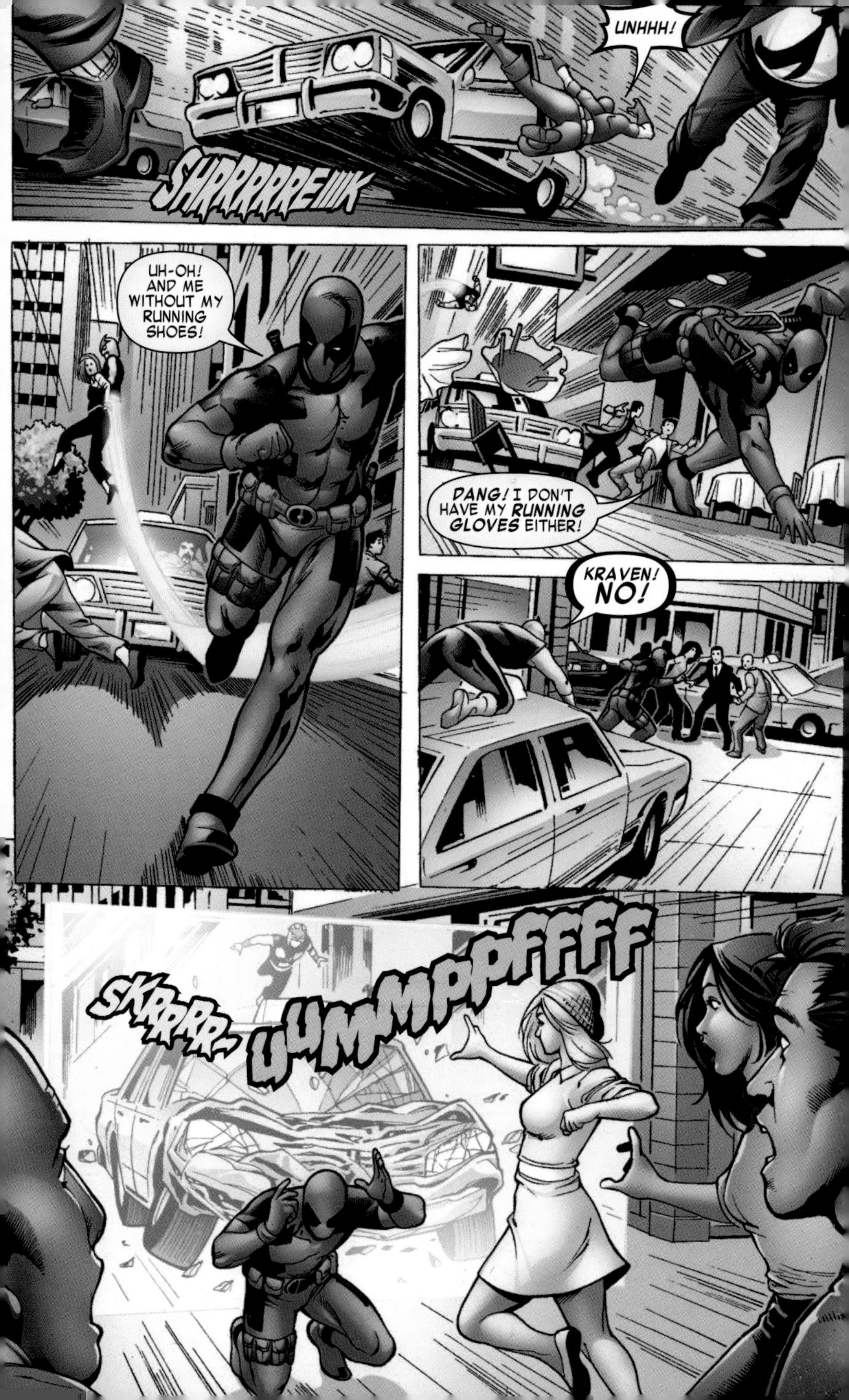
UNHHH!
SHRRRRREIIIK
UH-OH! AND ME WITHOUT MY RUNNING SHOES!
DANG! I DON'T HAVE MY RUNNING GLOVES EITHER!
KRAVEN! NO!
SKRRRR- UUMMPPFFFF

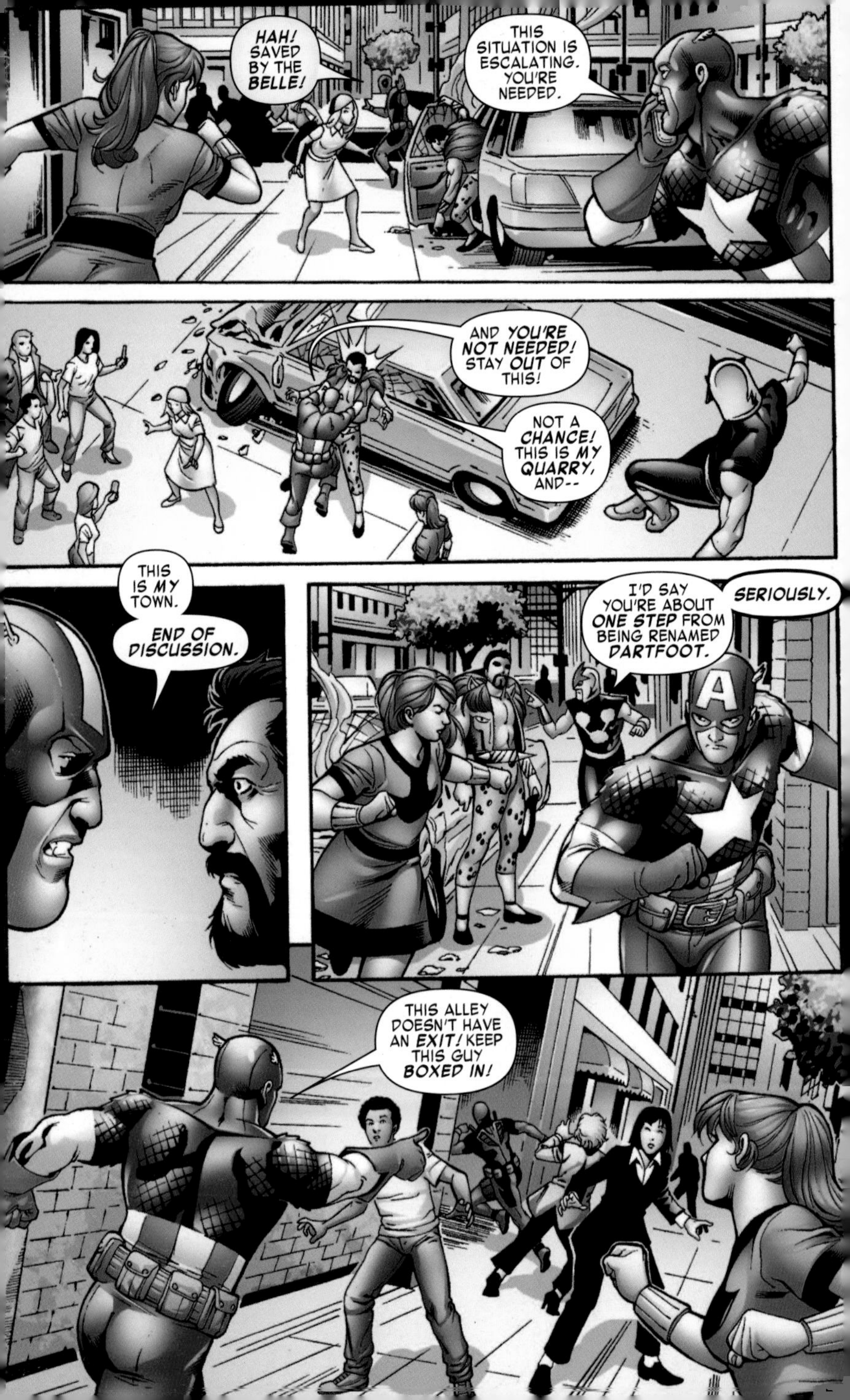
HAH! SAVED BY THE BELLE!
THIS SITUATION IS ESCALATING. YOU'RE NEEDED.
AND YOU'RE NOT NEEDED! STAY OUT OF THIS!
NOT A CHANCE! THIS IS MY QUARRY, AND--
THIS IS MY TOWN.
END OF DISCUSSION.
I'D SAY YOU'RE ABOUT ONE STEP FROM BEING RENAMED DARTFOOT.
SERIOUSLY.
THIS ALLEY DOESN'T HAVE AN EXIT! KEEP THIS GUY BOXED IN!

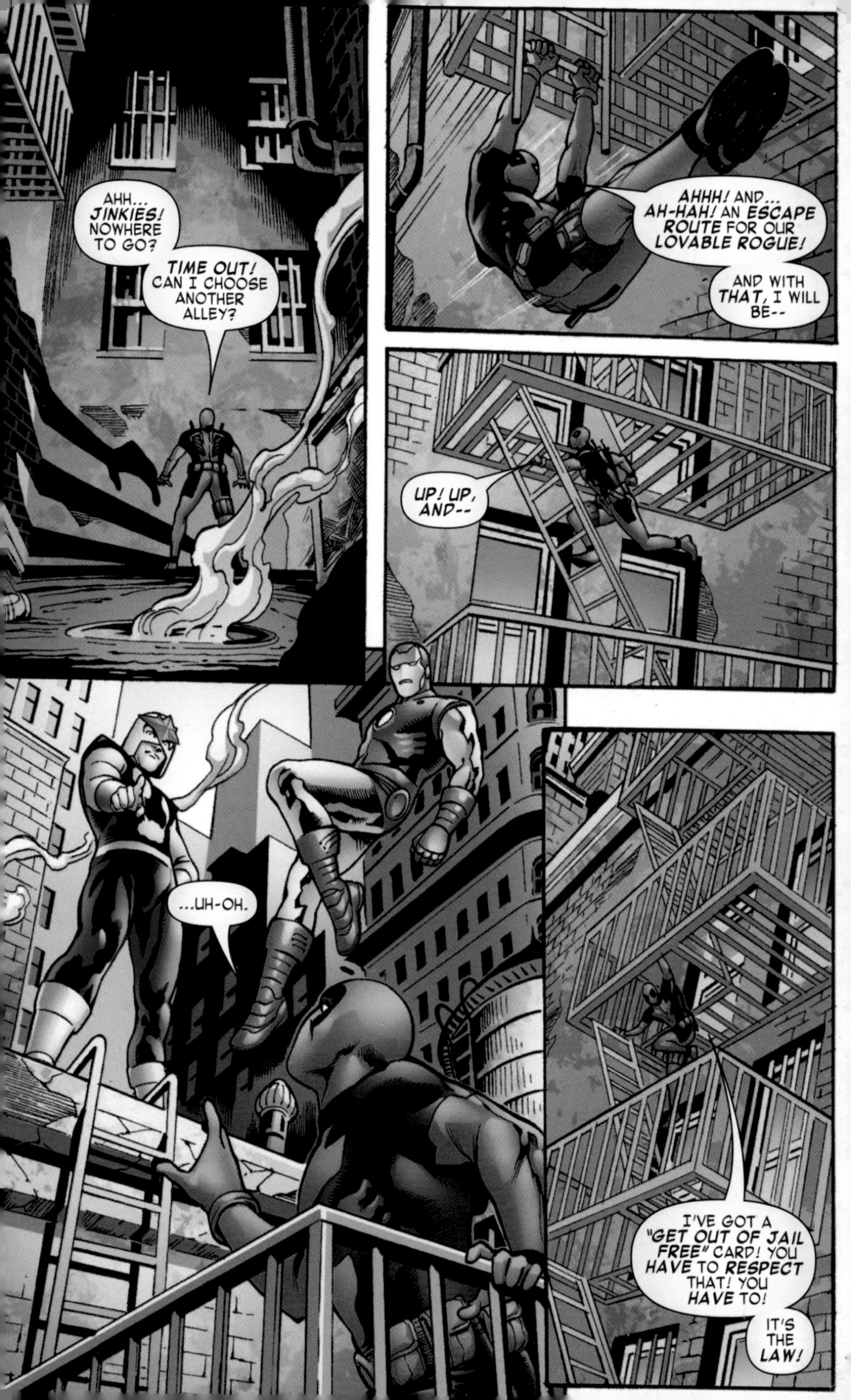
AHH... JINKIES! NOWHERE TO GO?
TIME OUT! CAN I CHOOSE ANOTHER ALLEY?
AHHH! AND... AH-HAH! AN ESCAPE ROUTE FOR OUR LOVABLE ROGUE!
AND WITH THAT, I WILL BE--
UP! UP, AND--
...UH-OH.
I'VE GOT A "GET OUT OF JAIL FREE" CARD! YOU HAVE TO RESPECT THAT! YOU HAVE TO!
IT'S THE LAW!

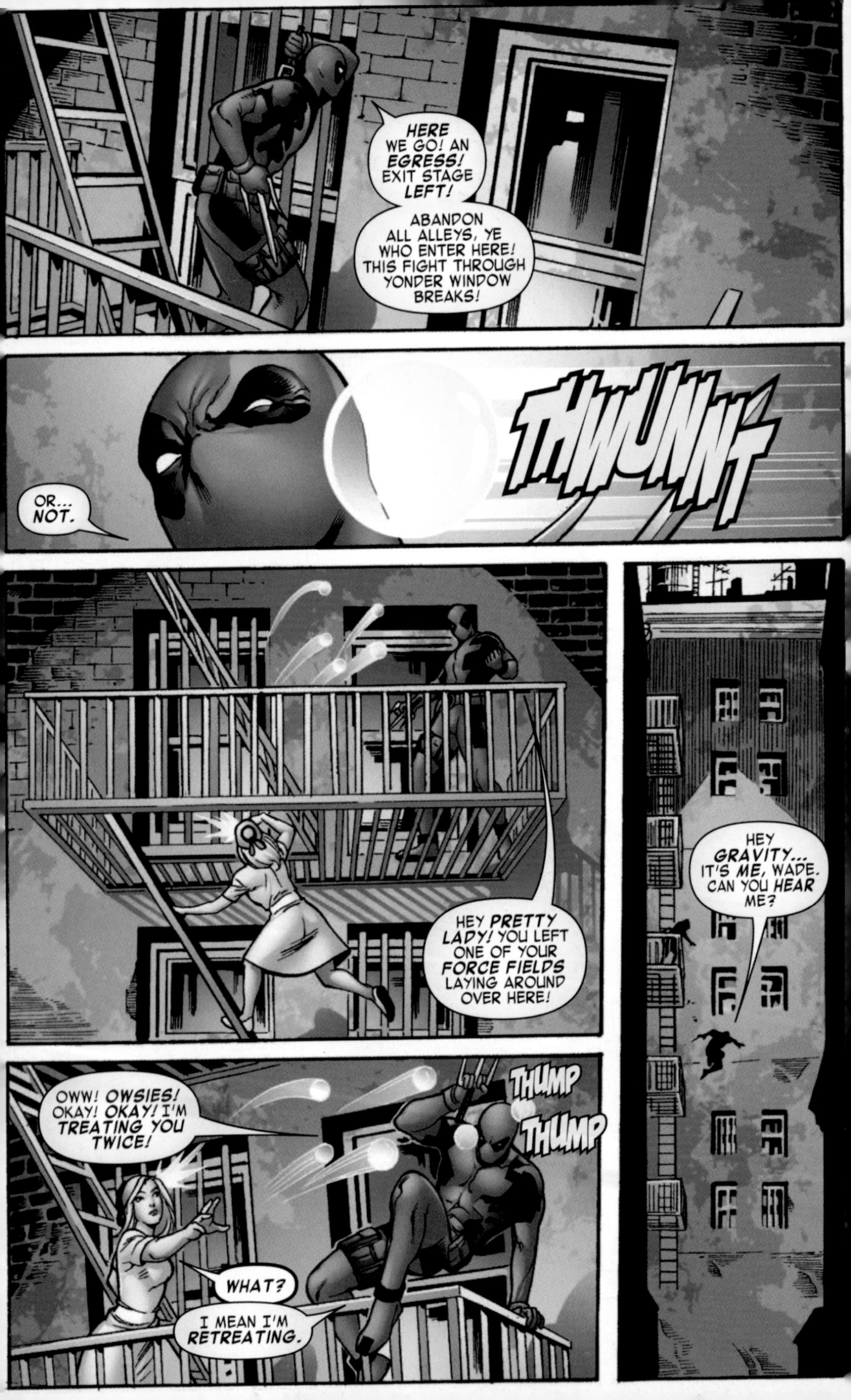
HERE WE GO! AN EGRESS! EXIT STAGE LEFT!
ABANDON ALL ALLEYS, YE WHO ENTER HERE! THIS FIGHT THROUGH YONDER WINDOW BREAKS!
OR... NOT.
THWUNNT
HEY PRETTY LADY! YOU LEFT ONE OF YOUR FORCE FIELDS LAYING AROUND OVER HERE!
OWW! OWSIES! OKAY! OKAY! I'M TREATING YOU TWICE!
THUMP
THUMP
WHAT?
I MEAN I'M RETREATING.
HEY GRAVITY... IT'S ME, WADE. CAN YOU HEAR ME?

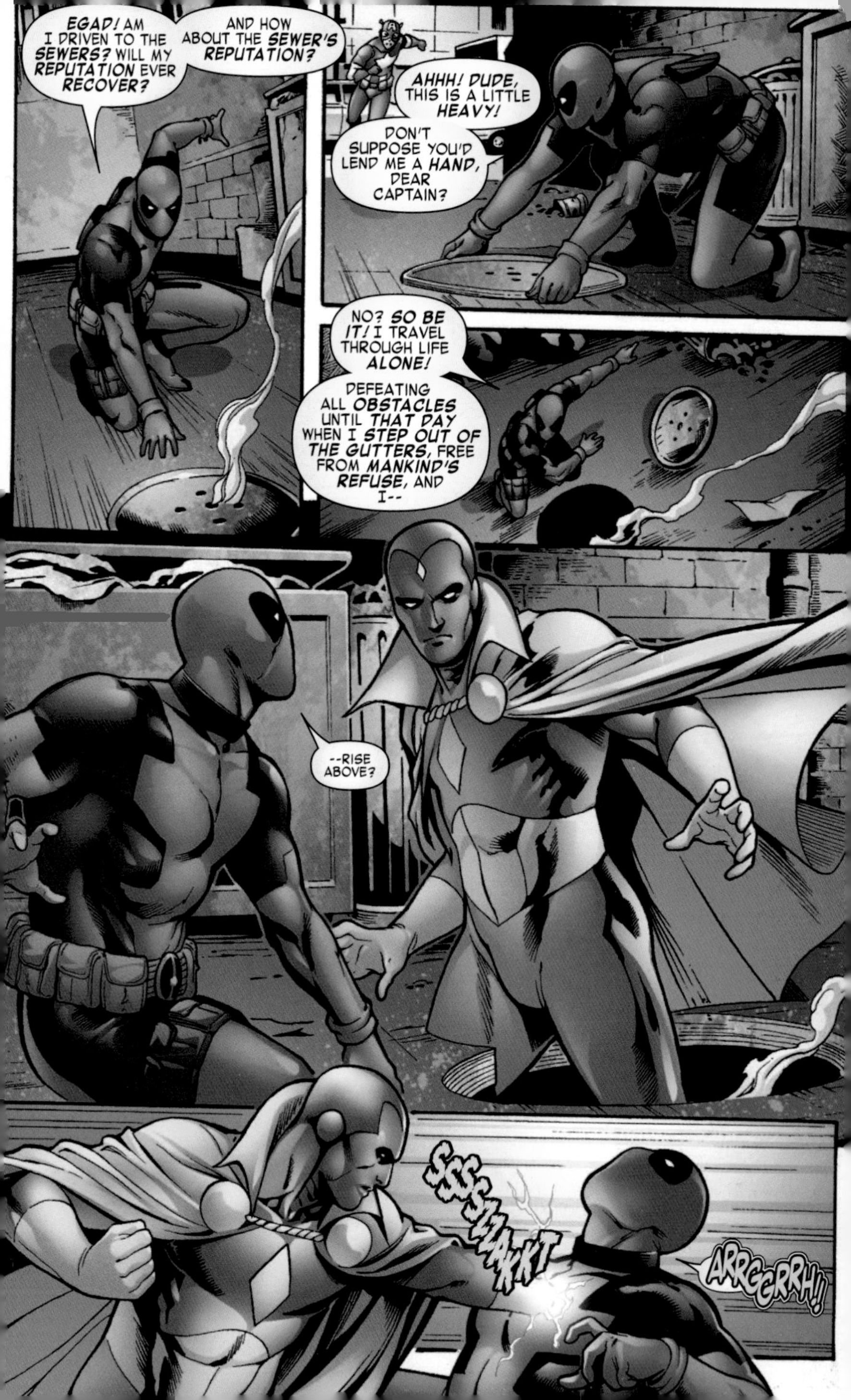
EGAD! AM I DRIVEN TO THE SEWERS? WILL MY REPUTATION EVER RECOVER?
AND HOW ABOUT THE SEWER'S REPUTATION?
AHHH! DUDE, THIS IS A LITTLE HEAVY!
DON'T SUPPOSE YOU'D LEND ME A HAND, DEAR CAPTAIN?
NO? SO BE IT! I TRAVEL THROUGH LIFE ALONE!
DEFEATING ALL OBSTACLES UNTIL THAT DAY WHEN I STEP OUT OF THE GUTTERS, FREE FROM MANKIND'S REFUSE, AND I--
--RISE ABOVE?
SSSZZAKKT
ARRGGRRH!!

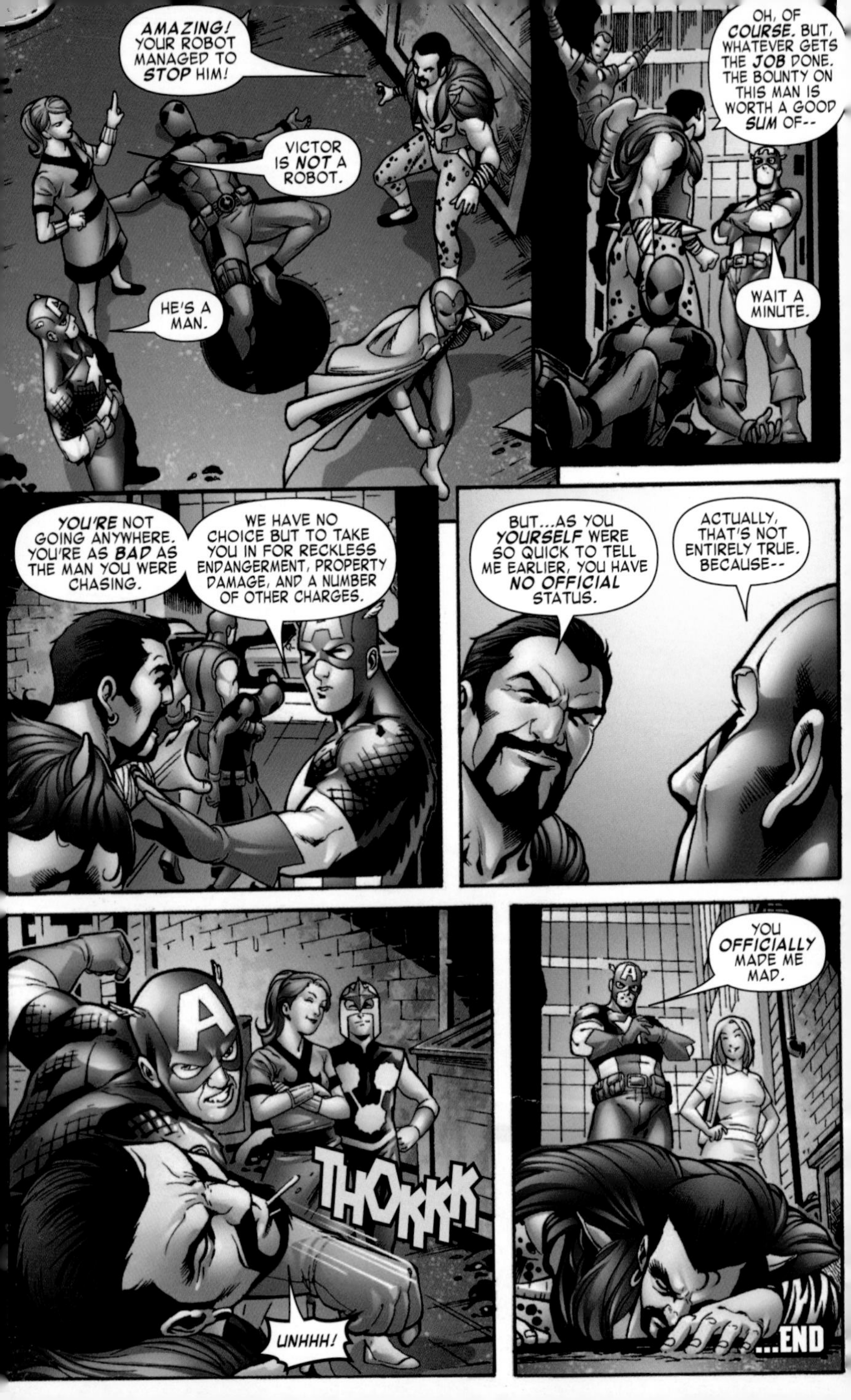
AMAZING! YOUR ROBOT MANAGED TO STOP HIM!
VICTOR IS NOT A ROBOT.
HE'S A MAN.
OH, OF COURSE. BUT, WHATEVER GETS THE JOB DONE. THE BOUNTY ON THIS MAN IS WORTH A GOOD SUM OF--
WAIT A MINUTE.
YOU'RE NOT GOING ANYWHERE. YOU'RE AS BAD AS THE MAN YOU WERE CHASING.
WE HAVE NO CHOICE BUT TO TAKE YOU IN FOR RECKLESS ENDANGERMENT, PROPERTY DAMAGE, AND A NUMBER OF OTHER CHARGES.
BUT...AS YOU YOURSELF WERE SO QUICK TO TELL ME EARLIER, YOU HAVE NO OFFICIAL STATUS.
ACTUALLY, THAT'S NOT ENTIRELY TRUE. BECAUSE--
THOKKK
UNHHH!
YOU OFFICIALLY MADE ME MAD.
...END

D-Pool
RULES!!
Spidey
drools!!

MARVEL UNIVERSE ULTIMATE
SPIDER-MAN: WEB WARRIORS 8

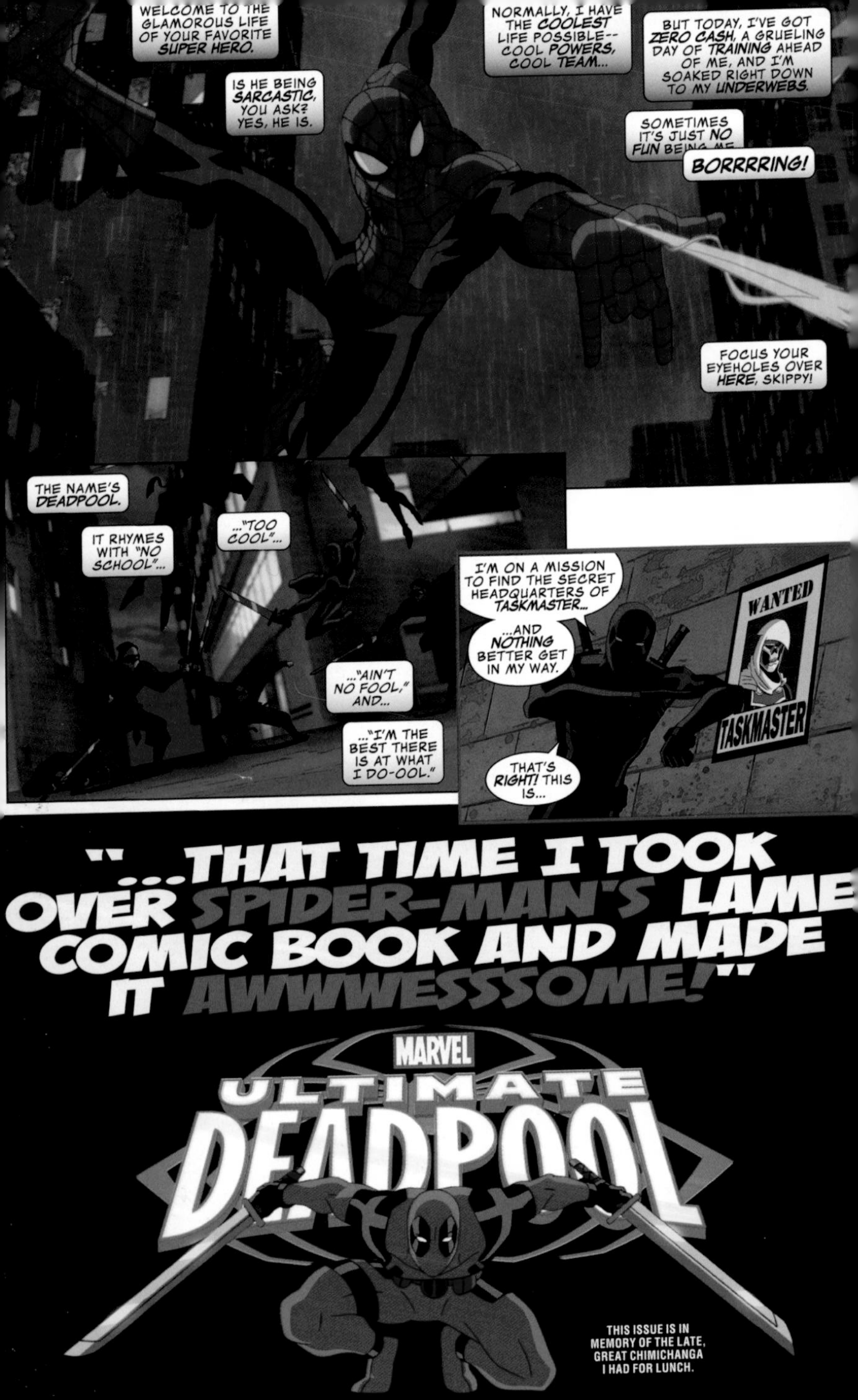
WELCOME TO THE GLAMOROUS LIFE OF YOUR FAVORITE SUPER HERO.
IS HE BEING SARCASTIC, YOU ASK? YES, HE IS.
NORMALLY, I HAVE THE COOLEST LIFE POSSIBLE-- COOL POWERS, COOL TEAM...
BUT TODAY, I'VE GOT ZERO CASH, A GRUELING DAY OF TRAINING AHEAD OF ME, AND I'M SOAKED RIGHT DOWN TO MY UNDERWEBS.
SOMETIMES IT'S JUST NO FUN BEING ME
BORRRRING!
FOCUS YOUR EYEHOLES OVER HERE, SKIPPY!
THE NAME'S DEADPOOL.
IT RHYMES WITH "NO SCHOOL"...
..."TOO COOL"...
..."AIN'T NO FOOL," AND...
..."I'M THE BEST THERE IS AT WHAT I DO-OOL."
I'M ON A MISSION TO FIND THE SECRET HEADQUARTERS OF TASKMASTER...
...AND NOTHING BETTER GET IN MY WAY.
WANTED
TASKMASTER
THAT'S RIGHT! THIS IS...
"...THAT TIME I TOOK OVER SPIDER-MAN'S LAME COMIC BOOK AND MADE IT AWWWESSSOME!"
MARVEL
ULTIMATE DEADPOOL
THIS ISSUE IS IN MEMORY OF THE LATE, GREAT CHIMICHANGA I HAD FOR LUNCH.

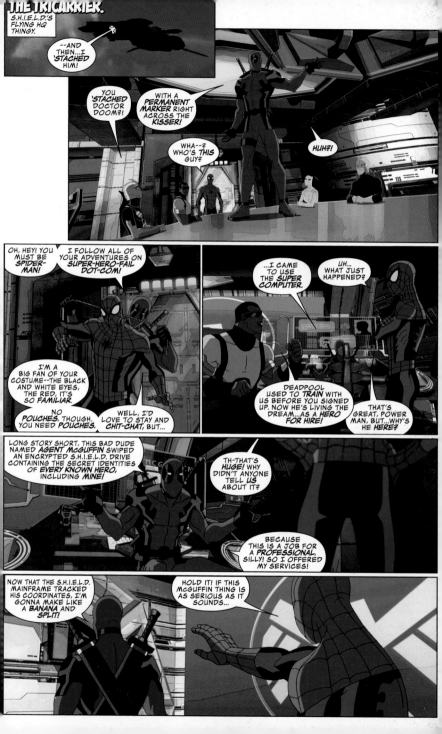

THE TRICARRIER.

S.H.I.E.L.D.'S FLYING HQ THINGY.

--AND THEN...I 'STACHED HIM!

YOU 'STACHED DOCTOR DOOM?!

WITH A PERMANENT MARKER RIGHT ACROSS THE KISSER!

WHA--? WHO'S THIS GUY?

HUH?!

OH, HEY! YOU MUST BE SPIDER-MAN!

I FOLLOW ALL OF YOUR ADVENTURES ON SUPER-HERO-FAIL DOT-COM!

...I CAME TO USE THE SUPER COMPUTER.

UH... WHAT JUST HAPPENED?

I'M A BIG FAN OF YOUR COSTUME--THE BLACK AND WHITE EYES, THE RED, IT'S SO FAMILIAR.

NO POUCHES, THOUGH. YOU NEED POUCHES.

WELL, I'D LOVE TO STAY AND CHIT-CHAT, BUT...

DEADPOOL USED TO TRAIN WITH US BEFORE YOU SIGNED UP. NOW HE'S LIVING THE DREAM...AS A HERO FOR HIRE!

THAT'S GREAT, POWER MAN, BUT...WHY'S HE HERE?

LONG STORY SHORT, THIS BAD DUDE NAMED AGENT McGUFFIN SWIPED AN ENCRYPTED S.H.I.E.L.D. DRIVE CONTAINING THE SECRET IDENTITIES OF EVERY KNOWN HERO, INCLUDING MINE!

TH-THAT'S HUGE! WHY DIDN'T ANYONE TELL US ABOUT IT?

BECAUSE THIS IS A JOB FOR A PROFESSIONAL, SILLY! SO I OFFERED MY SERVICES!

NOW THAT THE S.H.I.E.L.D. MAINFRAME TRACKED HIS COORDINATES, I'M GONNA MAKE LIKE A BANANA AND SPLIT!

HOLD IT! IF THIS McGUFFIN THING IS AS SERIOUS AS IT SOUNDS...

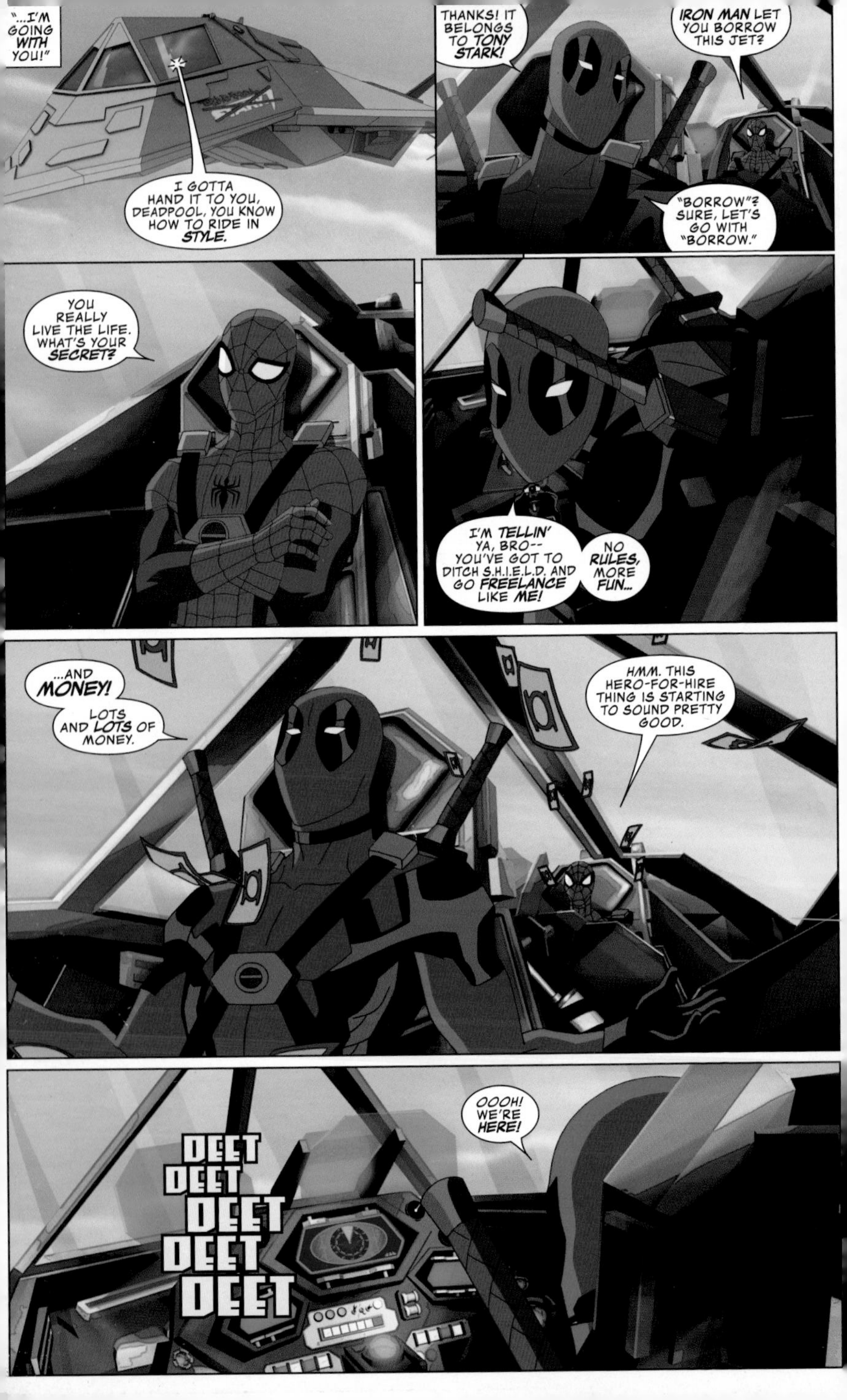
"...I'M GOING WITH YOU!"
I GOTTA HAND IT TO YOU, DEADPOOL, YOU KNOW HOW TO RIDE IN STYLE.
THANKS! IT BELONGS TO TONY STARK!
IRON MAN LET YOU BORROW THIS JET?
"BORROW"? SURE, LET'S GO WITH "BORROW."
YOU REALLY LIVE THE LIFE. WHAT'S YOUR SECRET?
I'M TELLIN' YA, BRO-- YOU'VE GOT TO DITCH S.H.I.E.L.D. AND GO FREELANCE LIKE ME!
NO RULES, MORE FUN...
...AND MONEY!
LOTS AND LOTS OF MONEY.
HMM. THIS HERO-FOR-HIRE THING IS STARTING TO SOUND PRETTY GOOD.
OOOH! WE'RE HERE!
DEET DEET DEET DEET DEET

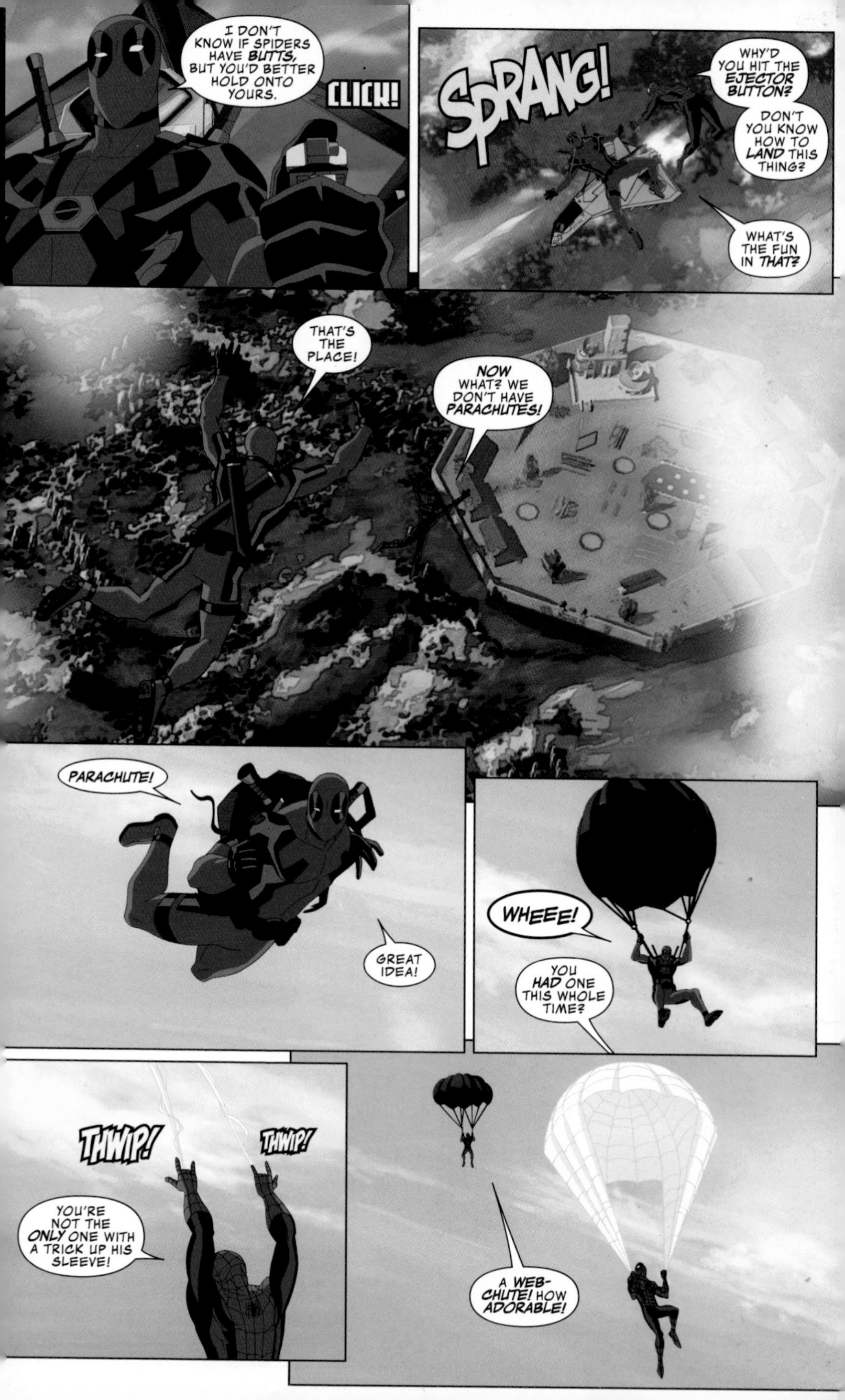
I DON'T KNOW IF SPIDERS HAVE BUTTS, BUT YOU'D BETTER HOLD ONTO YOURS.
CLICK!
SPRANG!
WHY'D YOU HIT THE EJECTOR BUTTON?
DON'T YOU KNOW HOW TO LAND THIS THING?
WHAT'S THE FUN IN THAT?
THAT'S THE PLACE!
NOW WHAT? WE DON'T HAVE PARACHUTES!
PARACHUTE!
GREAT IDEA!
WHEEE!
YOU HAD ONE THIS WHOLE TIME?
THWIP!
THWIP!
YOU'RE NOT THE ONLY ONE WITH A TRICK UP HIS SLEEVE!
A WEB-CHUTE! HOW ADORABLE!

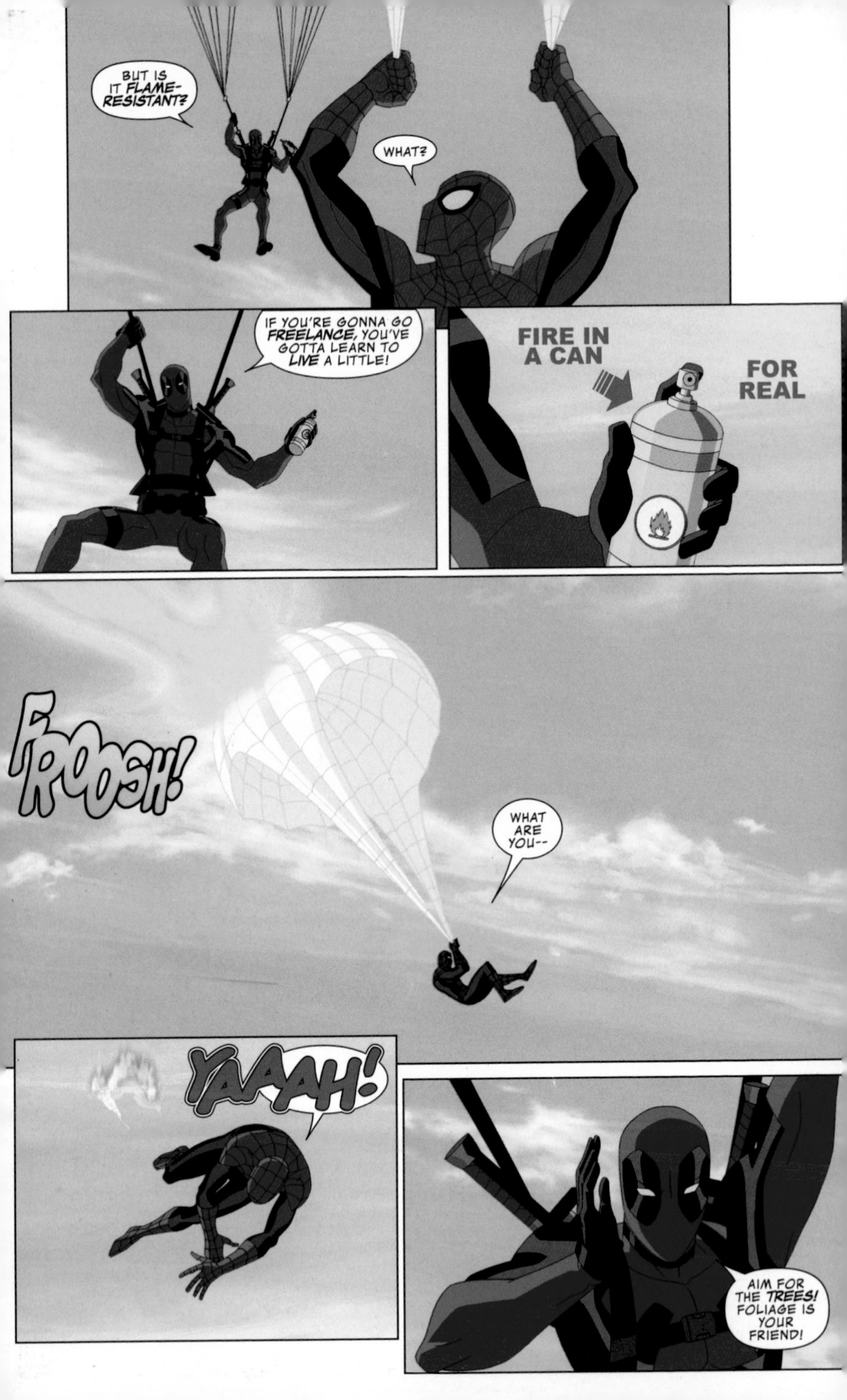
BUT IS IT FLAME-RESISTANT?
WHAT?
IF YOU'RE GONNA GO FREELANCE, YOU'VE GOTTA LEARN TO LIVE A LITTLE!
FIRE IN A CAN
FOR REAL
FROOSH!
WHAT ARE YOU--
YAAAH!
AIM FOR THE TREES! FOLIAGE IS YOUR FRIEND!

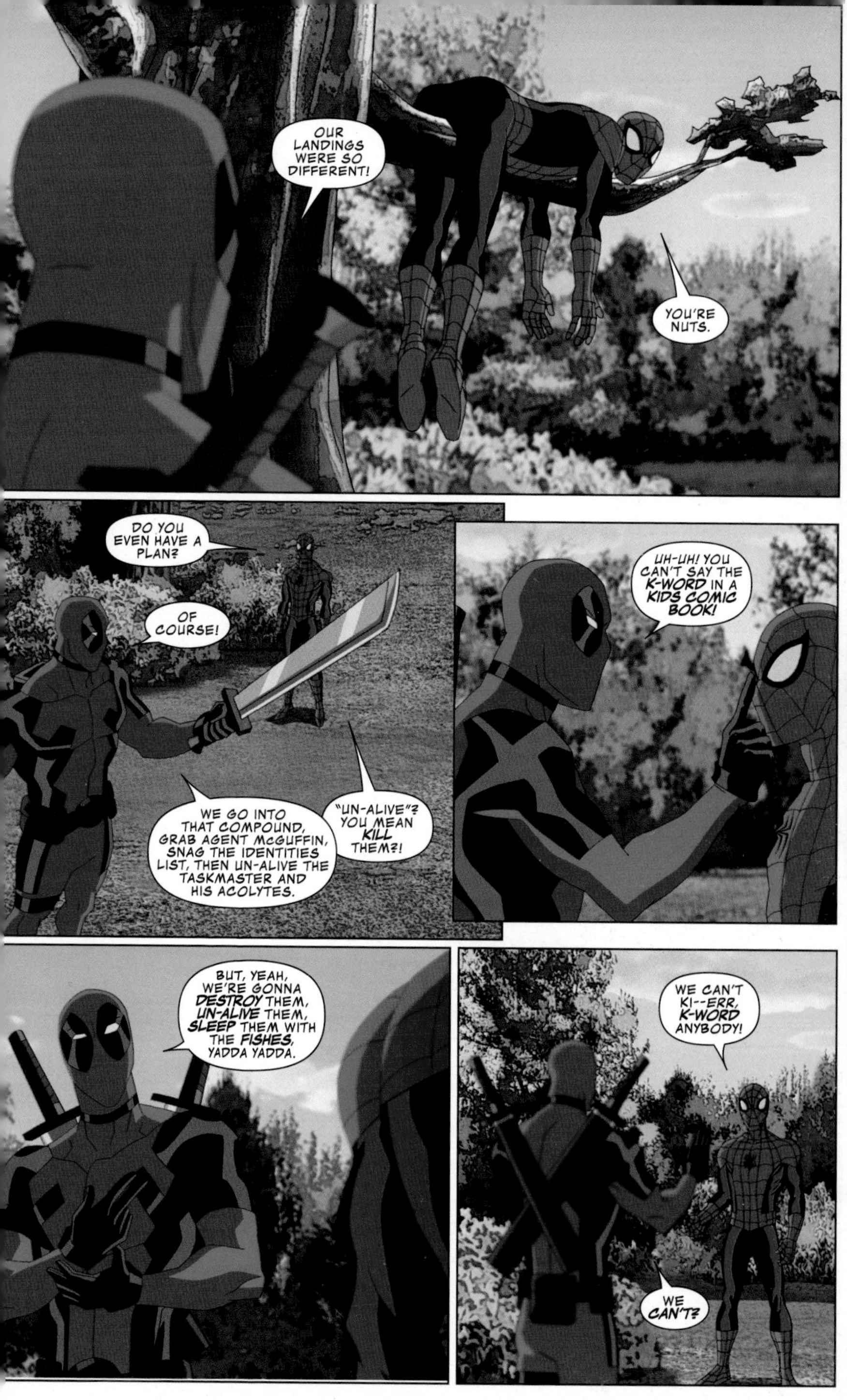
OUR LANDINGS WERE SO DIFFERENT!
YOU'RE NUTS.
DO YOU EVEN HAVE A PLAN?
OF COURSE!
WE GO INTO THAT COMPOUND, GRAB AGENT McGUFFIN, SNAG THE IDENTITIES LIST, THEN UN-ALIVE THE TASKMASTER AND HIS ACOLYTES.
"UN-ALIVE"? YOU MEAN KILL THEM?!
UH-UH! YOU CAN'T SAY THE K-WORD IN A KIDS COMIC BOOK!
BUT, YEAH, WE'RE GONNA DESTROY THEM, UN-ALIVE THEM, SLEEP THEM WITH THE FISHES, YADDA YADDA.
WE CAN'T KI--ERR, K-WORD ANYBODY!
WE CAN'T?

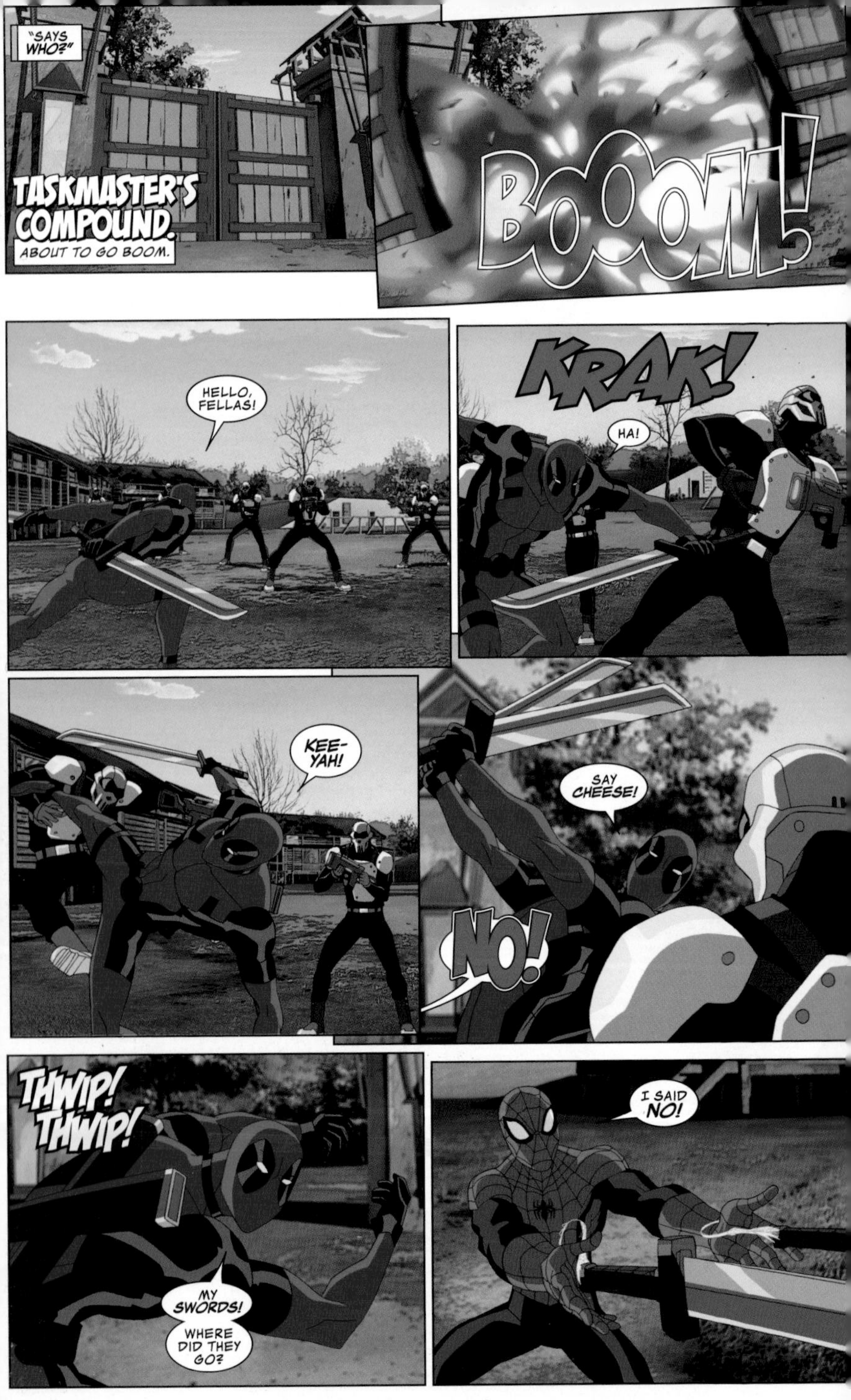
"SAYS WHO?"
TASKMASTER'S COMPOUND.
ABOUT TO GO BOOM.
BOOOM!
HELLO, FELLAS!
KRAK!
HA!
KEE-YAH!
SAY CHEESE!
NO!
THWIP! THWIP!
MY SWORDS!
WHERE DID THEY GO?
I SAID NO!

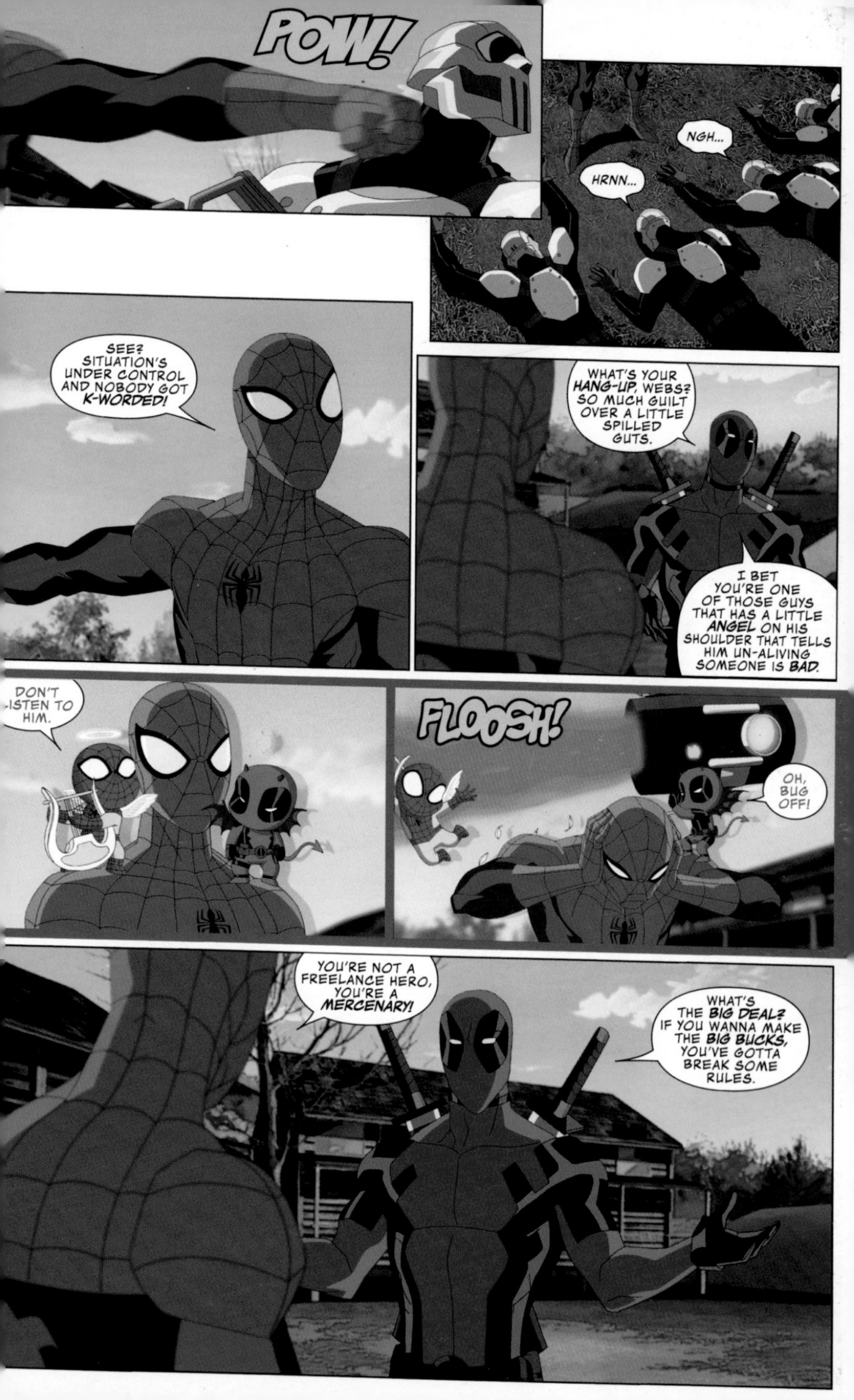
POW!
NGH...
HRNN...
SEE? SITUATION'S UNDER CONTROL AND NOBODY GOT K-WORDED!
WHAT'S YOUR HANG-UP, WEBS? SO MUCH GUILT OVER A LITTLE SPILLED GUTS.
I BET YOU'RE ONE OF THOSE GUYS THAT HAS A LITTLE ANGEL ON HIS SHOULDER THAT TELLS HIM UN-ALIVING SOMEONE IS BAD.
DON'T LISTEN TO HIM.
FLOOSH!
OH, BUG OFF!
YOU'RE NOT A FREELANCE HERO, YOU'RE A MERCENARY!
WHAT'S THE BIG DEAL? IF YOU WANNA MAKE THE BIG BUCKS, YOU'VE GOTTA BREAK SOME RULES.

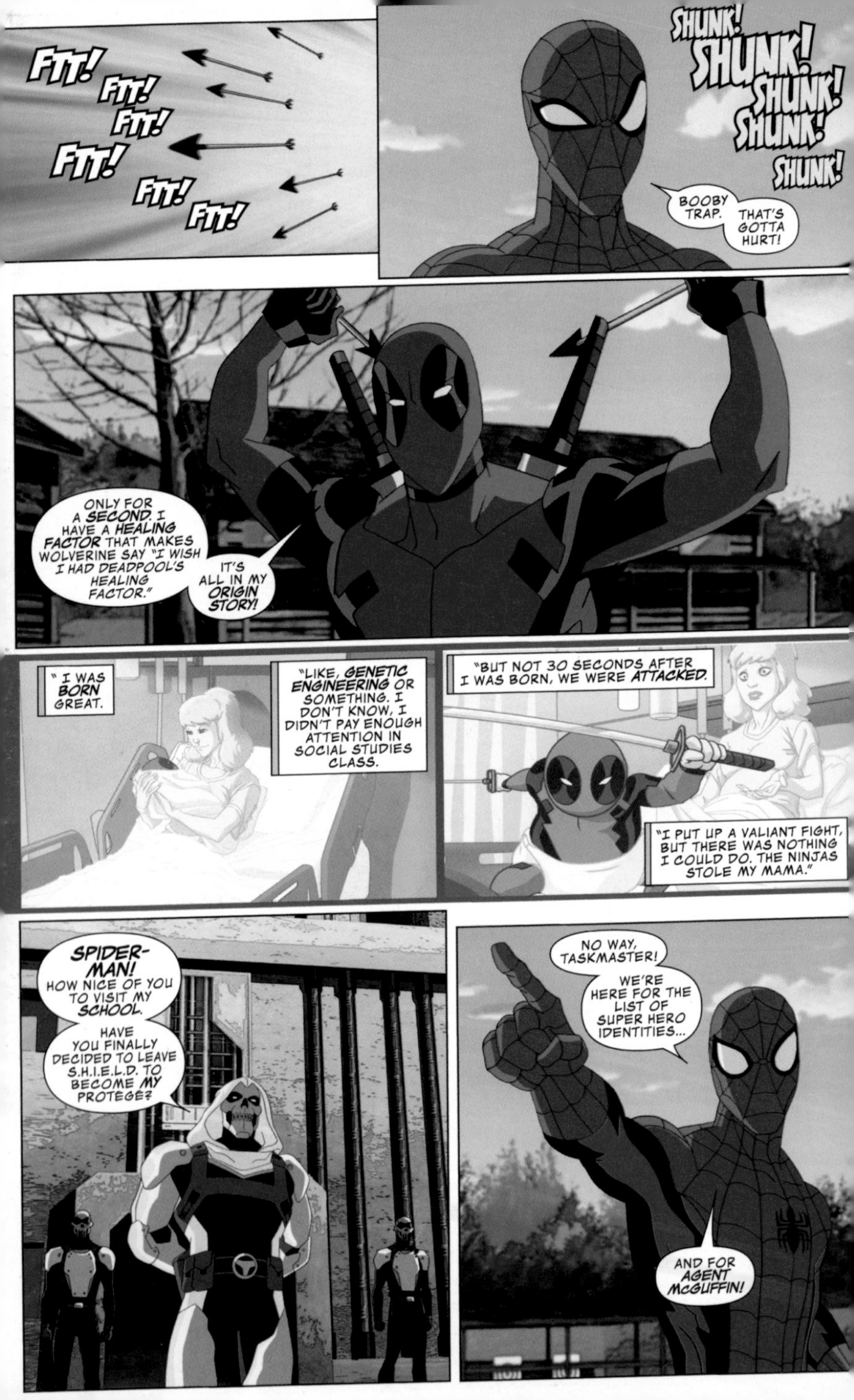
FTT!
FTT!
FTT!
FTT!
FTT!
FTT!
SHUNK!
SHUNK!
SHUNK!
SHUNK!
SHUNK!
BOOBY TRAP.
THAT'S GOTTA HURT!
ONLY FOR A SECOND. I HAVE A HEALING FACTOR THAT MAKES WOLVERINE SAY "I WISH I HAD DEADPOOL'S HEALING FACTOR."
IT'S ALL IN MY ORIGIN STORY!
"I WAS BORN GREAT.
"LIKE, GENETIC ENGINEERING OR SOMETHING. I DON'T KNOW, I DIDN'T PAY ENOUGH ATTENTION IN SOCIAL STUDIES CLASS.
"BUT NOT 30 SECONDS AFTER I WAS BORN, WE WERE ATTACKED.
"I PUT UP A VALIANT FIGHT, BUT THERE WAS NOTHING I COULD DO. THE NINJAS STOLE MY MAMA."
SPIDER-MAN! HOW NICE OF YOU TO VISIT MY SCHOOL.
HAVE YOU FINALLY DECIDED TO LEAVE S.H.I.E.L.D. TO BECOME MY PROTEGE?
NO WAY, TASKMASTER!
WE'RE HERE FOR THE LIST OF SUPER HERO IDENTITIES...
AND FOR AGENT McGUFFIN!

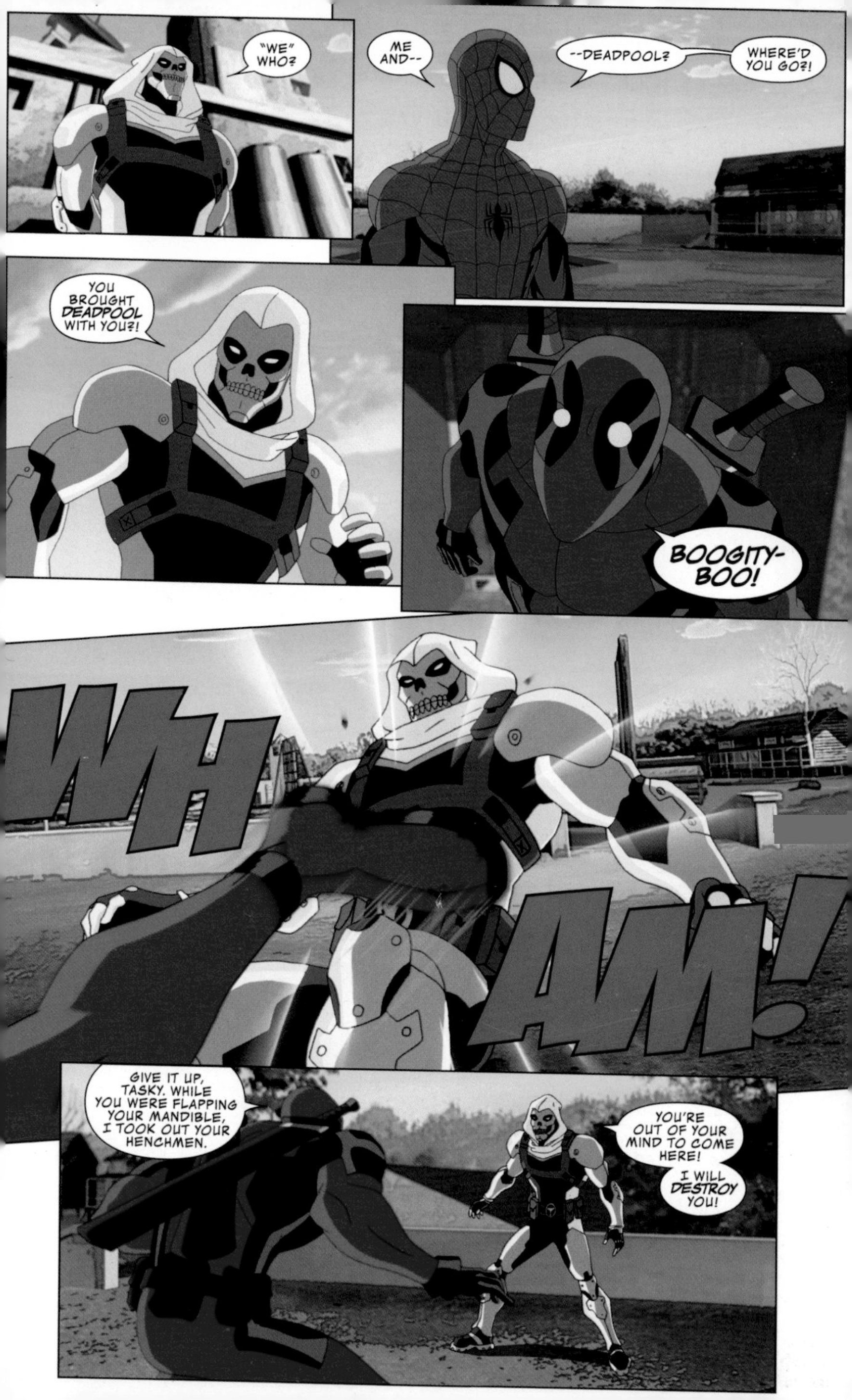
"WE" WHO?
ME AND--
--DEADPOOL?
WHERE'D YOU GO?!
YOU BROUGHT **DEADPOOL** WITH YOU?!
BOOGITY-BOO!
WHAM!
GIVE IT UP, TASKY. WHILE YOU WERE FLAPPING YOUR MANDIBLE, I TOOK OUT YOUR HENCHMEN.
YOU'RE OUT OF YOUR MIND TO COME HERE!
I WILL **DESTROY** YOU!

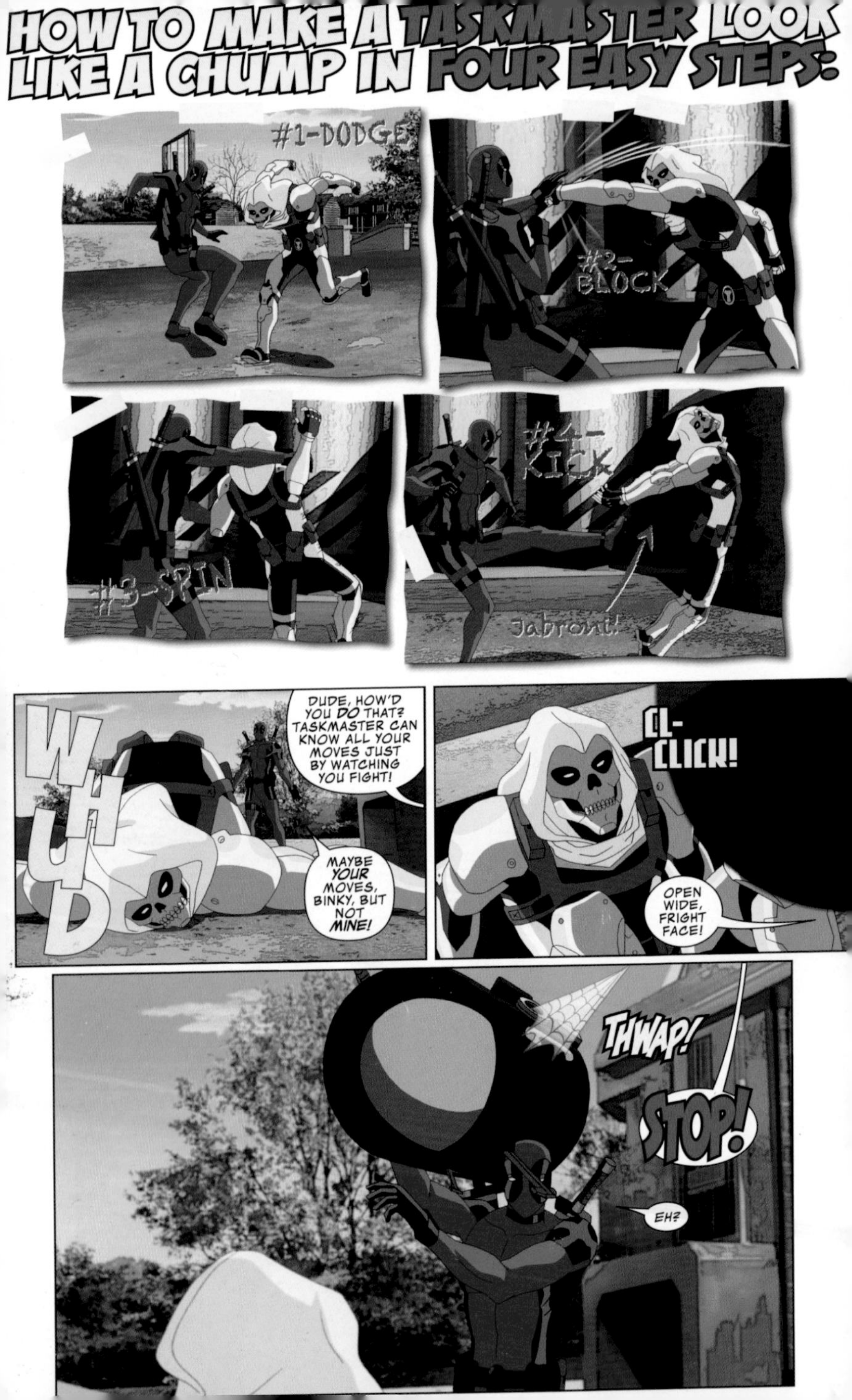
HOW TO MAKE A TASKMASTER LOOK LIKE A CHUMP IN FOUR EASY STEPS:
#1-DODGE
#2-BLOCK
#3-SPIN
#4-KICK
Jabroni!
WHUD
DUDE, HOW'D YOU DO THAT? TASKMASTER CAN KNOW ALL YOUR MOVES JUST BY WATCHING YOU FIGHT!
MAYBE YOUR MOVES, BINKY, BUT NOT MINE!
CL-CLICK!
OPEN WIDE, FRIGHT FACE!
THWAP!
STOP!
EH?

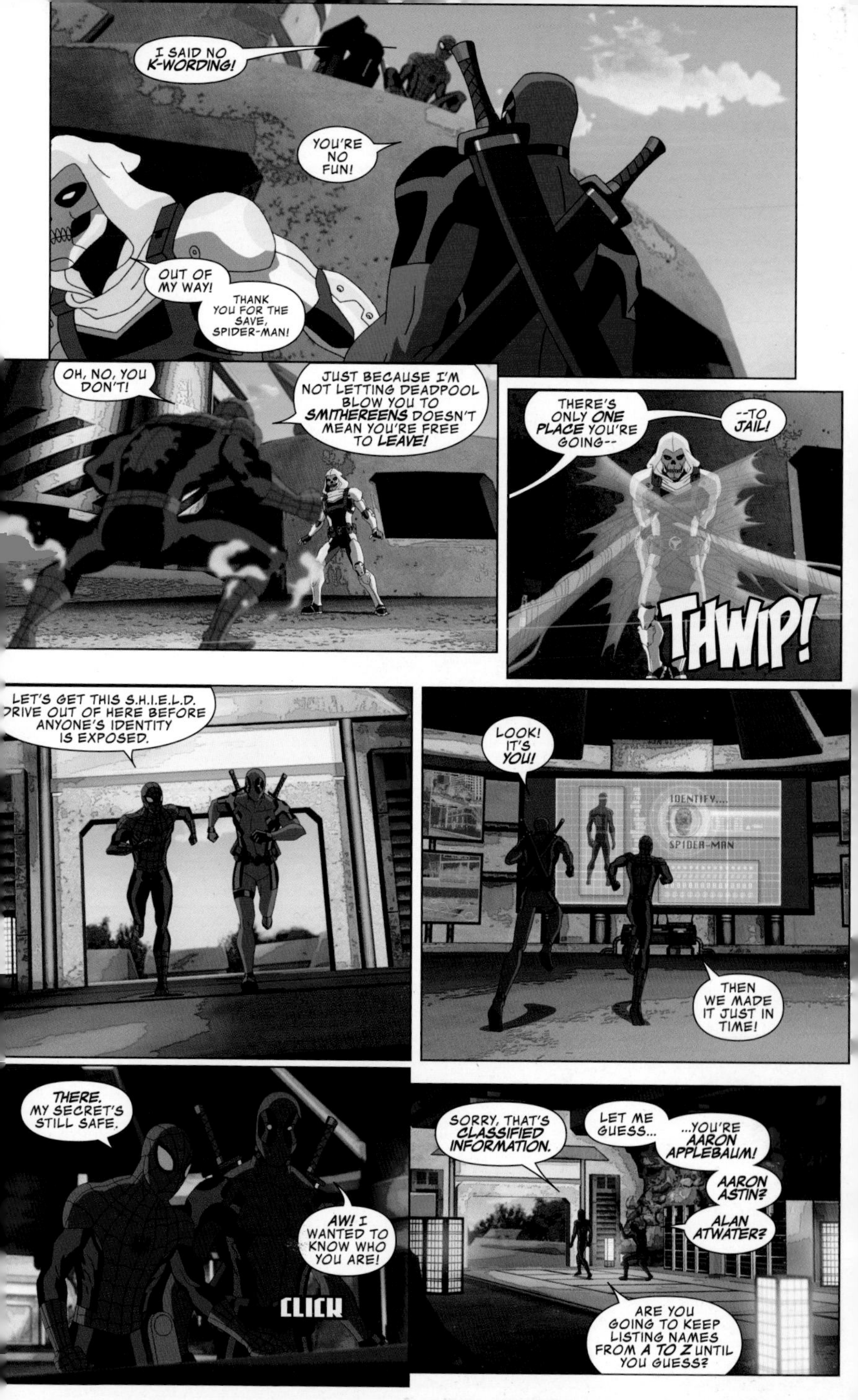
I SAID NO K-WORDING!
YOU'RE NO FUN!
OUT OF MY WAY!
THANK YOU FOR THE SAVE, SPIDER-MAN!
OH, NO, YOU DON'T!
JUST BECAUSE I'M NOT LETTING DEADPOOL BLOW YOU TO SMITHEREENS DOESN'T MEAN YOU'RE FREE TO LEAVE!
THERE'S ONLY ONE PLACE YOU'RE GOING--
--TO JAIL!
THWIP!
LET'S GET THIS S.H.I.E.L.D. DRIVE OUT OF HERE BEFORE ANYONE'S IDENTITY IS EXPOSED.
LOOK! IT'S YOU!
IDENTIFY....
SPIDER-MAN
THEN WE MADE IT JUST IN TIME!
THERE. MY SECRET'S STILL SAFE.
AW! I WANTED TO KNOW WHO YOU ARE!
CLICK
SORRY, THAT'S CLASSIFIED INFORMATION.
LET ME GUESS...
...YOU'RE AARON APPLEBAUM!
AARON ASTIN?
ALAN ATWATER?
ARE YOU GOING TO KEEP LISTING NAMES FROM A TO Z UNTIL YOU GUESS?

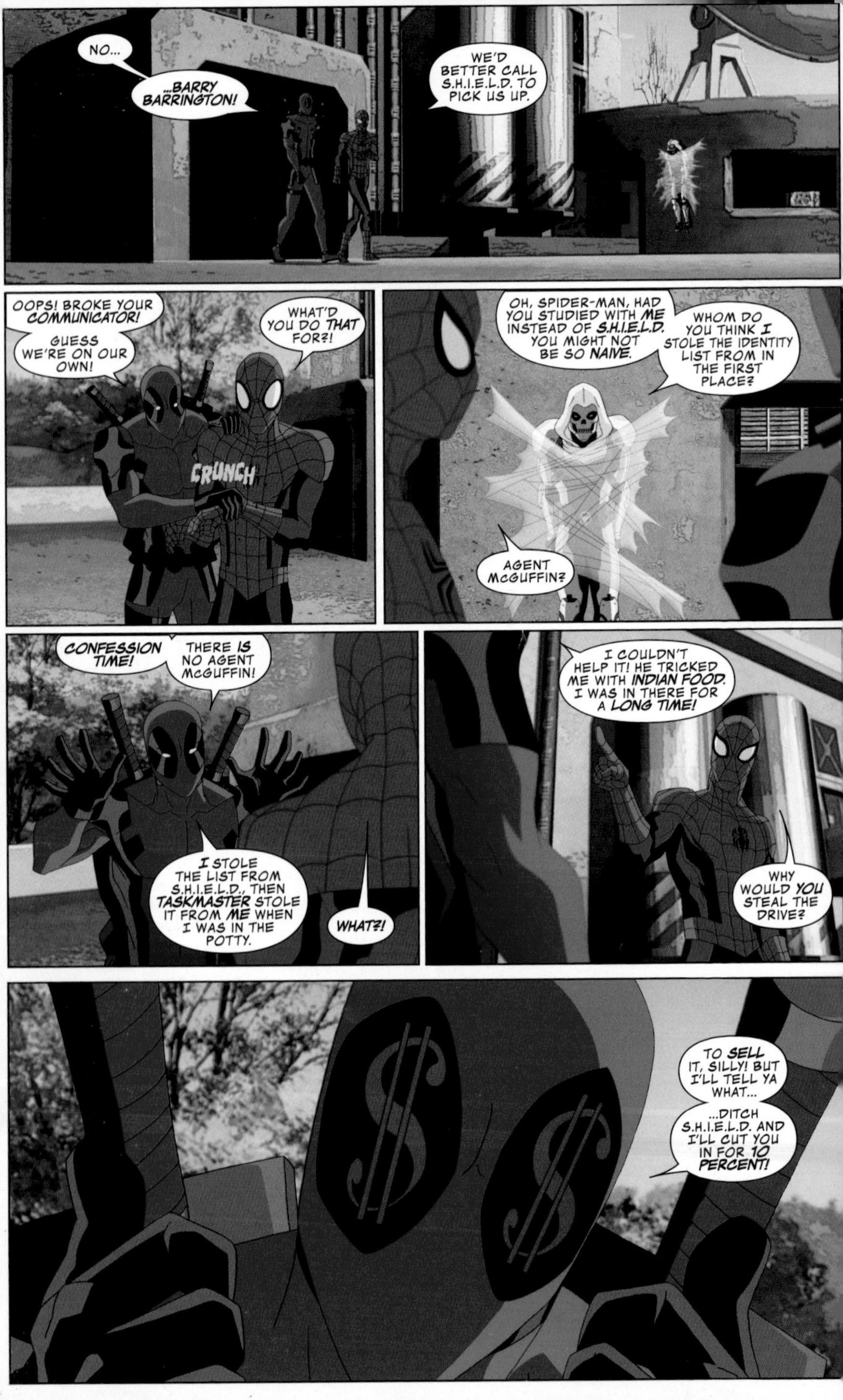
NO...
...BARRY BARRINGTON!
WE'D BETTER CALL S.H.I.E.L.D. TO PICK US UP.
OOPS! BROKE YOUR COMMUNICATOR!
GUESS WE'RE ON OUR OWN!
WHAT'D YOU DO THAT FOR?!
CRUNCH
OH, SPIDER-MAN, HAD YOU STUDIED WITH ME INSTEAD OF S.H.I.E.L.D. YOU MIGHT NOT BE SO NAIVE.
WHOM DO YOU THINK I STOLE THE IDENTITY LIST FROM IN THE FIRST PLACE?
AGENT McGUFFIN?
CONFESSION TIME!
THERE IS NO AGENT McGUFFIN!
I STOLE THE LIST FROM S.H.I.E.L.D., THEN TASKMASTER STOLE IT FROM ME WHEN I WAS IN THE POTTY.
WHAT?!
I COULDN'T HELP IT! HE TRICKED ME WITH INDIAN FOOD. I WAS IN THERE FOR A LONG TIME!
WHY WOULD YOU STEAL THE DRIVE?
TO SELL IT, SILLY! BUT I'LL TELL YA WHAT...
...DITCH S.H.I.E.L.D. AND I'LL CUT YOU IN FOR 10 PERCENT!

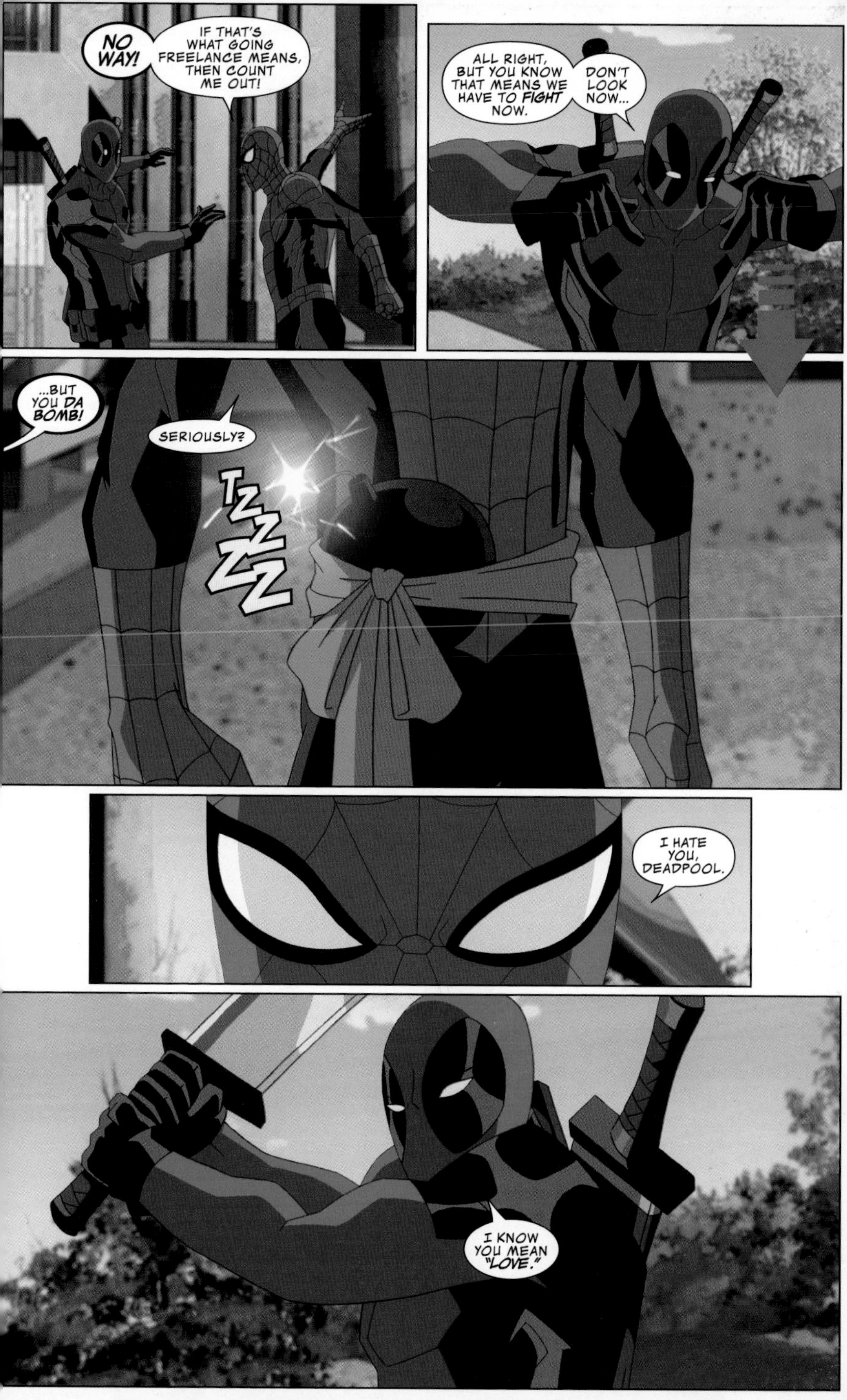
NO WAY!
IF THAT'S WHAT GOING FREELANCE MEANS, THEN COUNT ME OUT!
ALL RIGHT, BUT YOU KNOW THAT MEANS WE HAVE TO FIGHT NOW.
DON'T LOOK NOW...
...BUT YOU DA BOMB!
SERIOUSLY?
TZZZZ
I HATE YOU, DEADPOOL.
I KNOW YOU MEAN "LOVE."

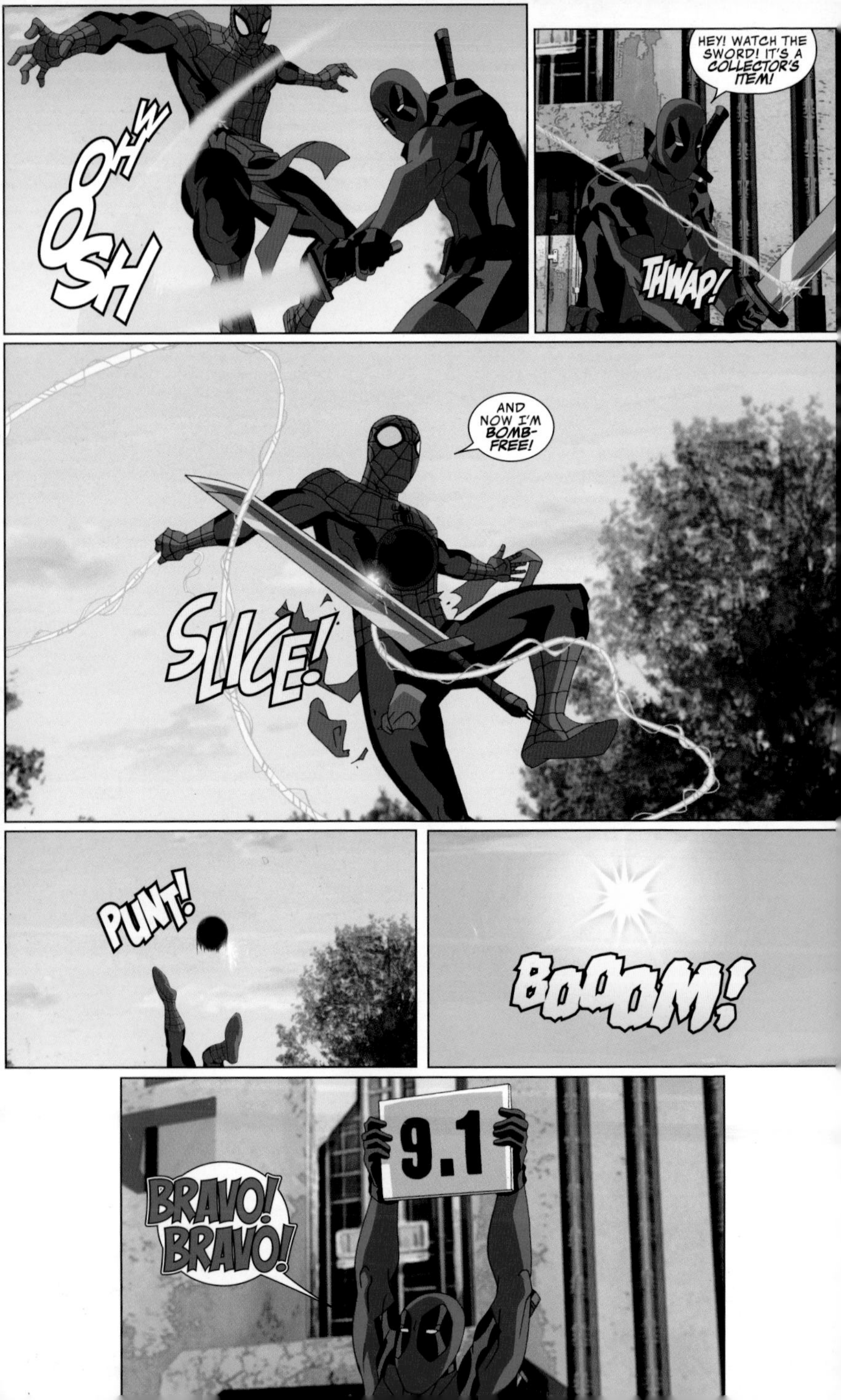
WHOOSH
HEY! WATCH THE SWORD! IT'S A COLLECTOR'S ITEM!
THWAP!
AND NOW I'M BOMB-FREE!
SLICE!
PUNT!
BOOOM!
9.1
BRAVO! BRAVO!

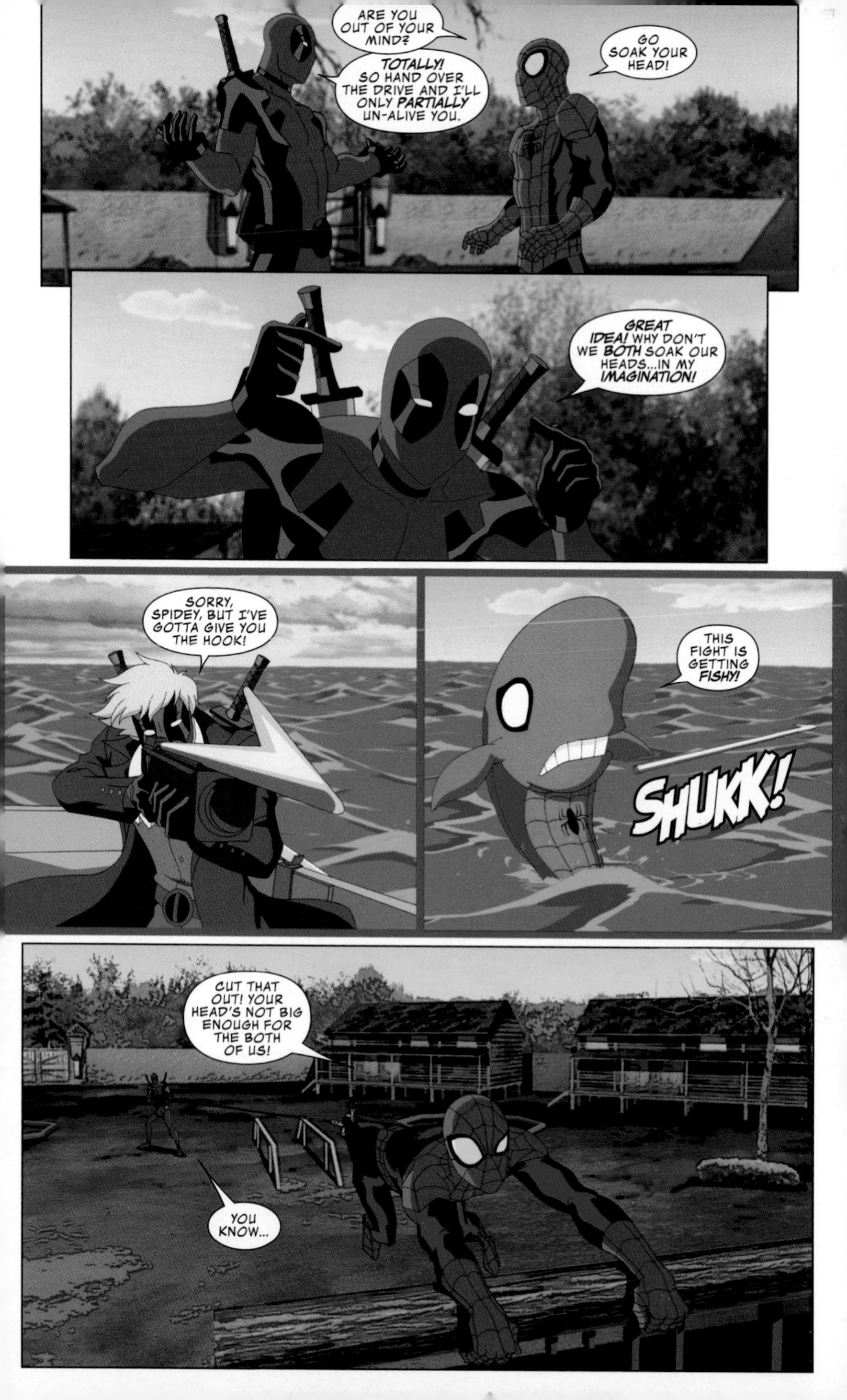
ARE YOU OUT OF YOUR MIND?
GO SOAK YOUR HEAD!
TOTALLY! SO HAND OVER THE DRIVE AND I'LL ONLY PARTIALLY UN-ALIVE YOU.
GREAT IDEA! WHY DON'T WE BOTH SOAK OUR HEADS...IN MY IMAGINATION!
SORRY, SPIDEY, BUT I'VE GOTTA GIVE YOU THE HOOK!
THIS FIGHT IS GETTING FISHY!
SHUKK!
CUT THAT OUT! YOUR HEAD'S NOT BIG ENOUGH FOR THE BOTH OF US!
YOU KNOW...

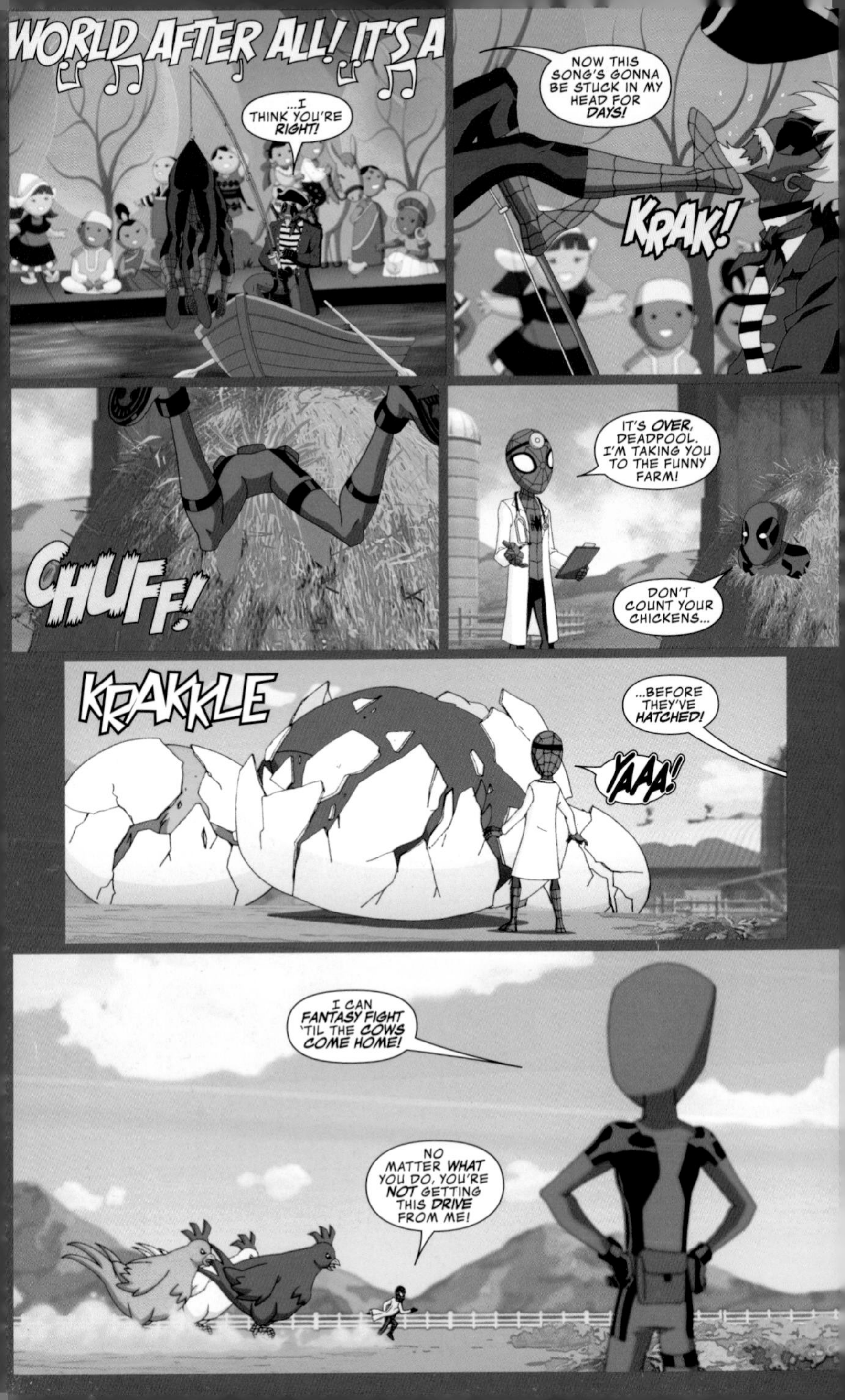
WORLD AFTER ALL! IT'S A
...I THINK YOU'RE RIGHT!
NOW THIS SONG'S GONNA BE STUCK IN MY HEAD FOR DAYS!
KRAK!
CHUFF!
IT'S OVER, DEADPOOL. I'M TAKING YOU TO THE FUNNY FARM!
DON'T COUNT YOUR CHICKENS...
KRAKKLE
...BEFORE THEY'VE HATCHED!
YAAA!
I CAN FANTASY FIGHT 'TIL THE COWS COME HOME!
NO MATTER WHAT YOU DO, YOU'RE NOT GETTING THIS DRIVE FROM ME!

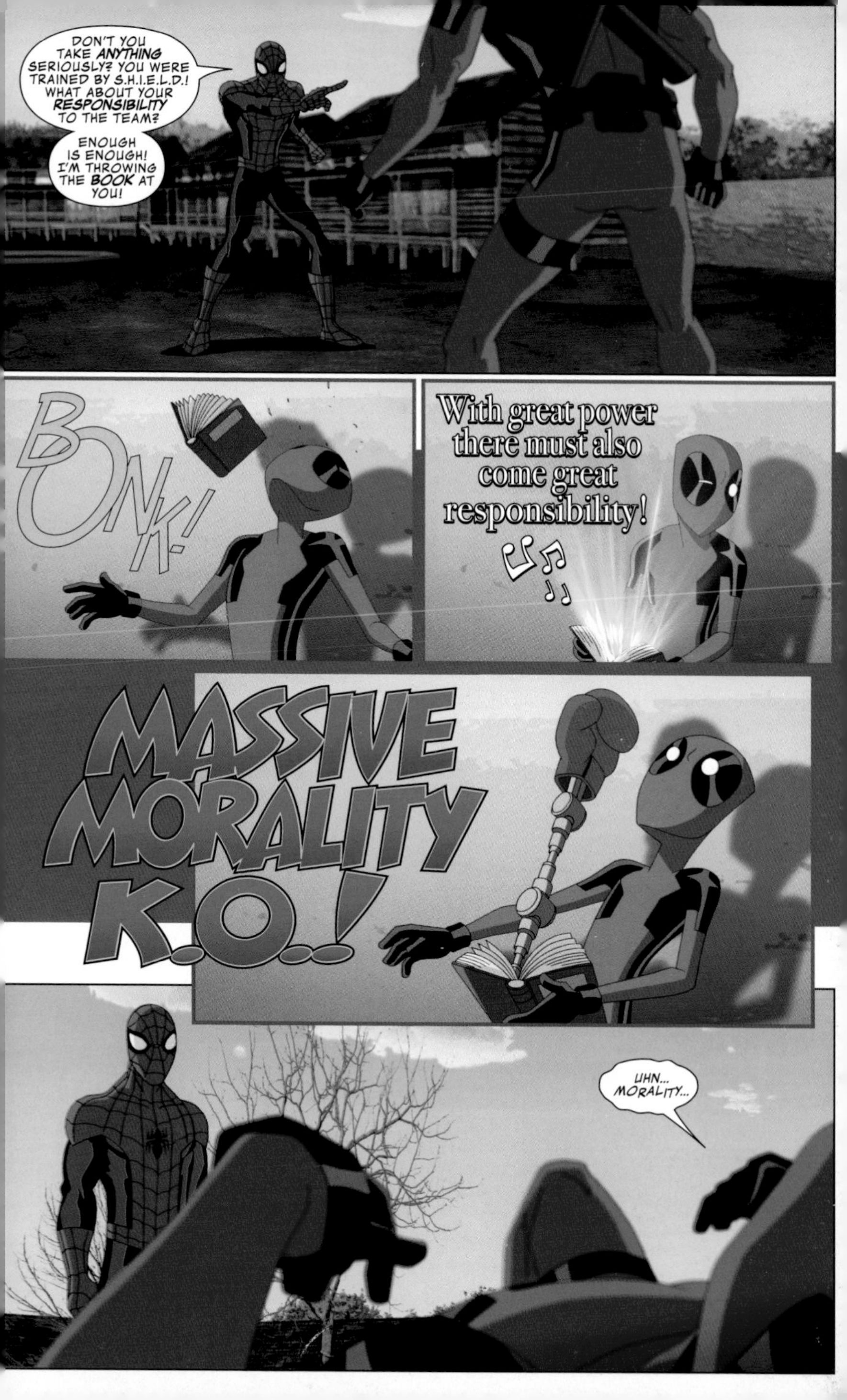

DON'T YOU TAKE ANYTHING SERIOUSLY? YOU WERE TRAINED BY S.H.I.E.L.D.! WHAT ABOUT YOUR RESPONSIBILITY TO THE TEAM?
ENOUGH IS ENOUGH! I'M THROWING THE BOOK AT YOU!
BONK!
With great power there must also come great responsibility!
MASSIVE MORALITY K.O.!
UHN... MORALITY...

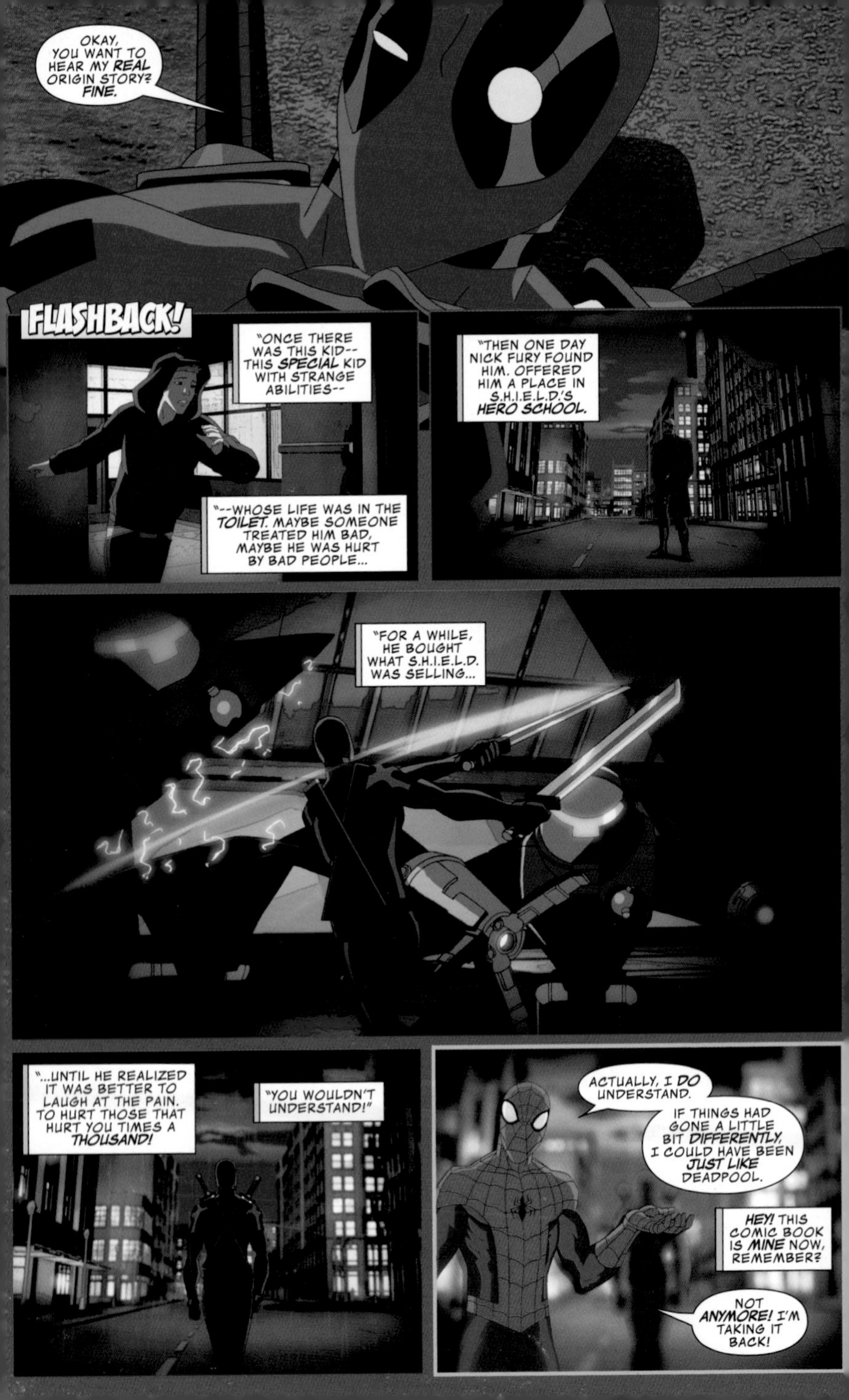
OKAY, YOU WANT TO HEAR MY REAL ORIGIN STORY? FINE.
FLASHBACK!
"ONCE THERE WAS THIS KID-- THIS SPECIAL KID WITH STRANGE ABILITIES--
"--WHOSE LIFE WAS IN THE TOILET. MAYBE SOMEONE TREATED HIM BAD, MAYBE HE WAS HURT BY BAD PEOPLE...
"THEN ONE DAY NICK FURY FOUND HIM. OFFERED HIM A PLACE IN S.H.I.E.L.D.'S HERO SCHOOL.
"FOR A WHILE, HE BOUGHT WHAT S.H.I.E.L.D. WAS SELLING...
"...UNTIL HE REALIZED IT WAS BETTER TO LAUGH AT THE PAIN. TO HURT THOSE THAT HURT YOU TIMES A THOUSAND!
"YOU WOULDN'T UNDERSTAND!"
ACTUALLY, I DO UNDERSTAND.
IF THINGS HAD GONE A LITTLE BIT DIFFERENTLY, I COULD HAVE BEEN JUST LIKE DEADPOOL.
HEY! THIS COMIC BOOK IS MINE NOW, REMEMBER?
NOT ANYMORE! I'M TAKING IT BACK!

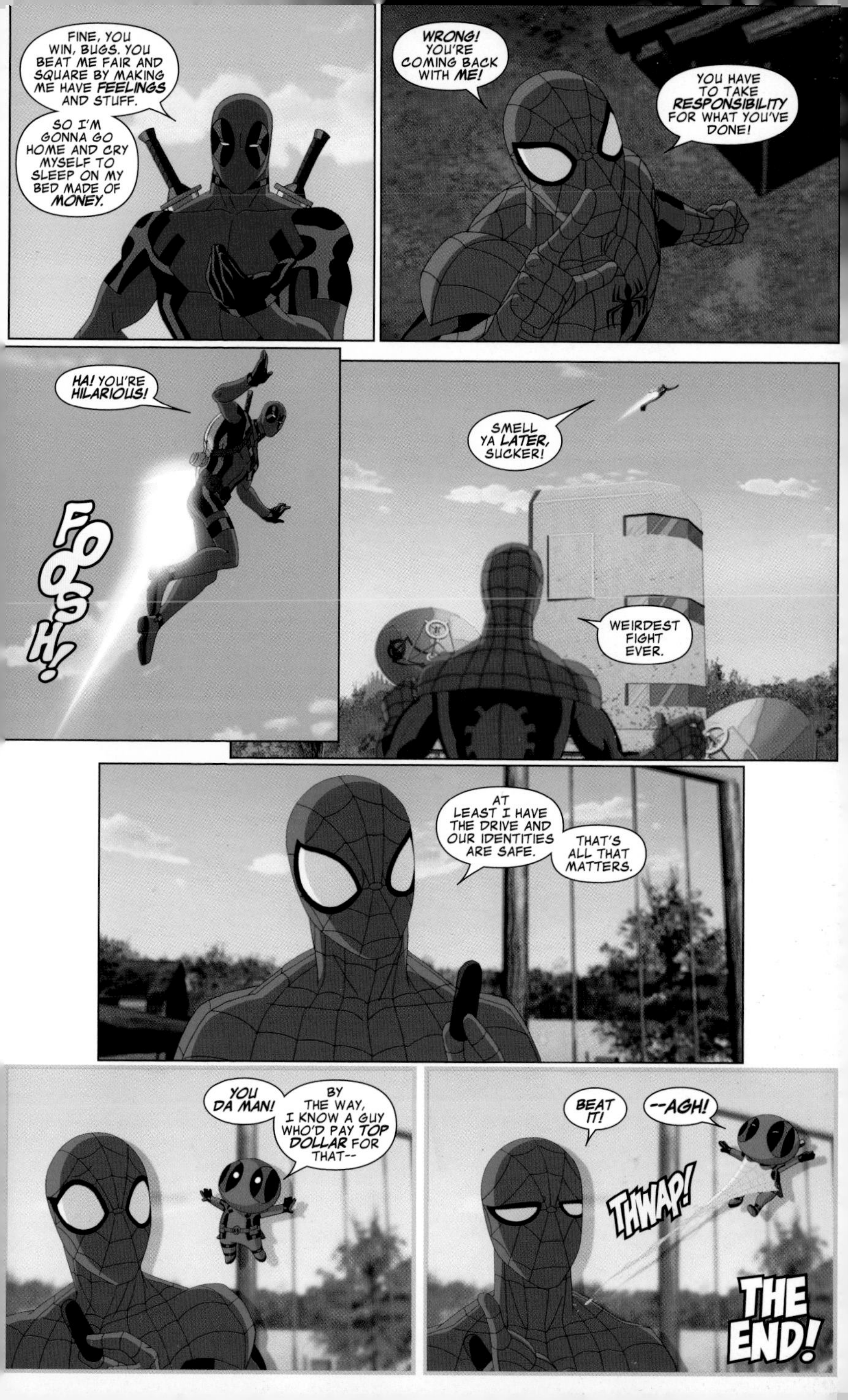
FINE, YOU WIN, BUGS. YOU BEAT ME FAIR AND SQUARE BY MAKING ME HAVE FEELINGS AND STUFF.
SO I'M GONNA GO HOME AND CRY MYSELF TO SLEEP ON MY BED MADE OF MONEY.
WRONG! YOU'RE COMING BACK WITH ME!
YOU HAVE TO TAKE RESPONSIBILITY FOR WHAT YOU'VE DONE!
HA! YOU'RE HILARIOUS!
FOOSH!
SMELL YA LATER, SUCKER!
WEIRDEST FIGHT EVER.
AT LEAST I HAVE THE DRIVE AND OUR IDENTITIES ARE SAFE.
THAT'S ALL THAT MATTERS.
YOU DA MAN!
BY THE WAY, I KNOW A GUY WHO'D PAY TOP DOLLAR FOR THAT--
BEAT IT!
--AGH!
THWAP!
THE END!

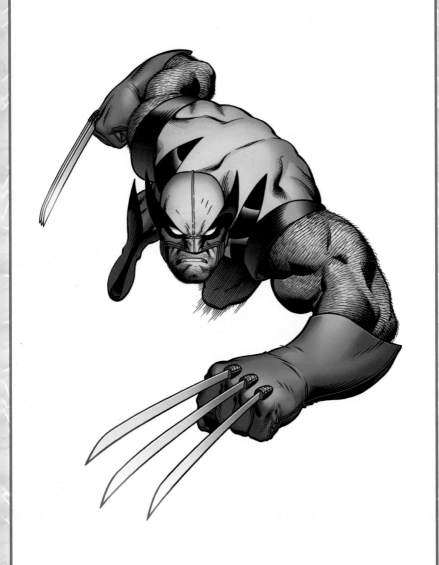

WOLVERINE: ORIGIN OF AN X-MAN

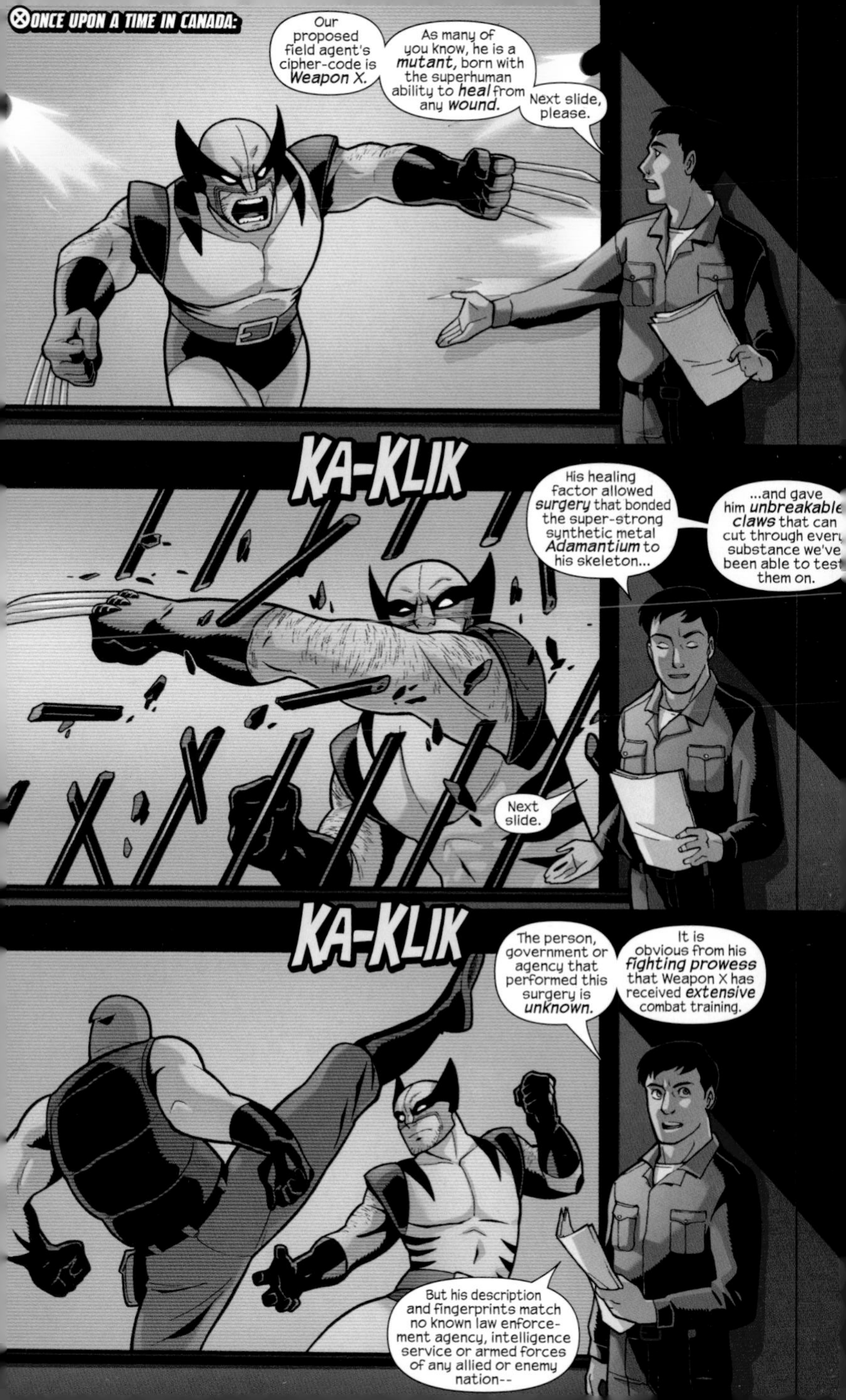
ONCE UPON A TIME IN CANADA:
Our proposed field agent's cipher-code is Weapon X.
As many of you know, he is a mutant, born with the superhuman ability to heal from any wound.
Next slide, please.
KA-KLIK
His healing factor allowed surgery that bonded the super-strong synthetic metal Adamantium to his skeleton...
...and gave him unbreakable claws that can cut through every substance we've been able to test them on.
Next slide.
KA-KLIK
The person, government or agency that performed this surgery is unknown.
It is obvious from his fighting prowess that Weapon X has received extensive combat training.
But his description and fingerprints match no known law enforcement agency, intelligence service or armed forces of any allied or enemy nation--

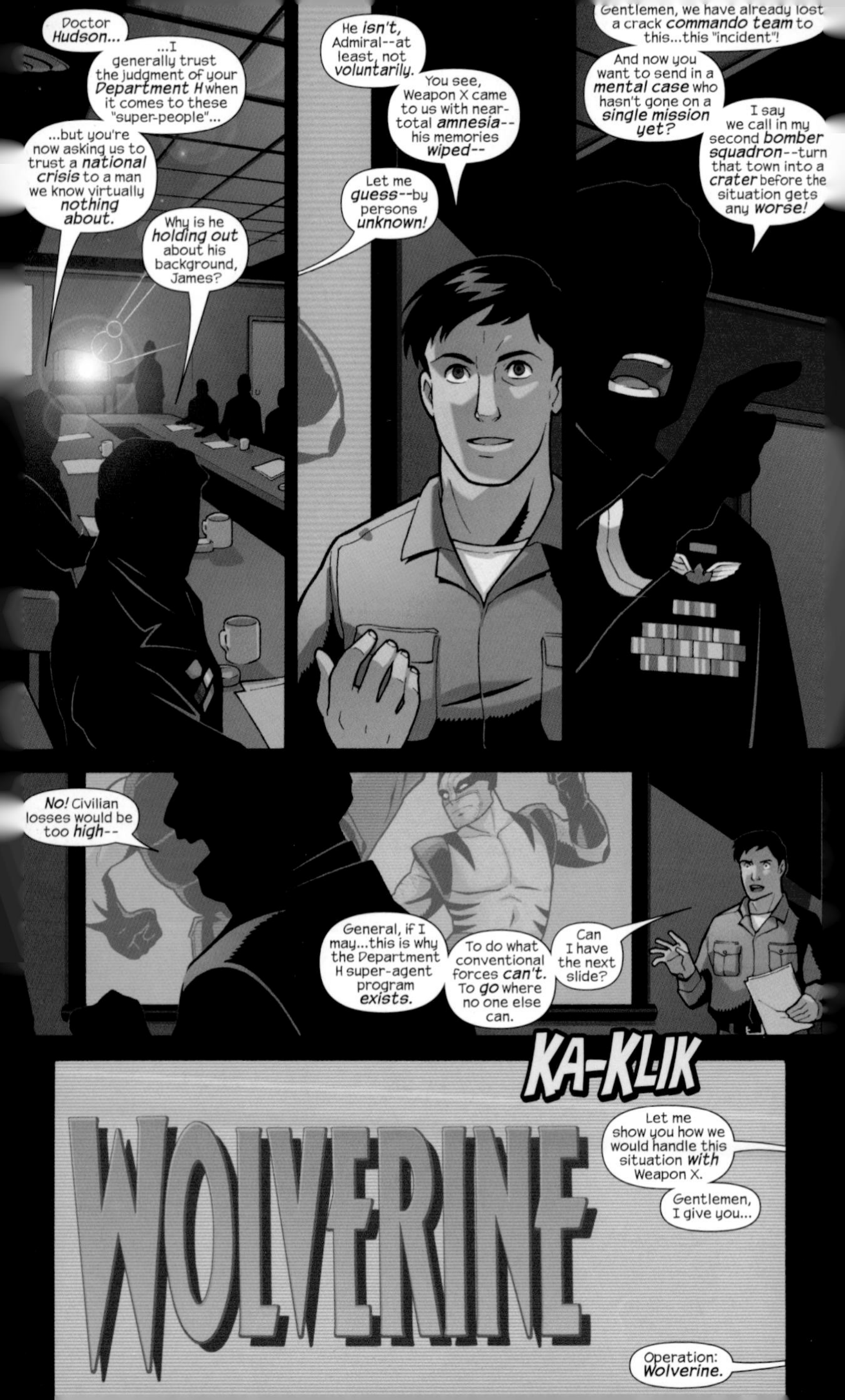
Doctor Hudson...
...I generally trust the judgment of your Department H when it comes to these "super-people"...
...but you're now asking us to trust a national crisis to a man we know virtually nothing about.
Why is he holding out about his background, James?
He isn't, Admiral--at least, not voluntarily.
You see, Weapon X came to us with near-total amnesia--his memories wiped--
Let me guess--by persons unknown!
Gentlemen, we have already lost a crack commando team to this...this "incident"!
And now you want to send in a mental case who hasn't gone on a single mission yet?
I say we call in my second bomber squadron--turn that town into a crater before the situation gets any worse!
No! Civilian losses would be too high--
General, if I may...this is why the Department H super-agent program exists.
To do what conventional forces can't. To go where no one else can.
Can I have the next slide?
KA-KLIK
WOLVERINE
Let me show you how we would handle this situation with Weapon X.
Gentlemen, I give you...
Operation: Wolverine.

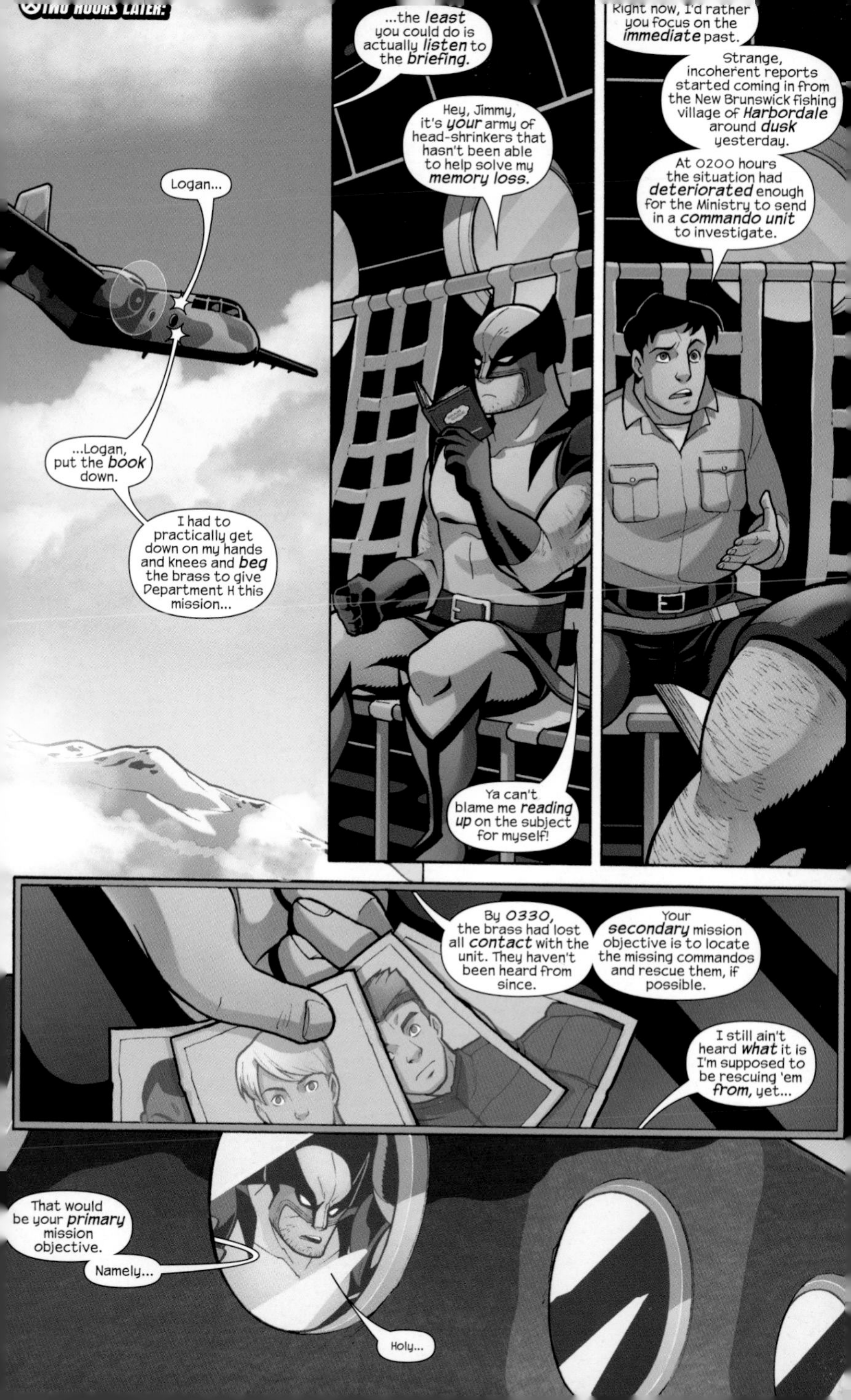
TWO HOURS LATER:
Logan...
...Logan, put the book down.
I had to practically get down on my hands and knees and beg the brass to give Department H this mission...
...the least you could do is actually listen to the briefing.
Hey, Jimmy, it's your army of head-shrinkers that hasn't been able to help solve my memory loss.
Ya can't blame me reading up on the subject for myself!
Right now, I'd rather you focus on the immediate past.
Strange, incoherent reports started coming in from the New Brunswick fishing village of Harbordale around dusk yesterday.
At 0200 hours the situation had deteriorated enough for the Ministry to send in a commando unit to investigate.
By 0330, the brass had lost all contact with the unit. They haven't been heard from since.
Your secondary mission objective is to locate the missing commandos and rescue them, if possible.
I still ain't heard what it is I'm supposed to be rescuing 'em from, yet...
That would be your primary mission objective.
Namely...
Holy...

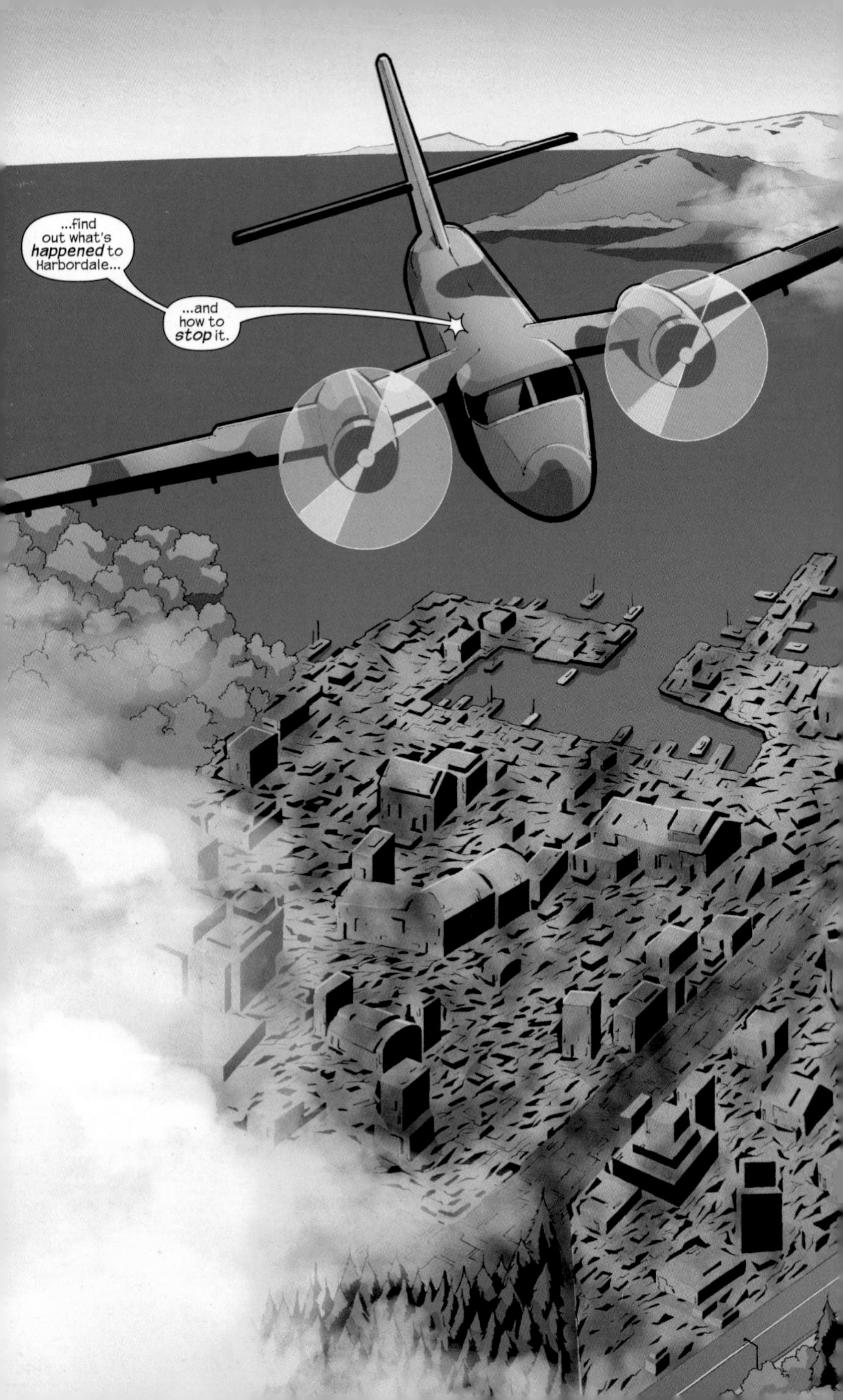
...find out what's *happened* to Harbordale...
...and how to *stop* it.

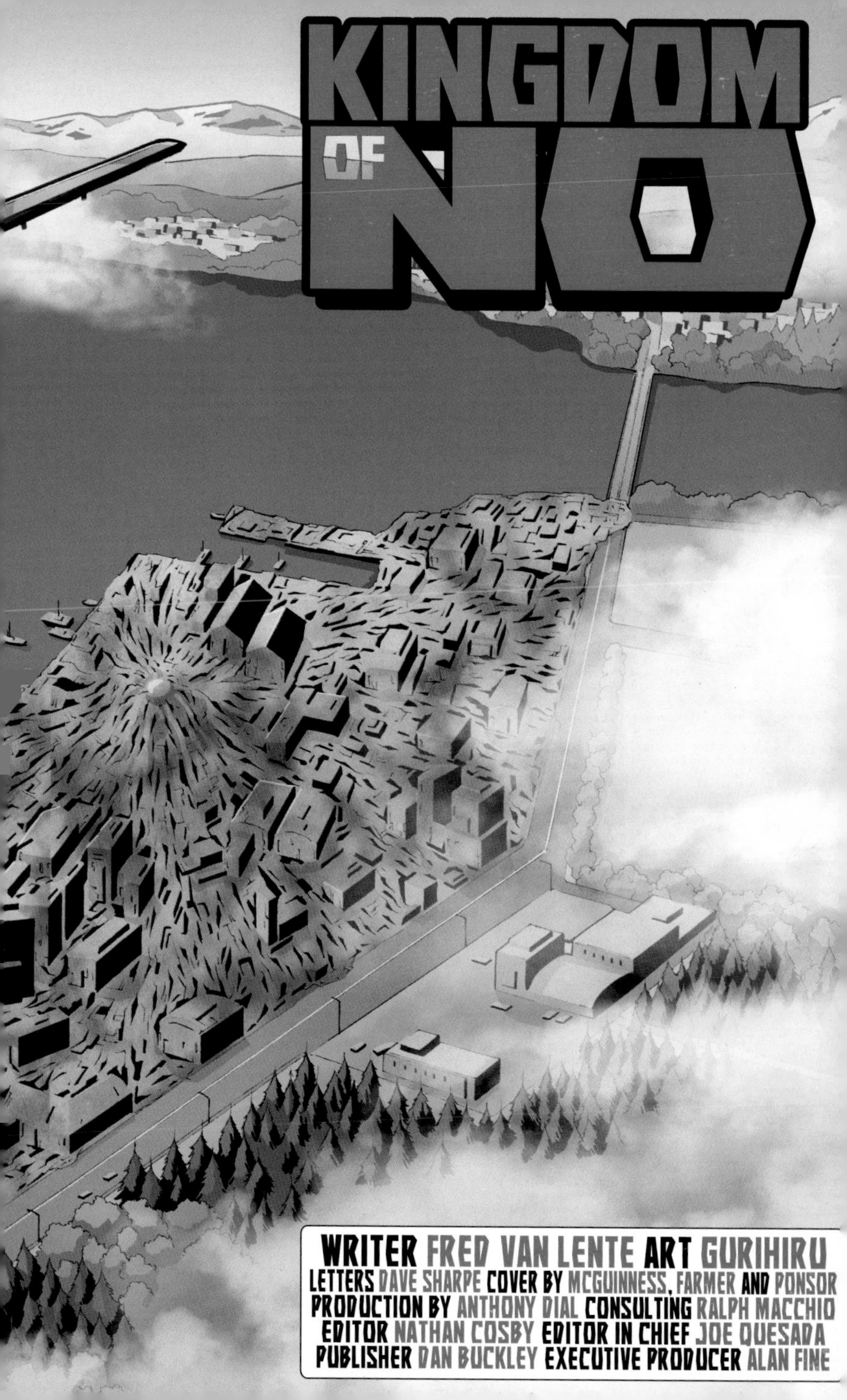
KINGDOM OF NO
WRITER FRED VAN LENTE ART GURIHIRU
LETTERS DAVE SHARPE COVER BY MCGUINNESS, FARMER AND PONSOR
PRODUCTION BY ANTHONY DIAL CONSULTING RALPH MACCHIO
EDITOR NATHAN COSBY EDITOR IN CHIEF JOE QUESADA
PUBLISHER DAN BUCKLEY EXECUTIVE PRODUCER ALAN FINE

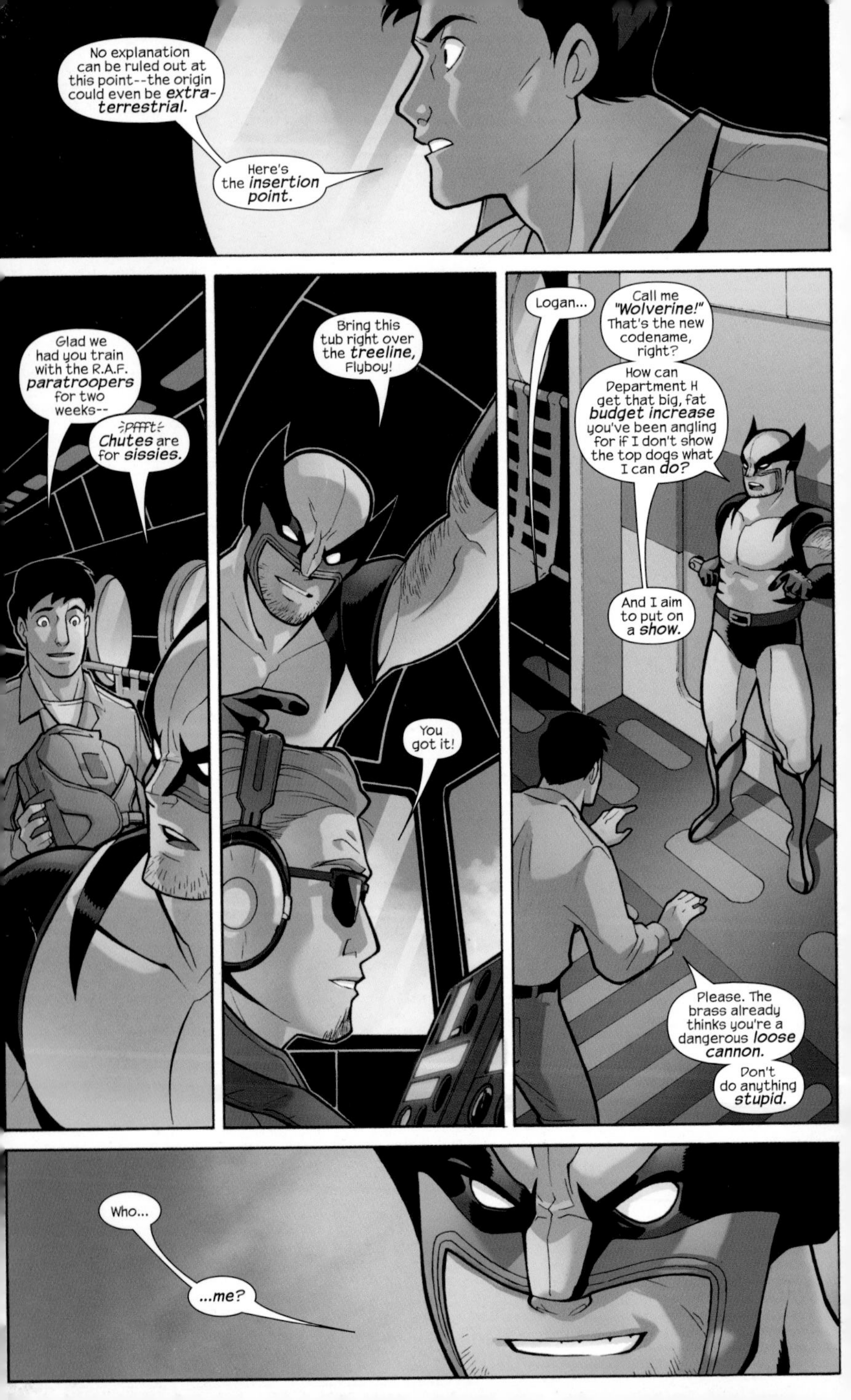
No explanation can be ruled out at this point--the origin could even be extra-terrestrial.
Here's the insertion point.
Glad we had you train with the R.A.F. paratroopers for two weeks--
Pffft Chutes are for sissies.
Bring this tub right over the treeline, Flyboy!
You got it!
Logan...
Call me "Wolverine!" That's the new codename, right?
How can Department H get that big, fat budget increase you've been angling for if I don't show the top dogs what I can do?
And I aim to put on a show.
Please. The brass already thinks you're a dangerous loose cannon.
Don't do anything stupid.
Who...
...me?

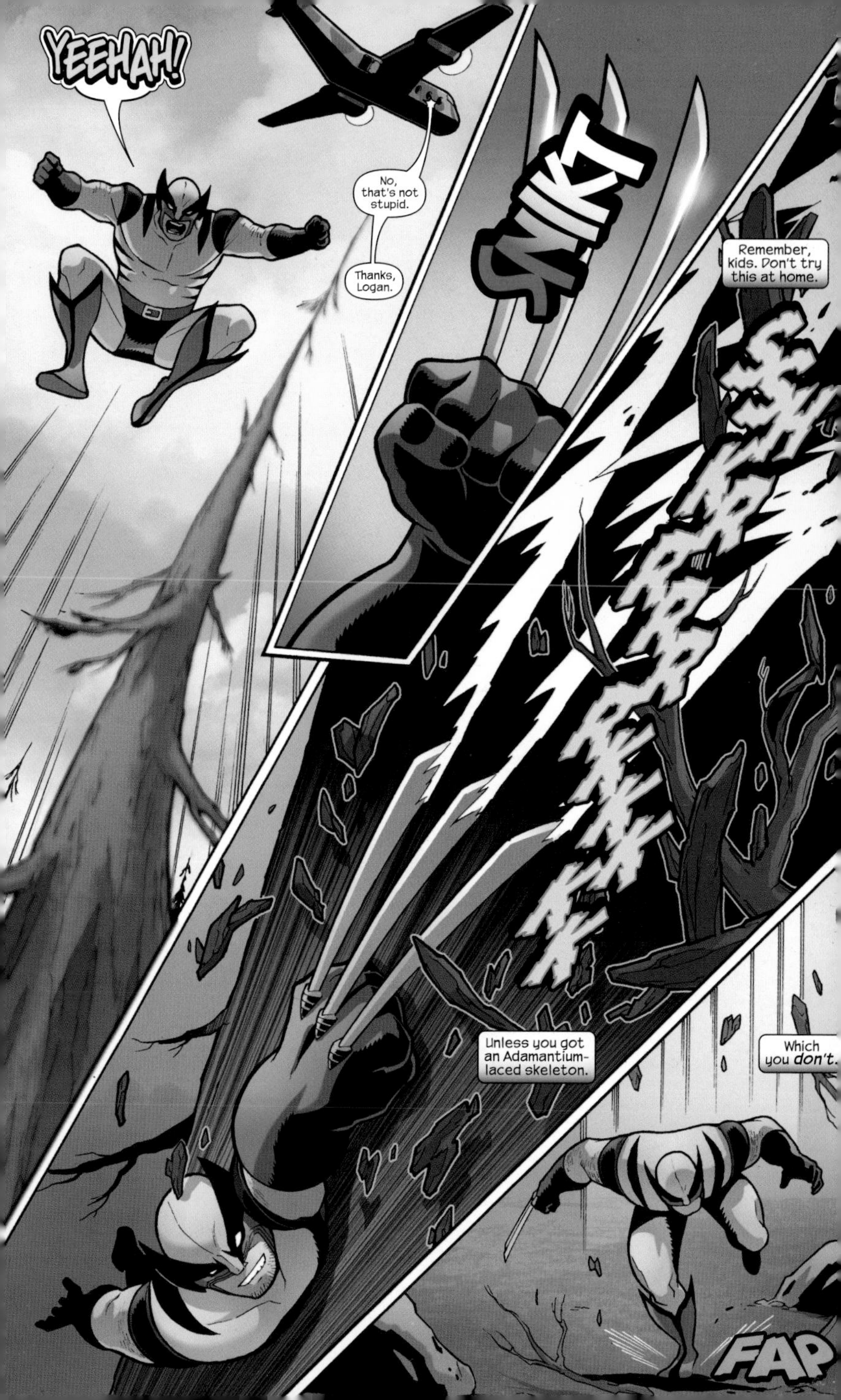
YEEHAH!
No, that's not stupid.
Thanks, Logan.
SNIKT
Remember, kids. Don't try this at home.
Unless you got an Adamantium-laced skeleton.
Which you don't.
FAP

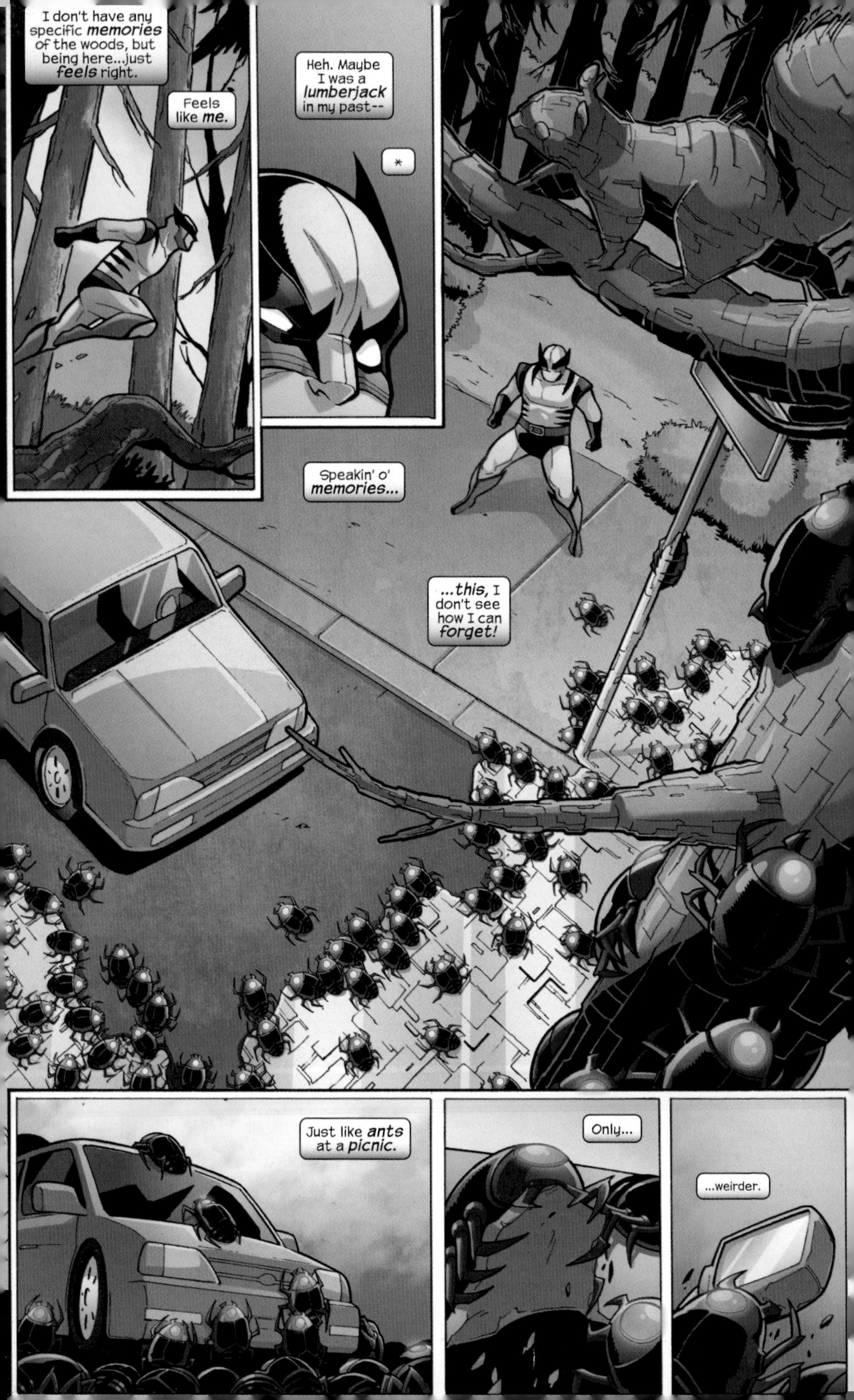
I don't have any specific memories of the woods, but being here...just feels right.
Feels like me.
Heh. Maybe I was a lumberjack in my past--
*
Speakin' o' memories...
...this, I don't see how I can forget!
Just like ants at a picnic.
Only...
...weirder.

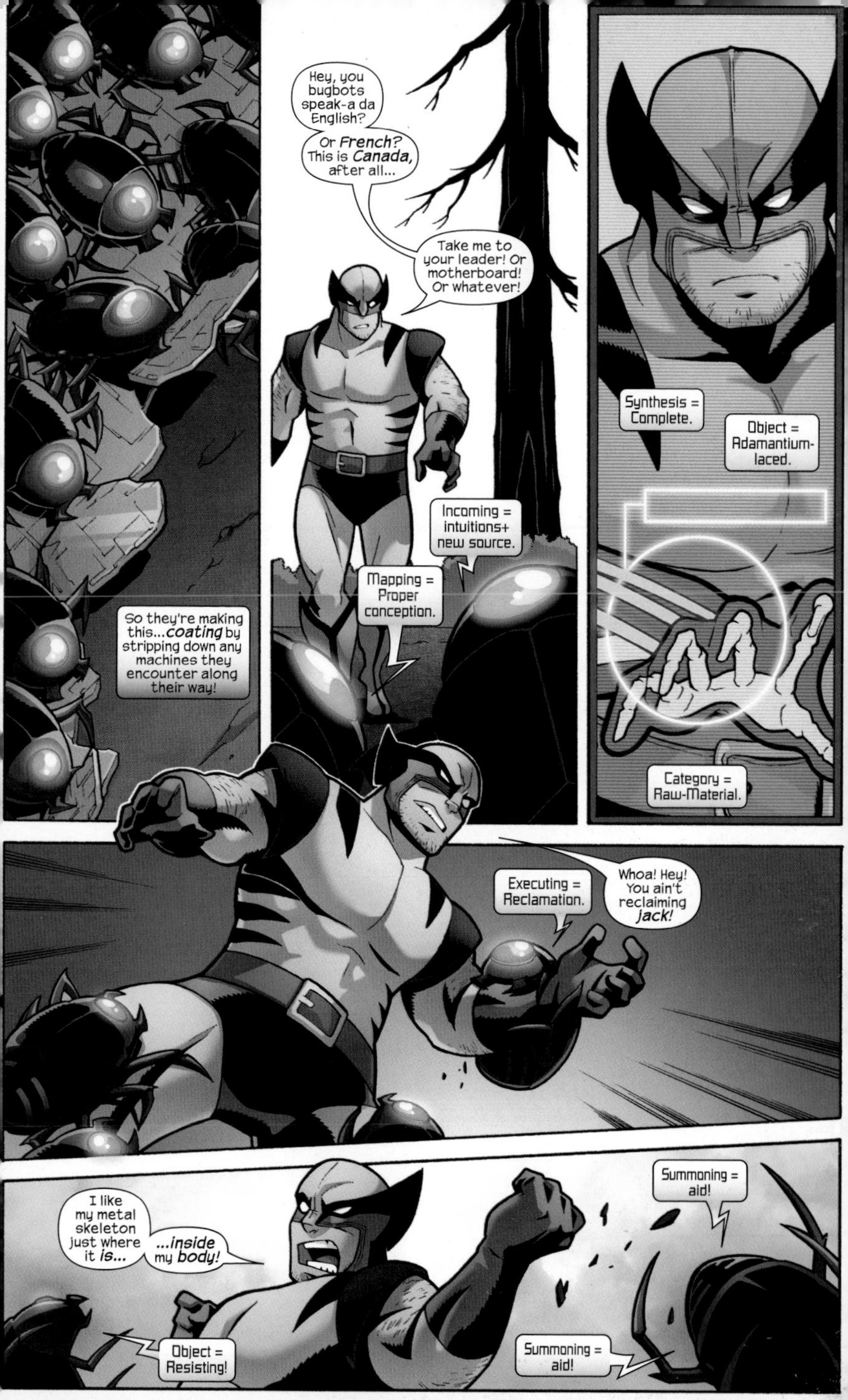

Hey, you bugbots speak-a da English?
Or French? This is Canada, after all...
Take me to your leader! Or motherboard! Or whatever!
Incoming = intuitions+ new source.
Mapping = Proper conception.
So they're making this...coating by stripping down any machines they encounter along their way!
Synthesis = Complete.
Object = Adamantium-laced.
Category = Raw-Material.
Executing = Reclamation.
Whoa! Hey! You ain't reclaiming jack!
I like my metal skeleton just where it is...
...inside my body!
Summoning = aid!
Object = Resisting!
Summoning = aid!

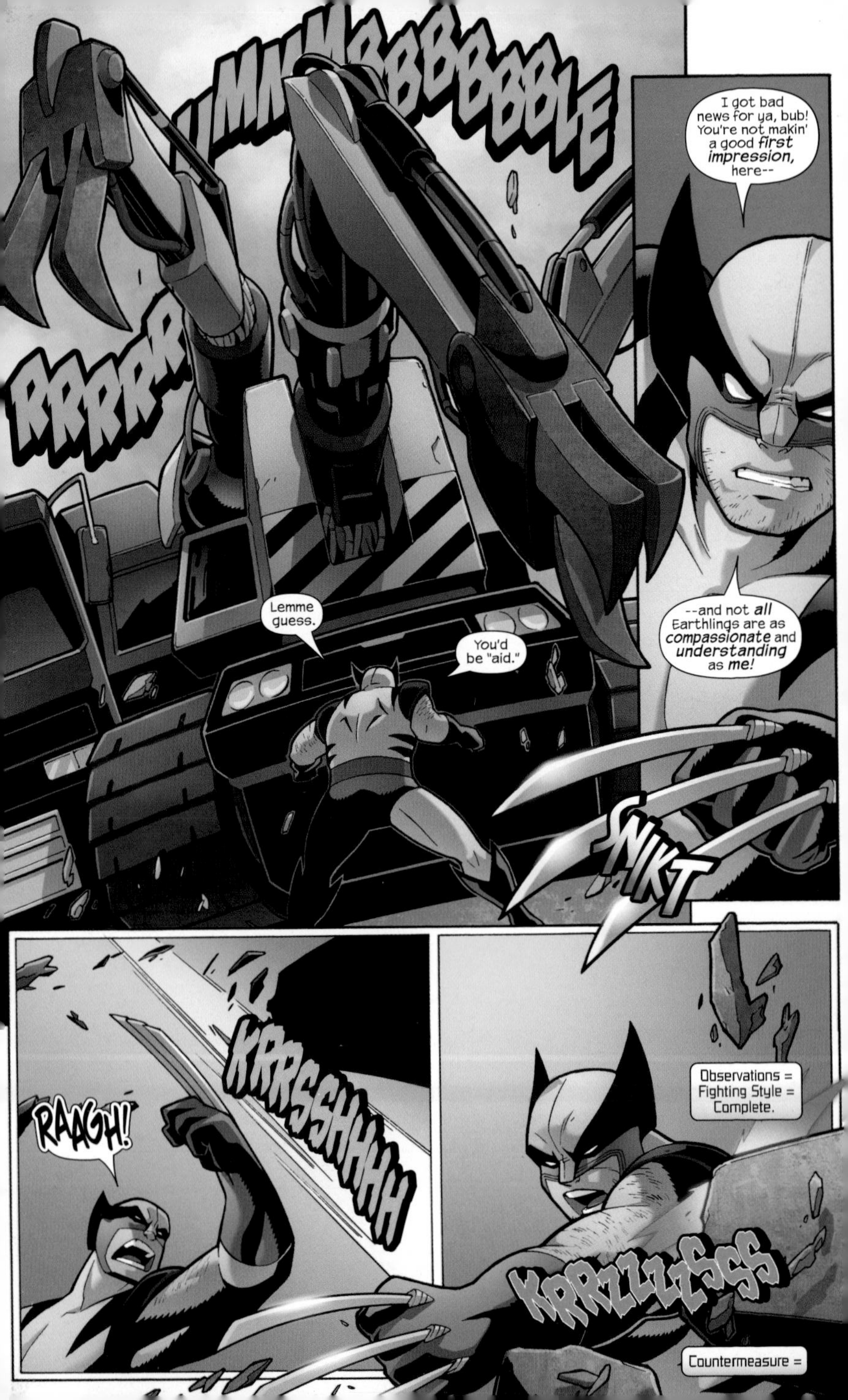
RRRR
BBBBBLE
I got bad news for ya, bub! You're not makin' a good *first impression,* here--
Lemme guess.
You'd be "aid."
--and not *all* Earthlings are as *compassionate* and *understanding* as *me!*
SNIKT
RAAGH!
KRRSSHHHHH
Observations = Fighting Style = Complete.
KRRZZZZSSS
Countermeasure =

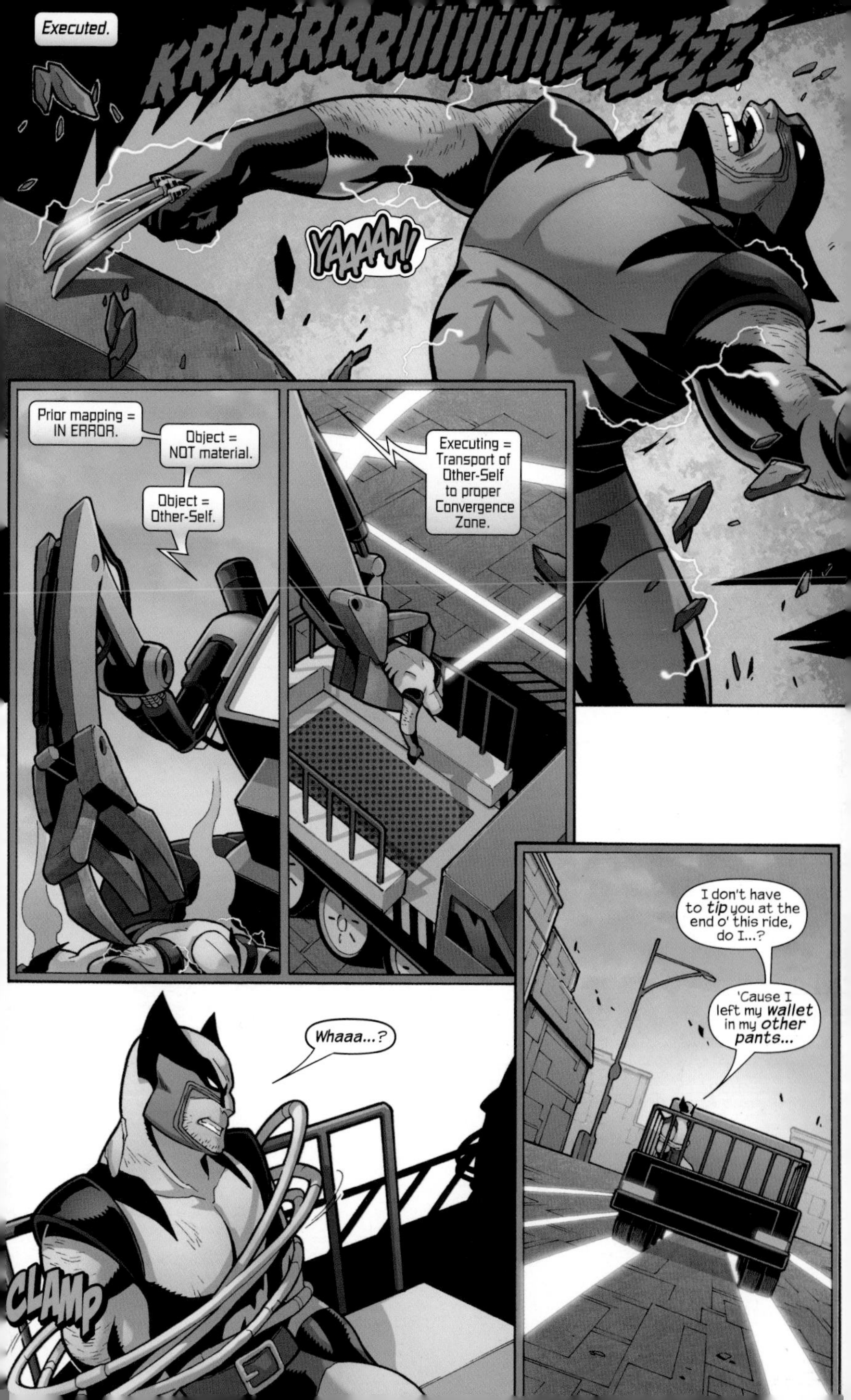
Executed.
KRRRRRRIIIIIIIIIIIZZZZZZ
YAAAAH!
Prior mapping = IN ERROR.
Object = NOT material.
Object = Other-Self.
Executing = Transport of Other-Self to proper Convergence Zone.
Whaaa...?
CLAMP
I don't have to *tip* you at the end o' this ride, do I...?
'Cause I left my *wallet* in my *other pants*...

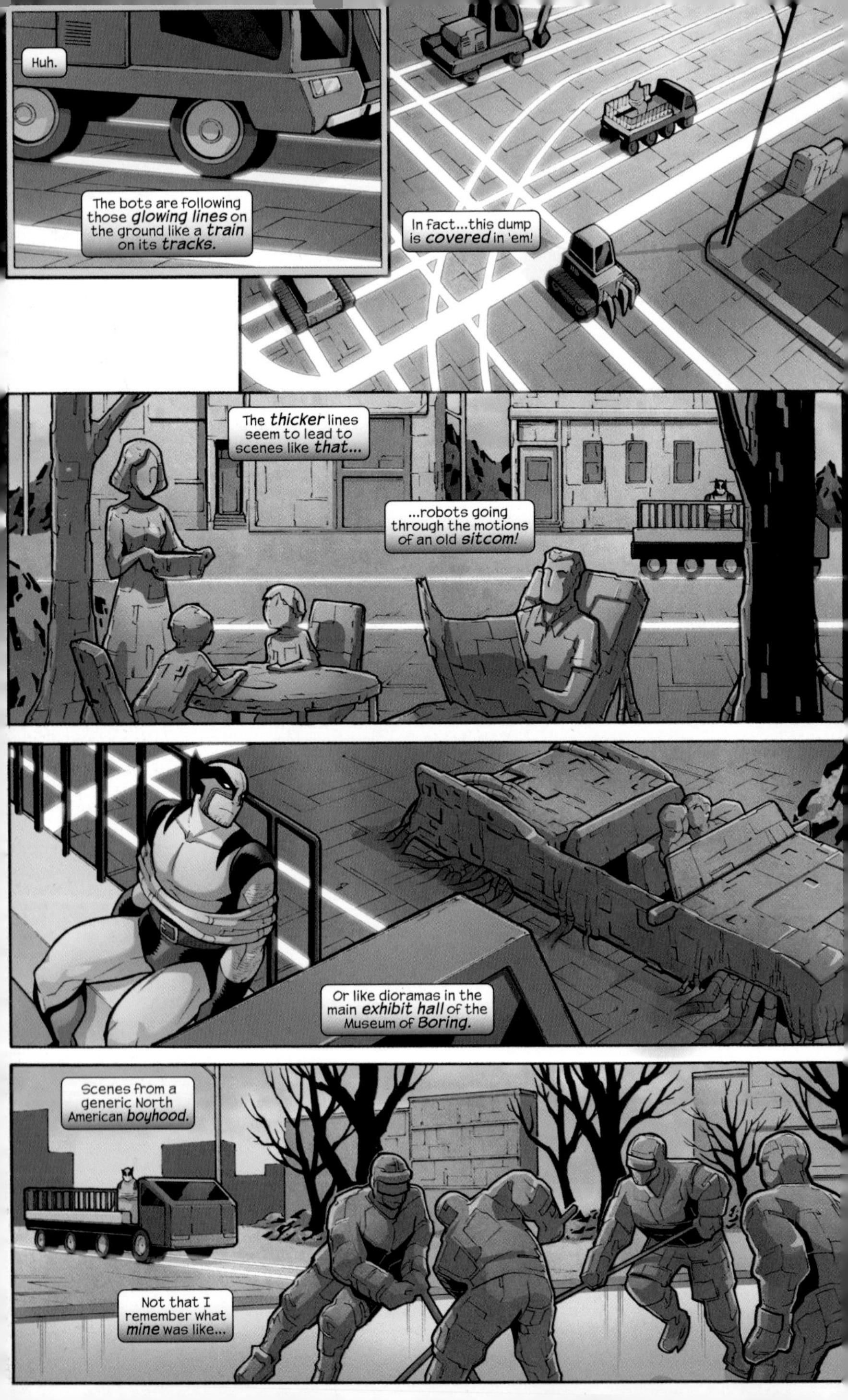
Huh.
The bots are following those glowing lines on the ground like a train on its tracks.
In fact...this dump is covered in 'em!
The thicker lines seem to lead to scenes like that...
...robots going through the motions of an old sitcom!
Or like dioramas in the main exhibit hall of the Museum of Boring.
Scenes from a generic North American boyhood.
Not that I remember what mine was like...

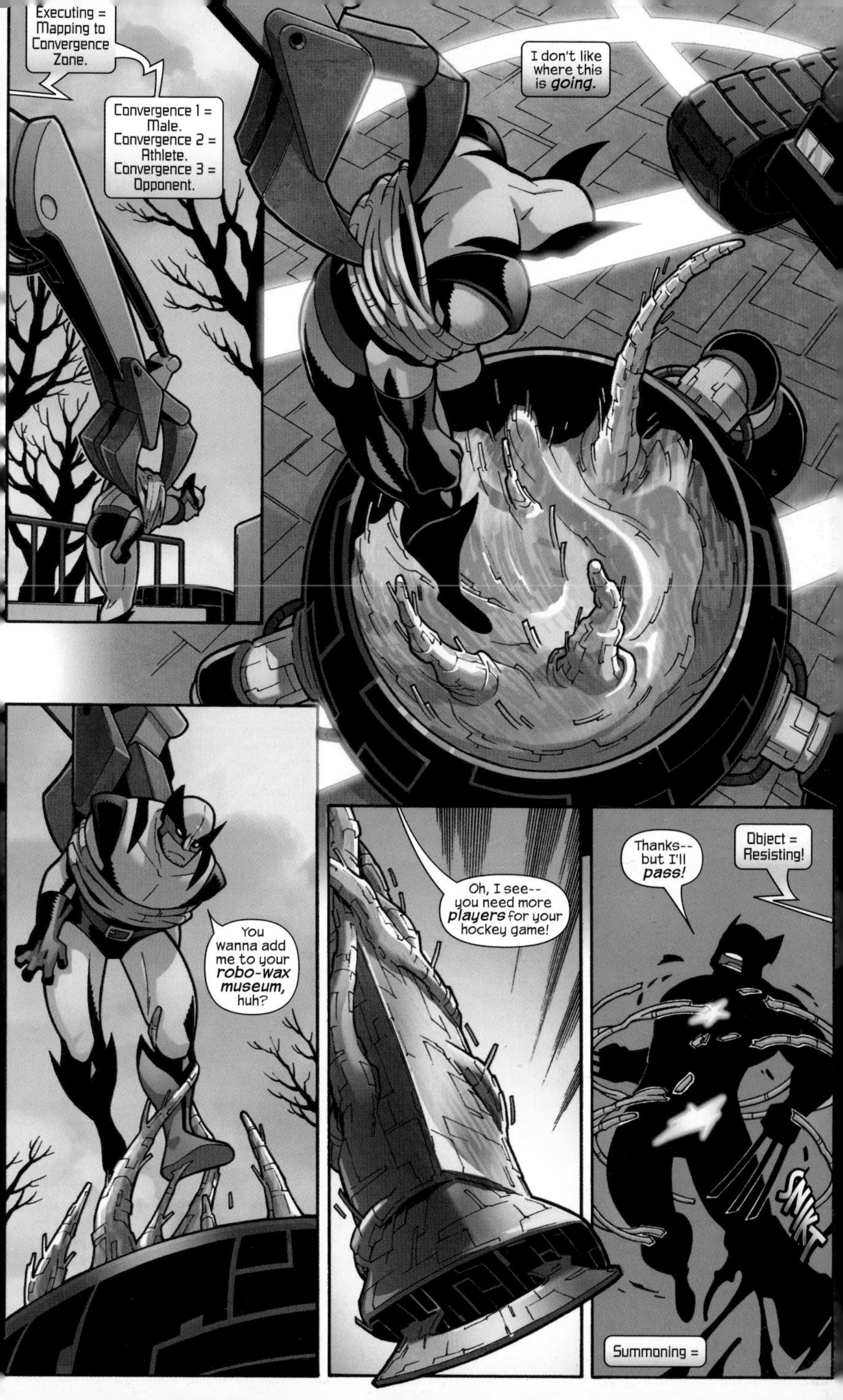
Executing = Mapping to Convergence Zone.
Convergence 1 = Male. Convergence 2 = Athlete. Convergence 3 = Opponent.
I don't like where this is *going.*
You wanna add me to your ***robo-wax museum,*** huh?
Oh, I see-- you need more ***players*** for your hockey game!
Thanks-- but I'll ***pass!***
Object = Resisting!
SNIKT
Summoning =

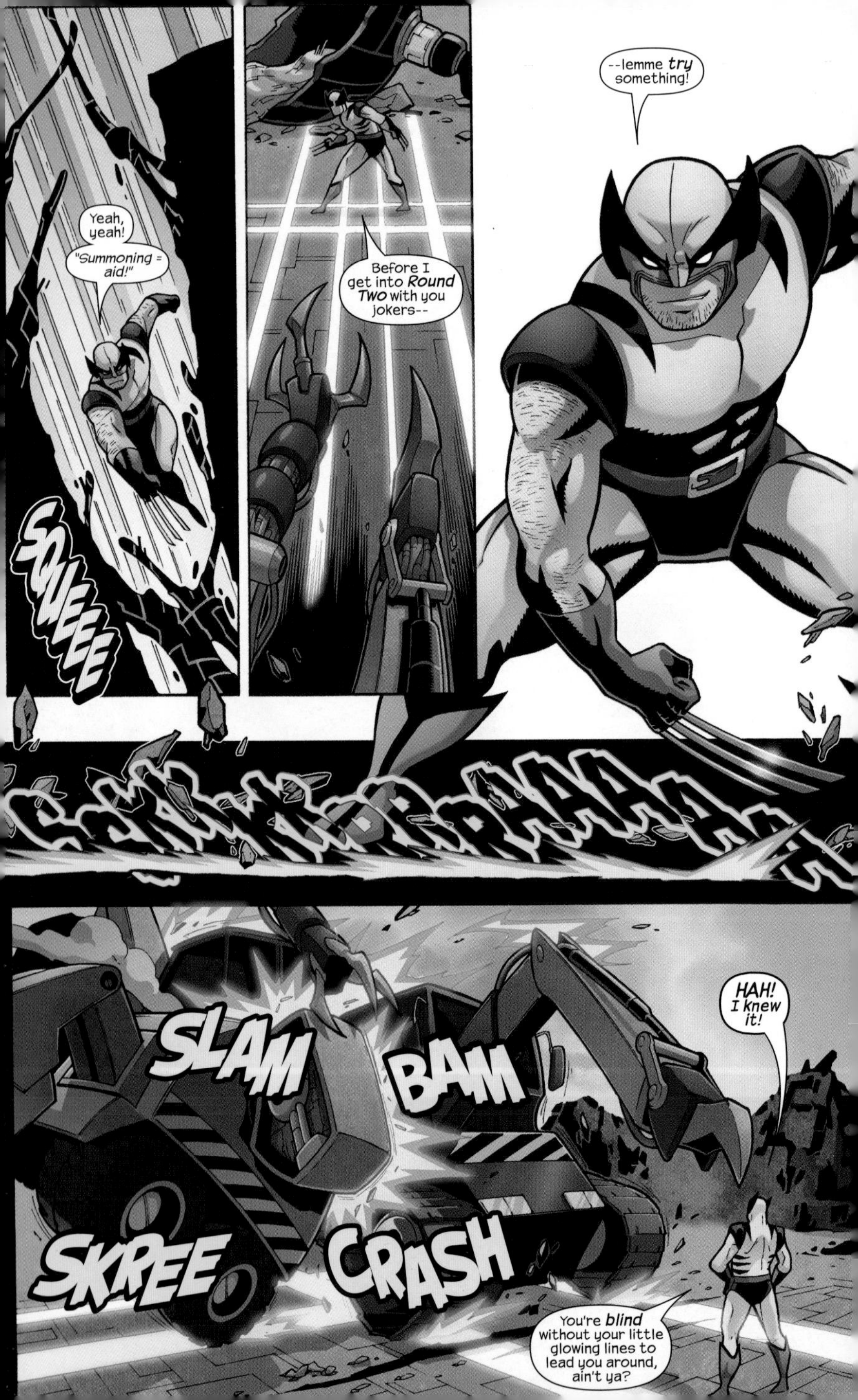
Yeah, yeah!
"Summoning = aid!"
SQUEEEE
Before I get into *Round Two* with you jokers--
--lemme *try* something!
SLAM
BAM
HAH! I knew it!
SKREE
CRASH
You're *blind* without your little glowing lines to lead you around, ain't ya?

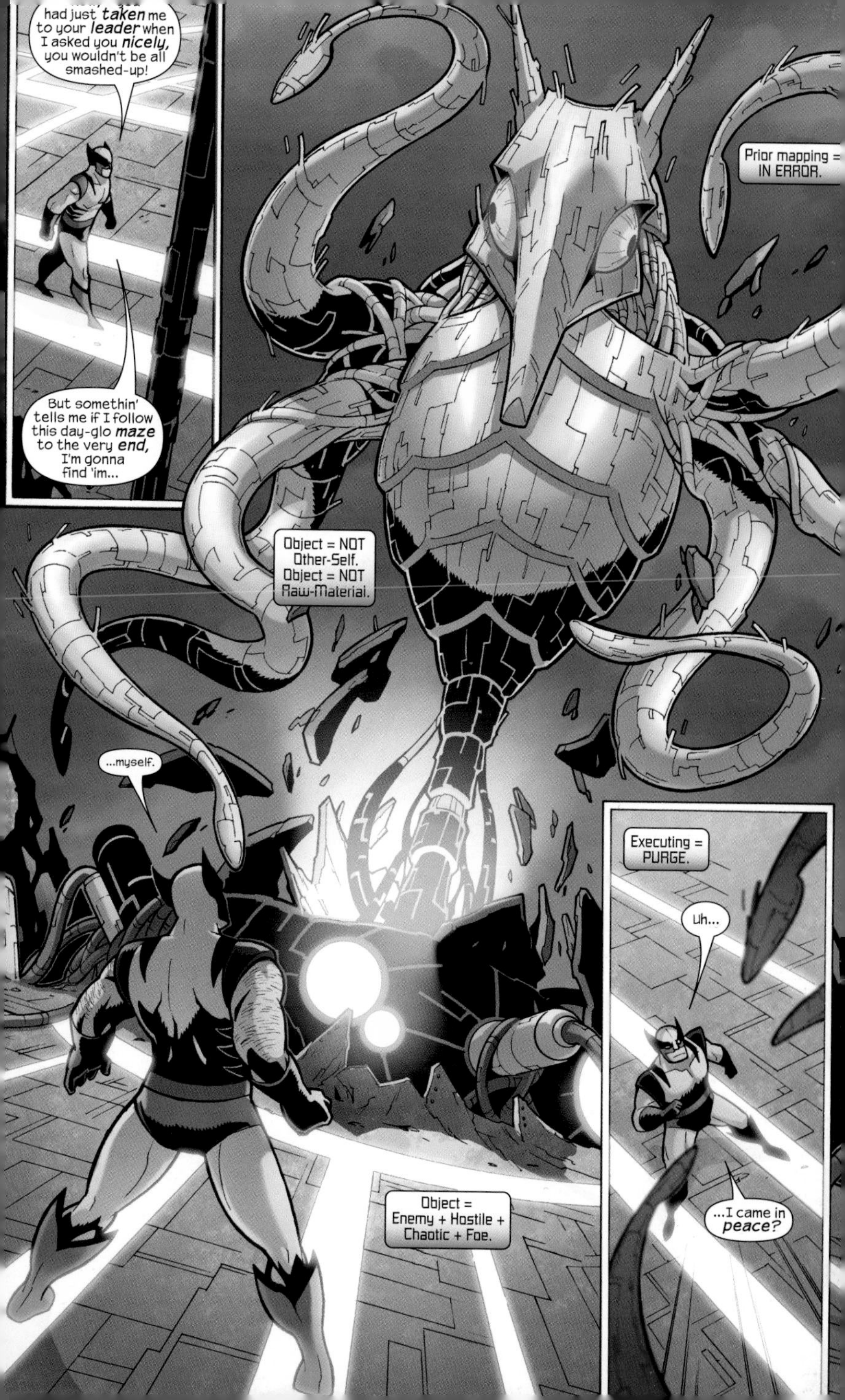

had just taken me to your leader when I asked you nicely, you wouldn't be all smashed-up!
But somethin' tells me if I follow this day-glo maze to the very end, I'm gonna find 'im...
Prior mapping = IN ERROR.
Object = NOT Other-Self. Object = NOT Raw-Material.
...myself.
Object = Enemy + Hostile + Chaotic + Foe.
Executing = PURGE.
uh...
...I came in peace?

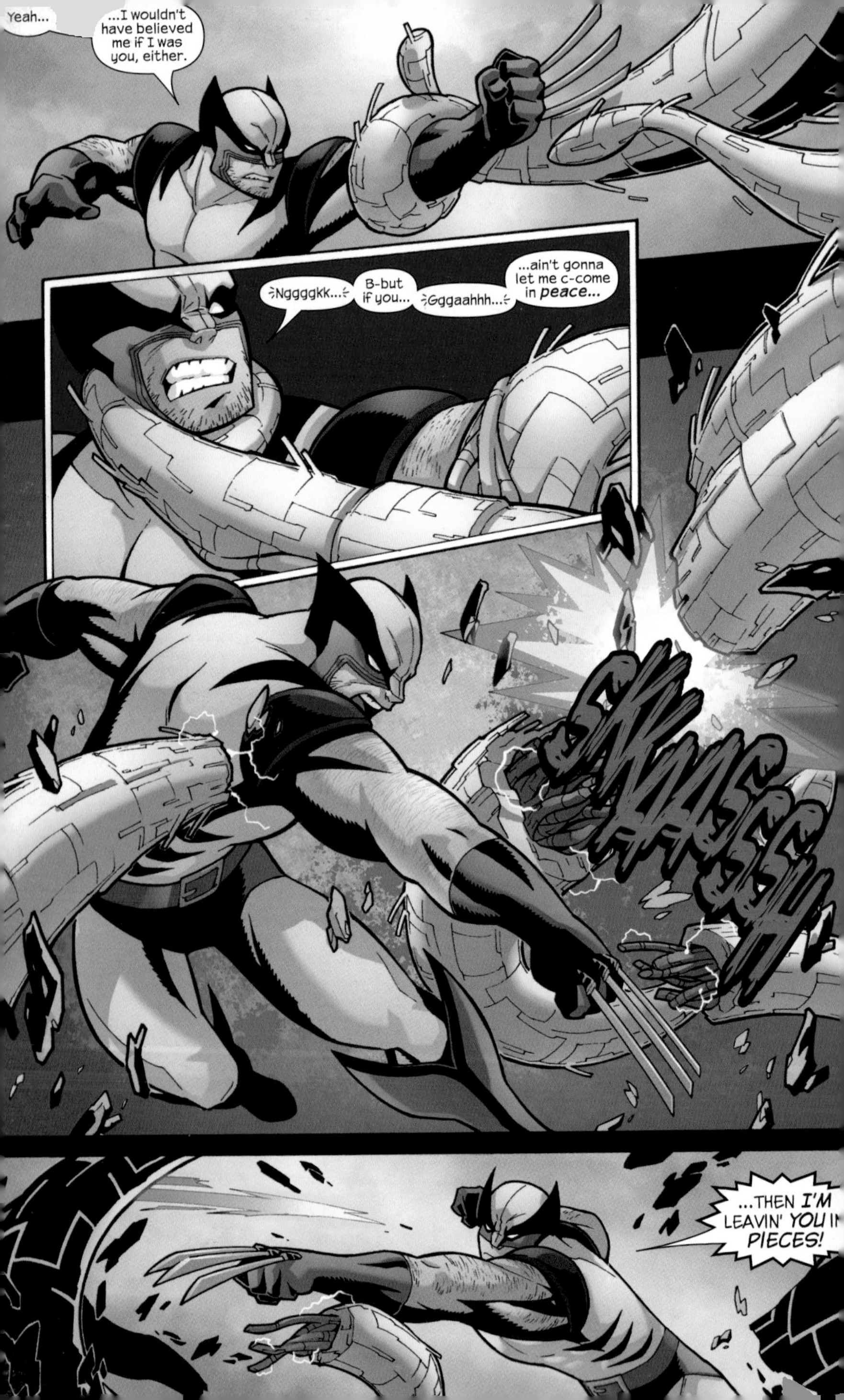
Yeah...
...I wouldn't have believed me if I was you, either.
Ngggkk...
B-but if you...
Gggaahhh...
...ain't gonna let me c-come in *peace*...
SKRASSSH
...THEN *I'M* LEAVIN' *YOU* IN *PIECES!*

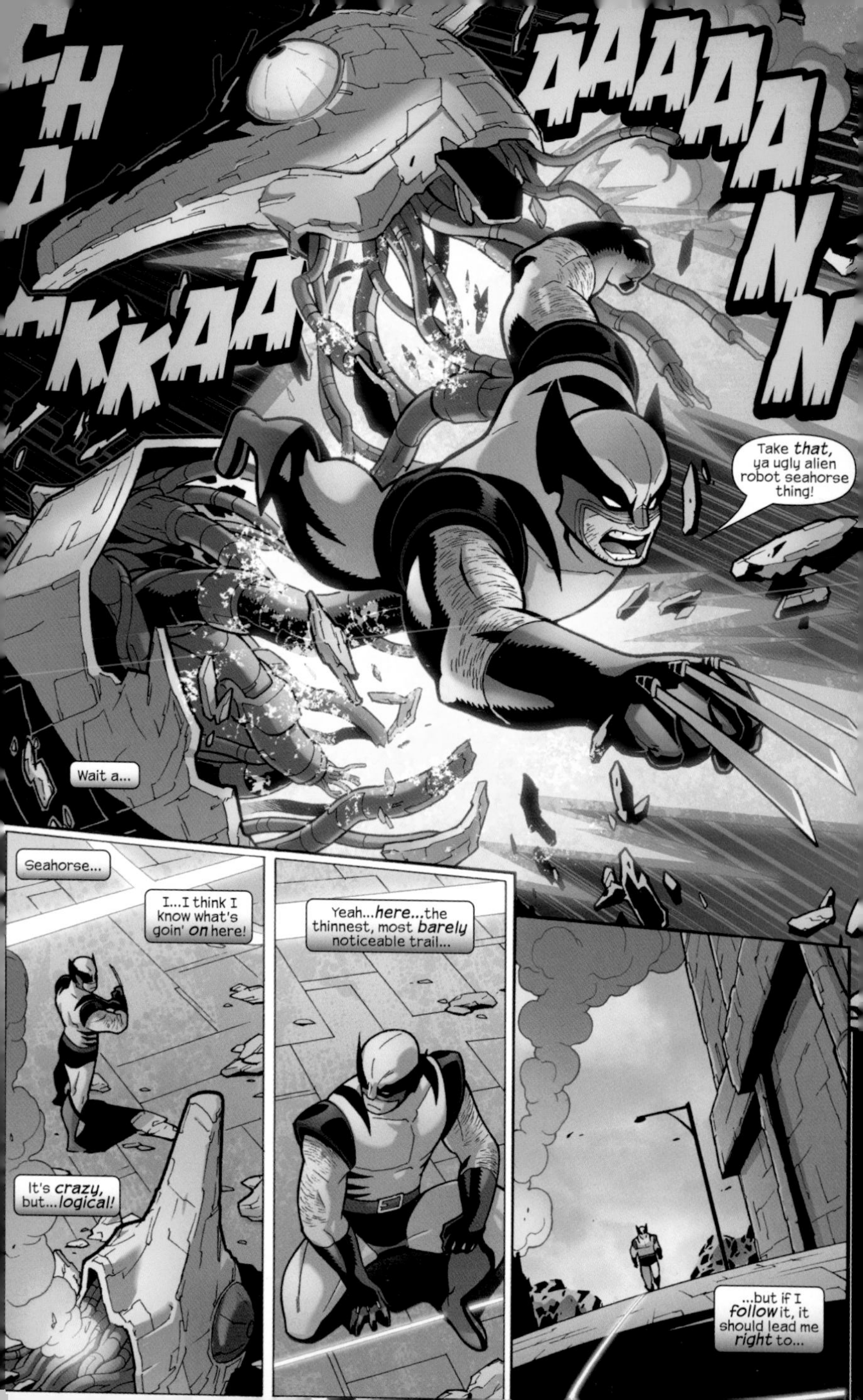

CHAKKAAAAAAAA-N-N
Take that, ya ugly alien robot seahorse thing!
Wait a...
Seahorse...
I...I think I know what's goin' on here!
It's crazy, but...logical!
Yeah...here...the thinnest, most barely noticeable trail...
...but if I follow it, it should lead me right to...

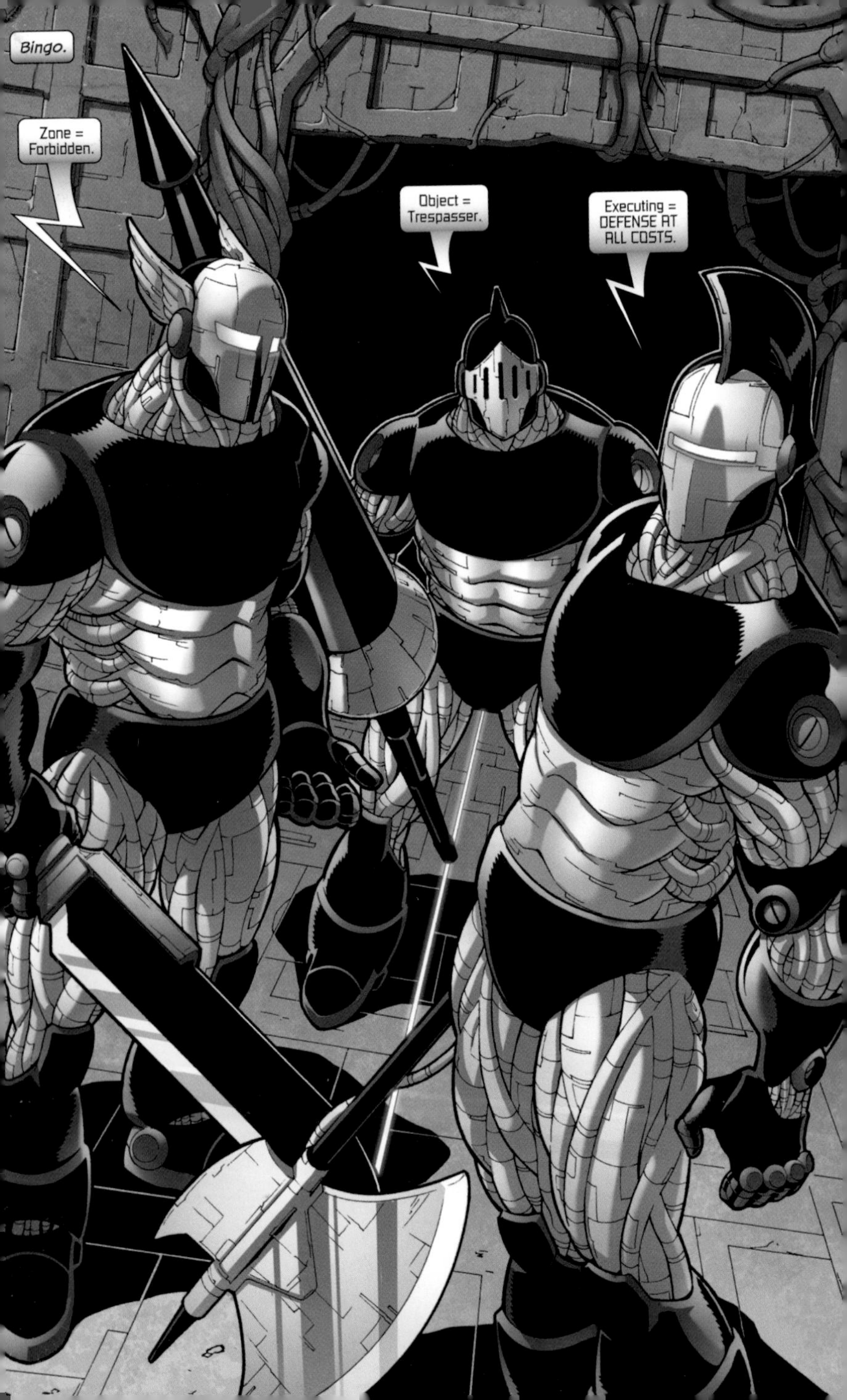

Bingo.
Zone = Forbidden.
Object = Trespasser.
Executing = DEFENSE AT ALL COSTS.

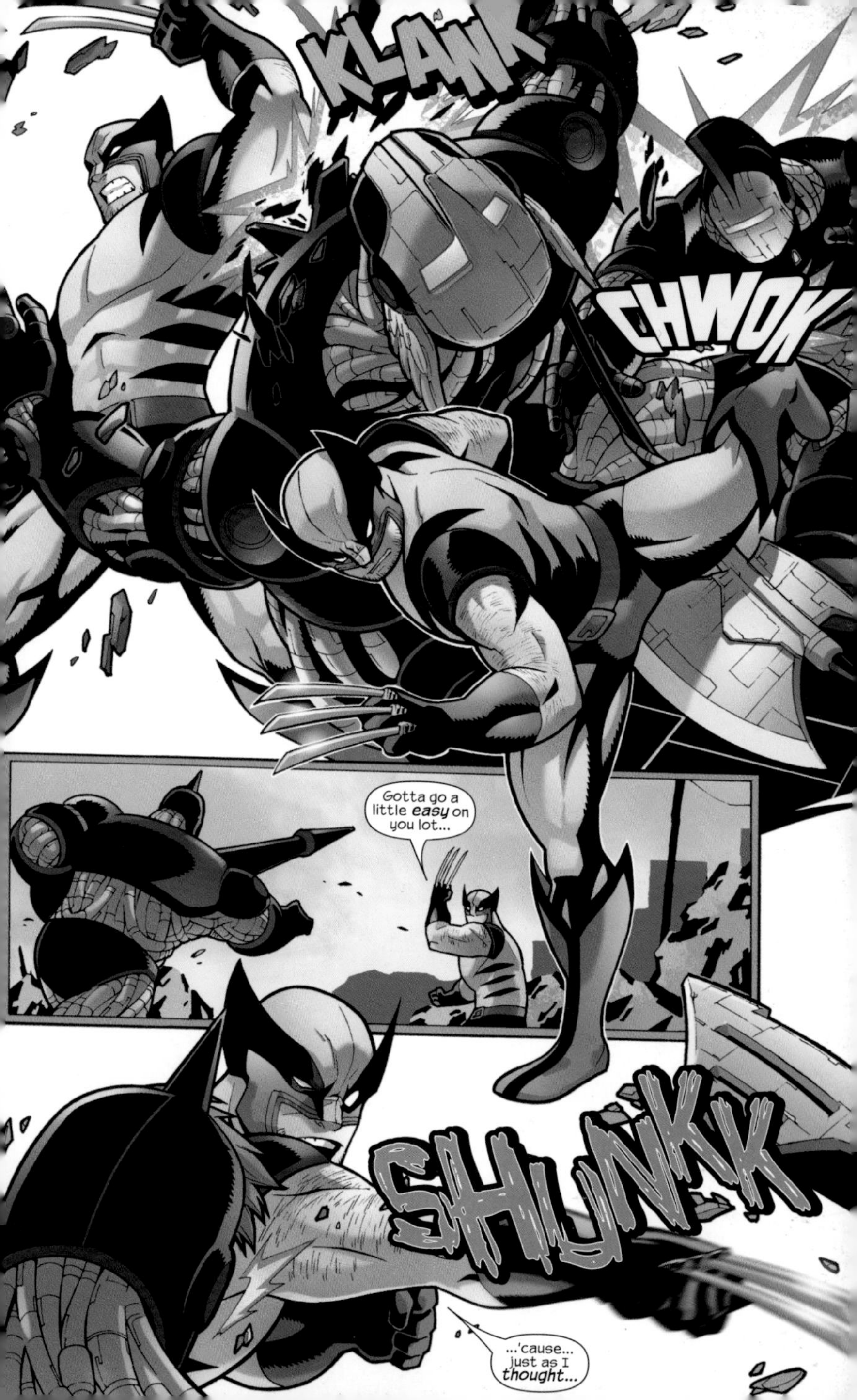
KLANK
CHWOK
Gotta go a little *easy* on you lot...
SHUNKK
...'cause... just as I *thought*...

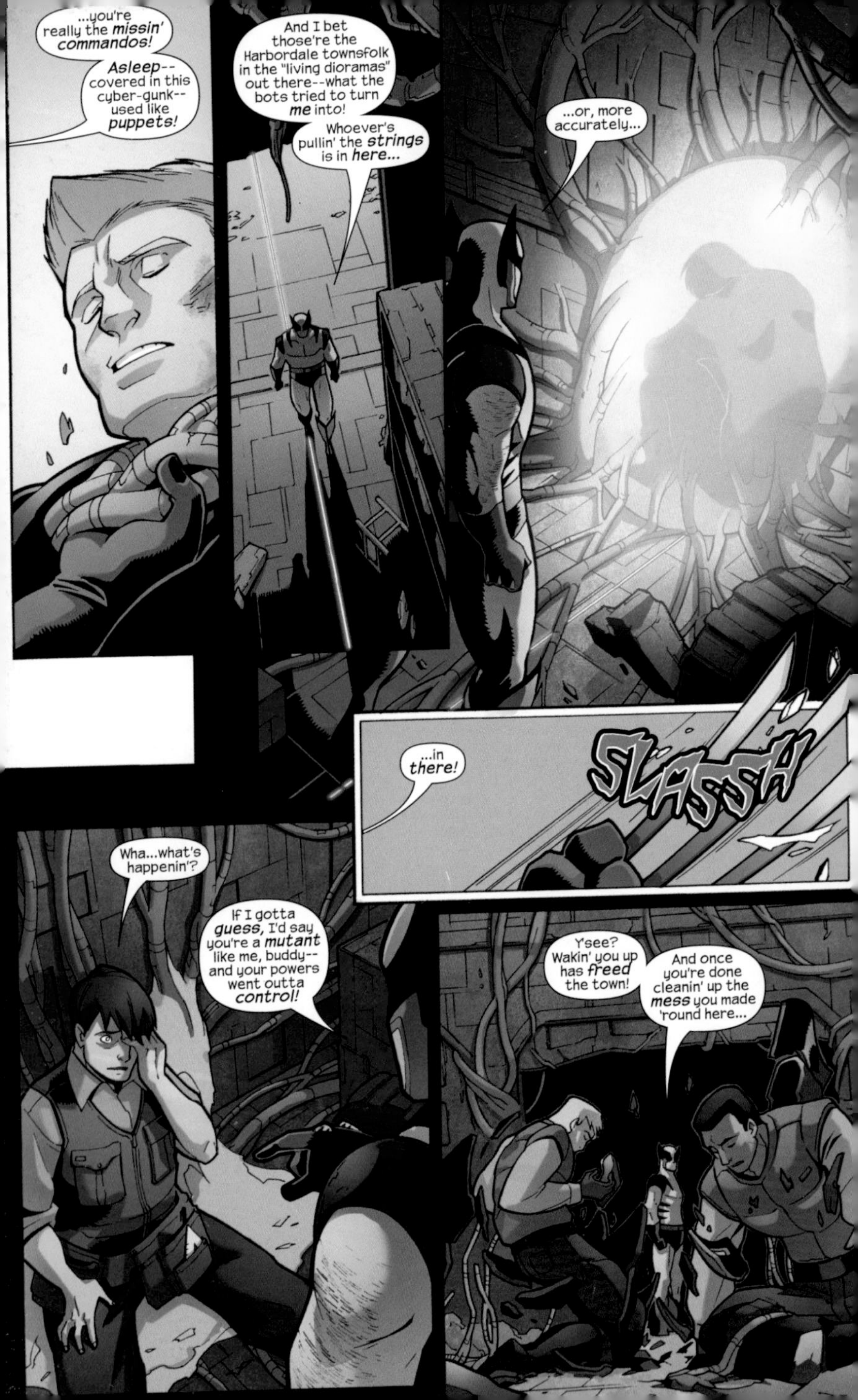
...you're really the missin' commandos!
Asleep--covered in this cyber-gunk--used like puppets!
And I bet those're the Harbordale townsfolk in the "living dioramas" out there--what the bots tried to turn me into!
Whoever's pullin' the strings is in here...
...or, more accurately...
...in there!
SLASSH
Wha...what's happenin'?
If I gotta guess, I'd say you're a mutant like me, buddy--and your powers went outta control!
Y'see? Wakin' you up has freed the town!
And once you're done cleanin' up the mess you made 'round here...

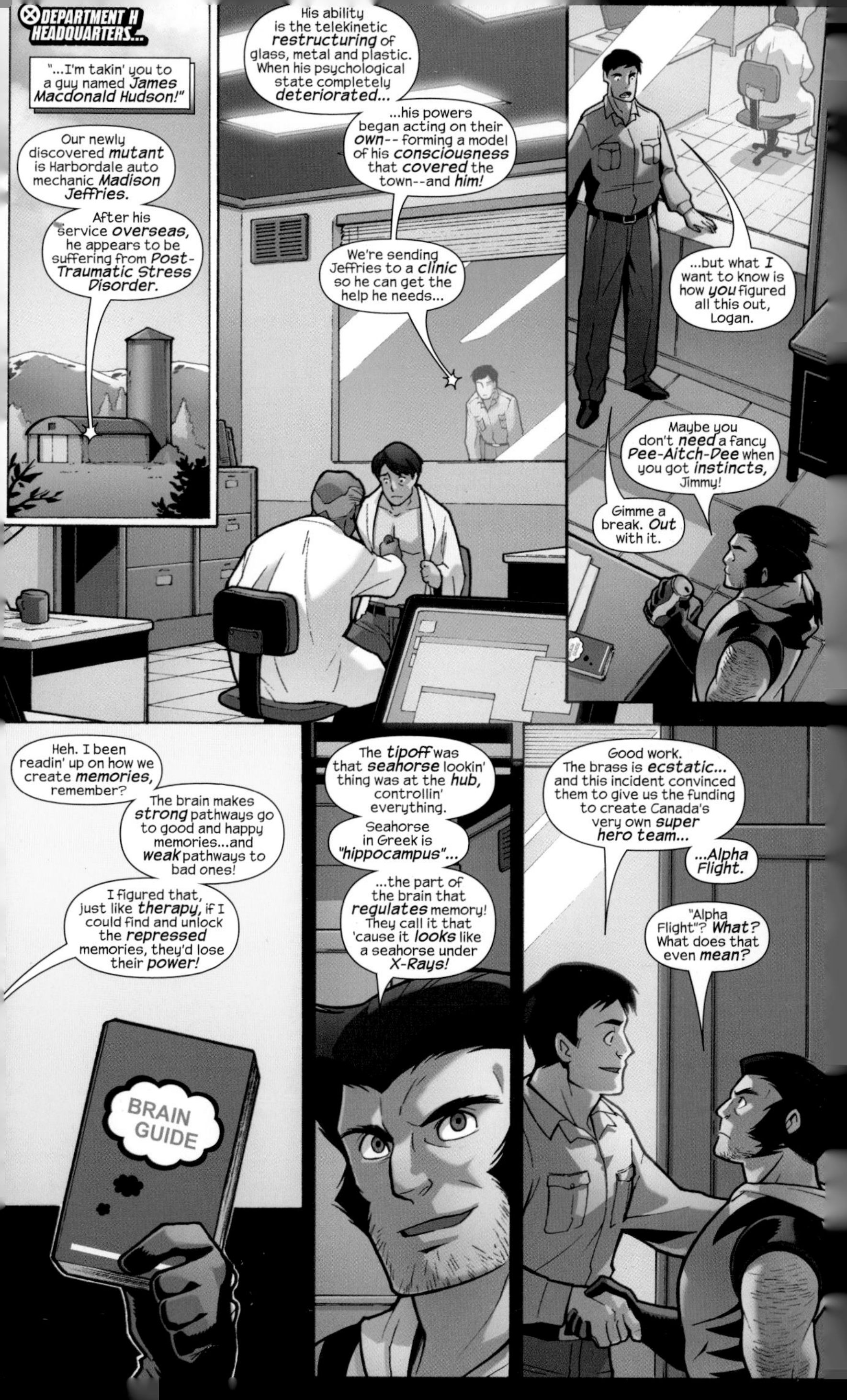
DEPARTMENT H HEADQUARTERS...
"...I'm takin' you to a guy named James Macdonald Hudson!"
Our newly discovered mutant is Harbordale auto mechanic Madison Jeffries.
After his service overseas, he appears to be suffering from Post-Traumatic Stress Disorder.
His ability is the telekinetic restructuring of glass, metal and plastic. When his psychological state completely deteriorated...
...his powers began acting on their own-- forming a model of his consciousness that covered the town--and him!
We're sending Jeffries to a clinic so he can get the help he needs...
...but what I want to know is how you figured all this out, Logan.
Maybe you don't need a fancy Pee-Aitch-Dee when you got instincts, Jimmy!
Gimme a break. Out with it.
Heh. I been readin' up on how we create memories, remember?
The brain makes strong pathways go to good and happy memories...and weak pathways to bad ones!
I figured that, just like therapy, if I could find and unlock the repressed memories, they'd lose their power!
BRAIN GUIDE
The tipoff was that seahorse lookin' thing was at the hub, controllin' everything.
Seahorse in Greek is "hippocampus"...
...the part of the brain that regulates memory! They call it that 'cause it looks like a seahorse under X-Rays!
Good work. The brass is ecstatic... and this incident convinced them to give us the funding to create Canada's very own super hero team...
...Alpha Flight.
"Alpha Flight"? What? What does that even mean?

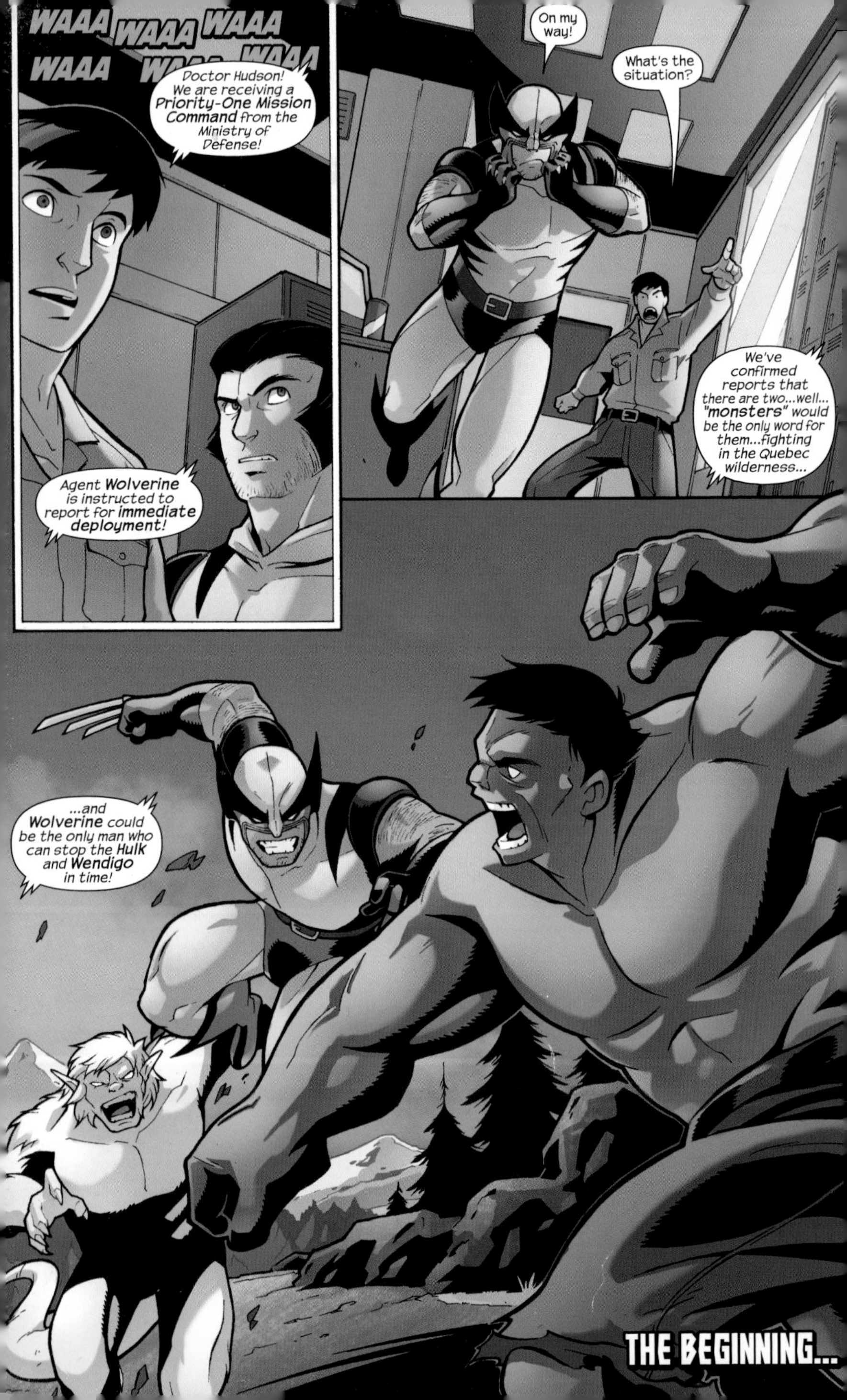
WAAA WAAA WAAA
WAAA
Doctor Hudson! We are receiving a Priority-One Mission Command from the Ministry of Defense!
Agent Wolverine is instructed to report for immediate deployment!
On my way!
What's the situation?
We've confirmed reports that there are two...well... "monsters" would be the only word for them...fighting in the Quebec wilderness...
...and Wolverine could be the only man who can stop the Hulk and Wendigo in time!
THE BEGINNING...

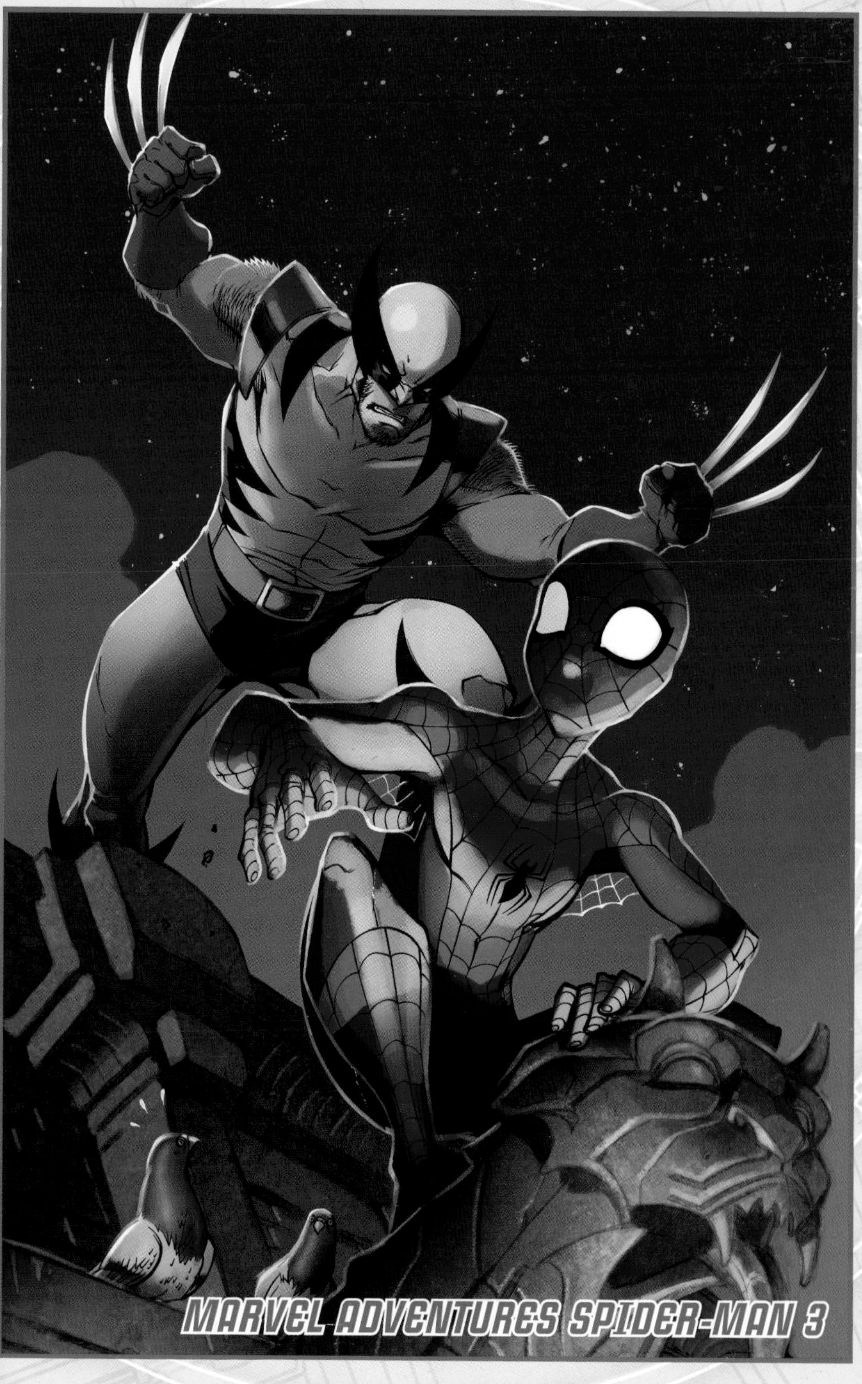
MARVEL ADVENTURES SPIDER-MAN 3

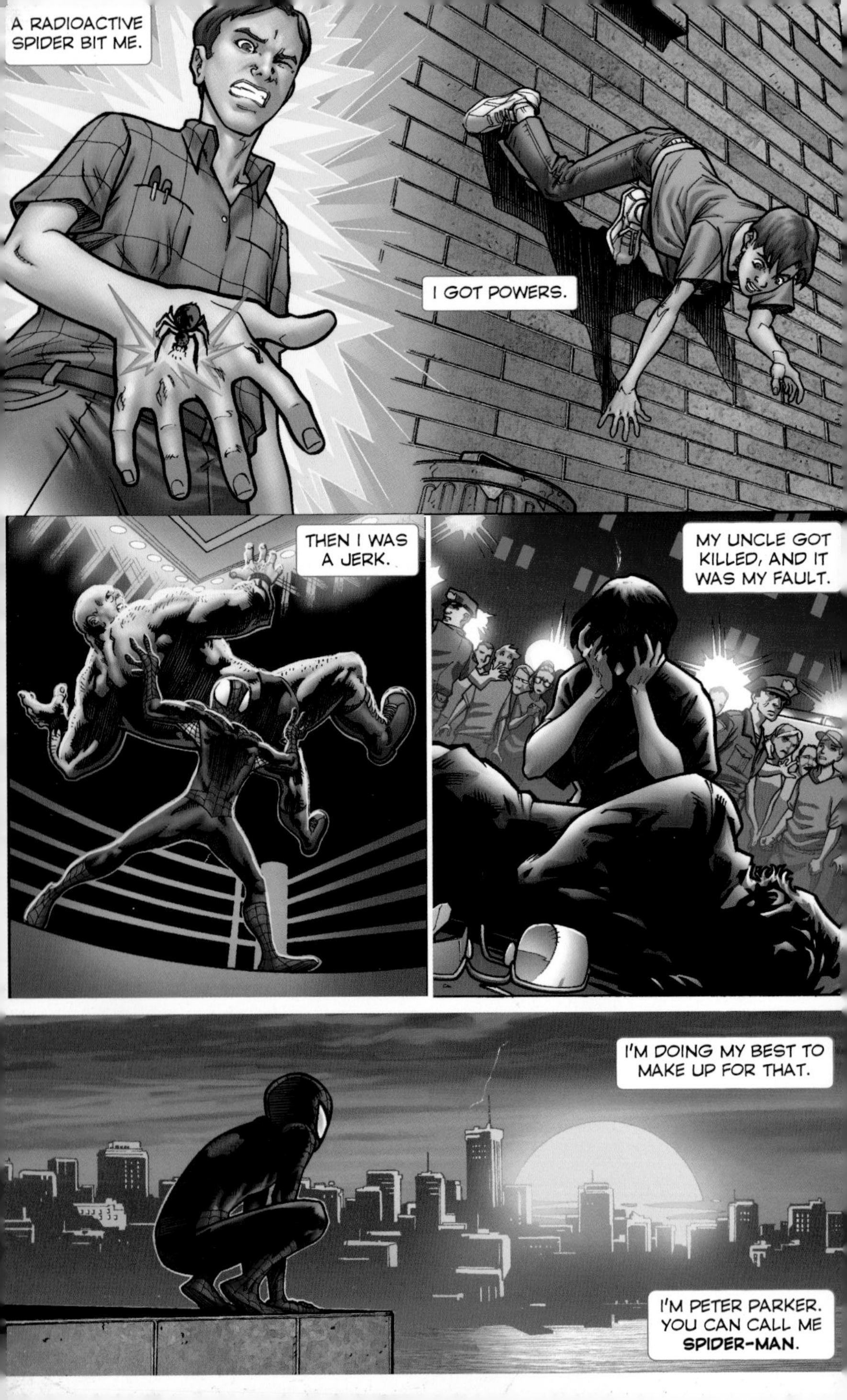
A RADIOACTIVE SPIDER BIT ME.
I GOT POWERS.
THEN I WAS A JERK.
MY UNCLE GOT KILLED, AND IT WAS MY FAULT.
I'M DOING MY BEST TO MAKE UP FOR THAT.
I'M PETER PARKER. YOU CAN CALL ME **SPIDER-MAN**.

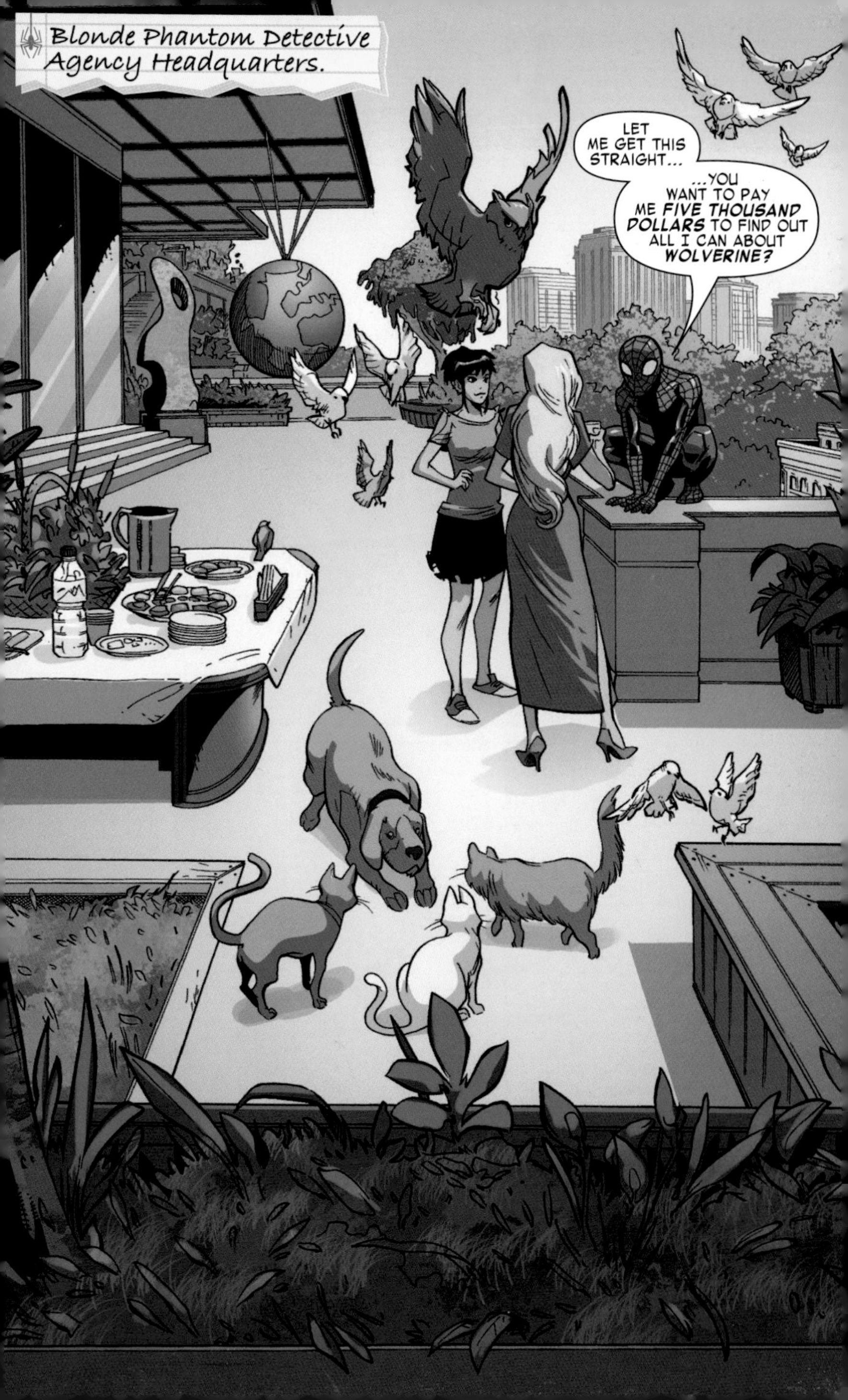
Blonde Phantom Detective Agency Headquarters.
LET ME GET THIS STRAIGHT...
...YOU WANT TO PAY ME FIVE THOUSAND DOLLARS TO FIND OUT ALL I CAN ABOUT WOLVERINE?

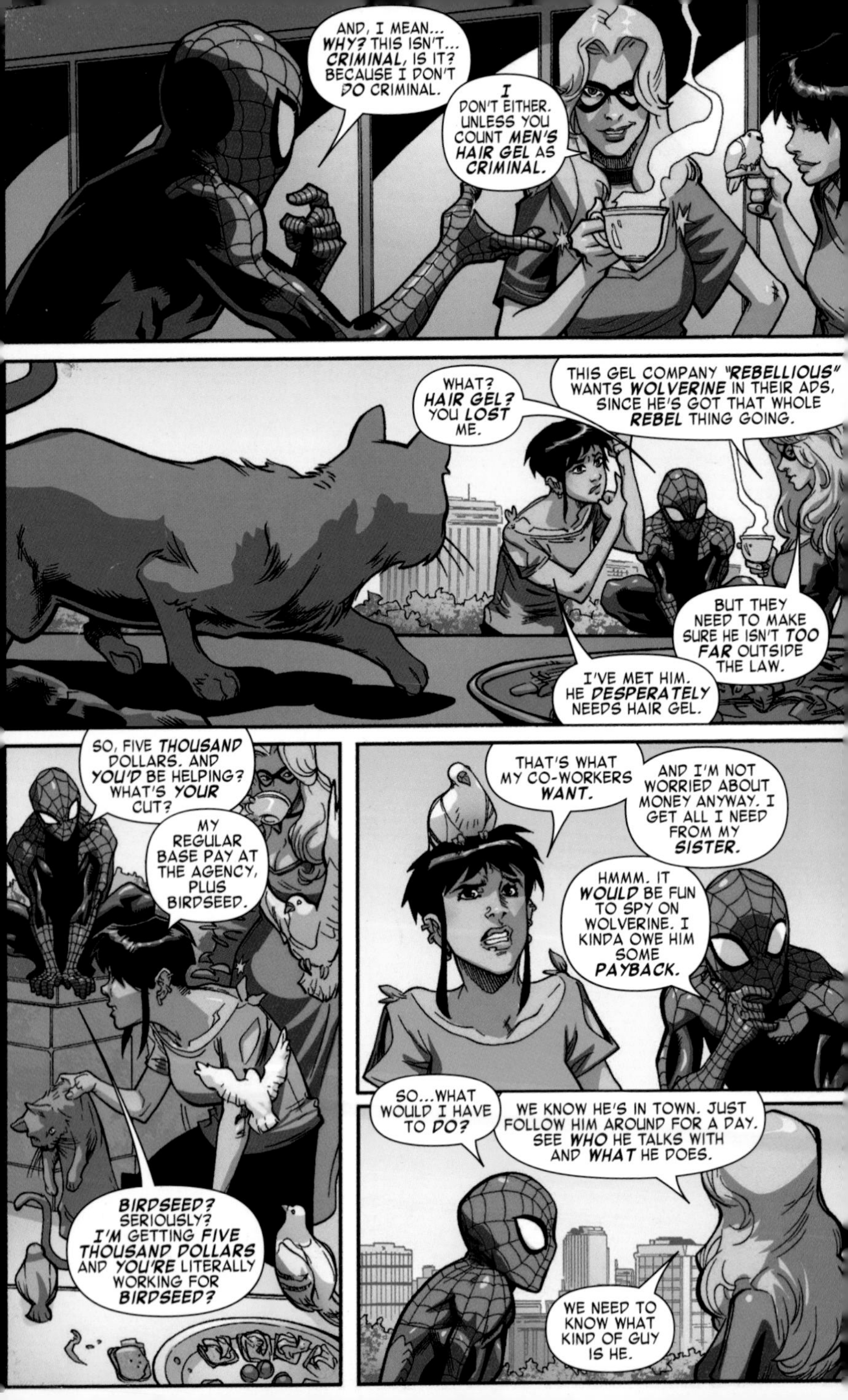
AND, I MEAN... WHY? THIS ISN'T... CRIMINAL, IS IT? BECAUSE I DON'T DO CRIMINAL.
I DON'T EITHER. UNLESS YOU COUNT MEN'S HAIR GEL AS CRIMINAL.
WHAT? HAIR GEL? YOU LOST ME.
THIS GEL COMPANY "REBELLIOUS" WANTS WOLVERINE IN THEIR ADS, SINCE HE'S GOT THAT WHOLE REBEL THING GOING.
BUT THEY NEED TO MAKE SURE HE ISN'T TOO FAR OUTSIDE THE LAW.
I'VE MET HIM. HE DESPERATELY NEEDS HAIR GEL.
SO, FIVE THOUSAND DOLLARS. AND YOU'D BE HELPING? WHAT'S YOUR CUT?
MY REGULAR BASE PAY AT THE AGENCY, PLUS BIRDSEED.
BIRDSEED? SERIOUSLY? I'M GETTING FIVE THOUSAND DOLLARS AND YOU'RE LITERALLY WORKING FOR BIRDSEED?
THAT'S WHAT MY CO-WORKERS WANT.
AND I'M NOT WORRIED ABOUT MONEY ANYWAY. I GET ALL I NEED FROM MY SISTER.
HMMM. IT WOULD BE FUN TO SPY ON WOLVERINE. I KINDA OWE HIM SOME PAYBACK.
SO...WHAT WOULD I HAVE TO DO?
WE KNOW HE'S IN TOWN. JUST FOLLOW HIM AROUND FOR A DAY. SEE WHO HE TALKS WITH AND WHAT HE DOES.
WE NEED TO KNOW WHAT KIND OF GUY IS HE.

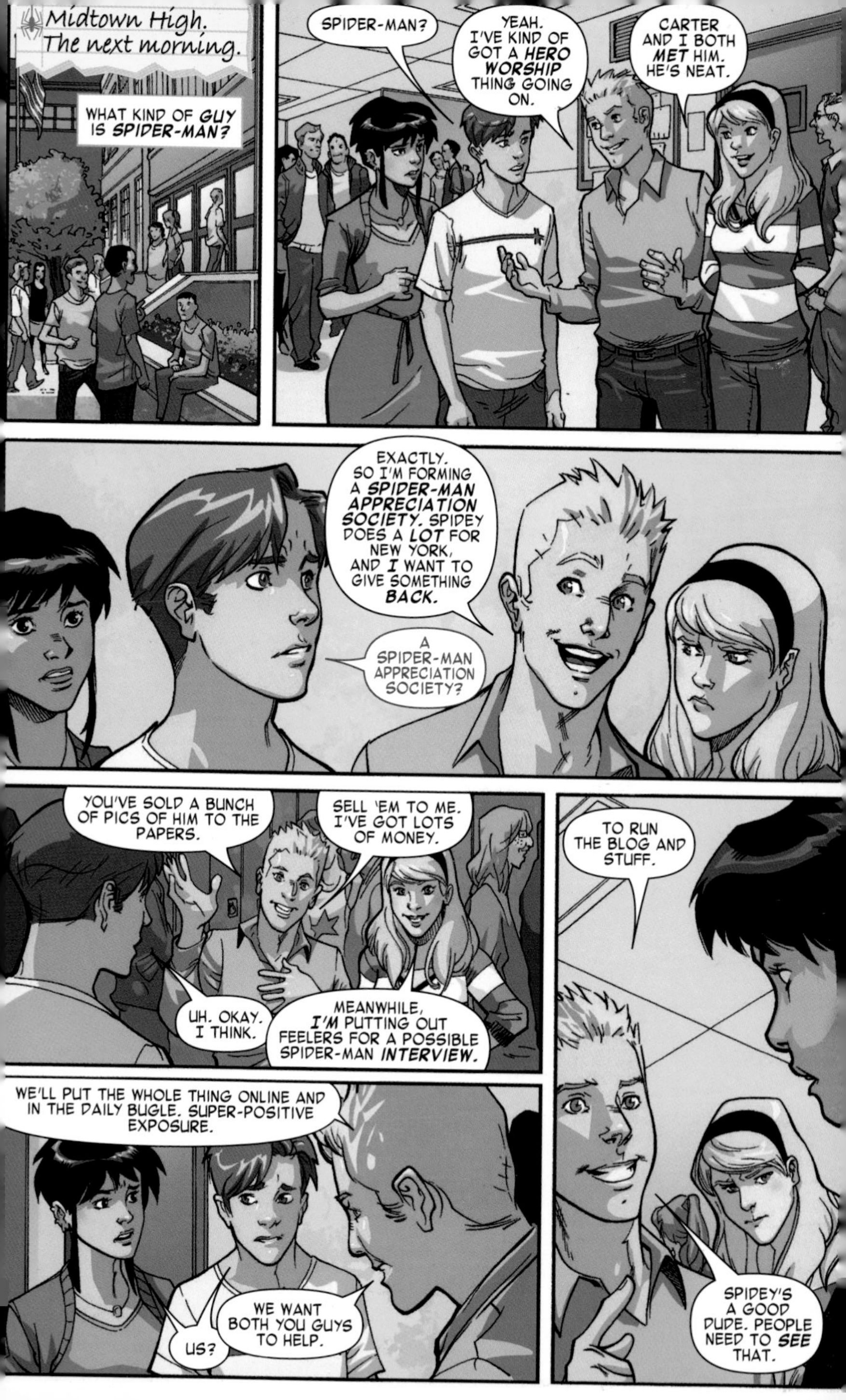
Midtown High. The next morning.
WHAT KIND OF GUY IS SPIDER-MAN?
SPIDER-MAN?
YEAH. I'VE KIND OF GOT A HERO WORSHIP THING GOING ON.
CARTER AND I BOTH MET HIM. HE'S NEAT.
EXACTLY. SO I'M FORMING A SPIDER-MAN APPRECIATION SOCIETY. SPIDEY DOES A LOT FOR NEW YORK, AND I WANT TO GIVE SOMETHING BACK.
A SPIDER-MAN APPRECIATION SOCIETY?
YOU'VE SOLD A BUNCH OF PICS OF HIM TO THE PAPERS.
SELL 'EM TO ME. I'VE GOT LOTS OF MONEY.
UH. OKAY. I THINK.
MEANWHILE, I'M PUTTING OUT FEELERS FOR A POSSIBLE SPIDER-MAN INTERVIEW.
WE'LL PUT THE WHOLE THING ONLINE AND IN THE DAILY BUGLE. SUPER-POSITIVE EXPOSURE.
WE WANT BOTH YOU GUYS TO HELP.
US?
TO RUN THE BLOG AND STUFF.
SPIDEY'S A GOOD DUDE. PEOPLE NEED TO SEE THAT.

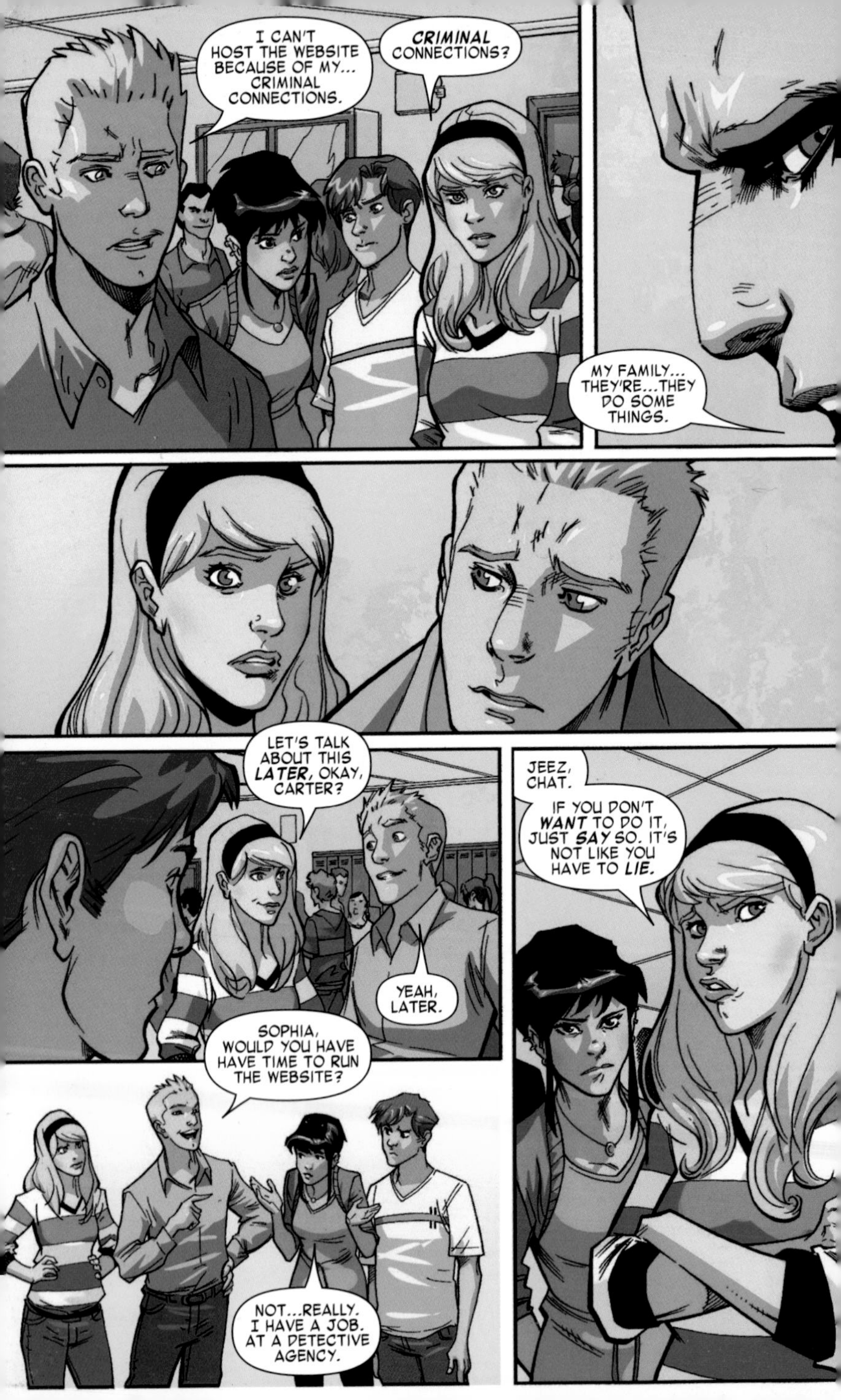
I CAN'T HOST THE WEBSITE BECAUSE OF MY... CRIMINAL CONNECTIONS.
CRIMINAL CONNECTIONS?
MY FAMILY... THEY'RE...THEY DO SOME THINGS.
LET'S TALK ABOUT THIS LATER, OKAY, CARTER?
YEAH, LATER.
SOPHIA, WOULD YOU HAVE HAVE TIME TO RUN THE WEBSITE?
NOT...REALLY. I HAVE A JOB. AT A DETECTIVE AGENCY.
JEEZ, CHAT.
IF YOU DON'T WANT TO DO IT, JUST SAY SO. IT'S NOT LIKE YOU HAVE TO LIE.

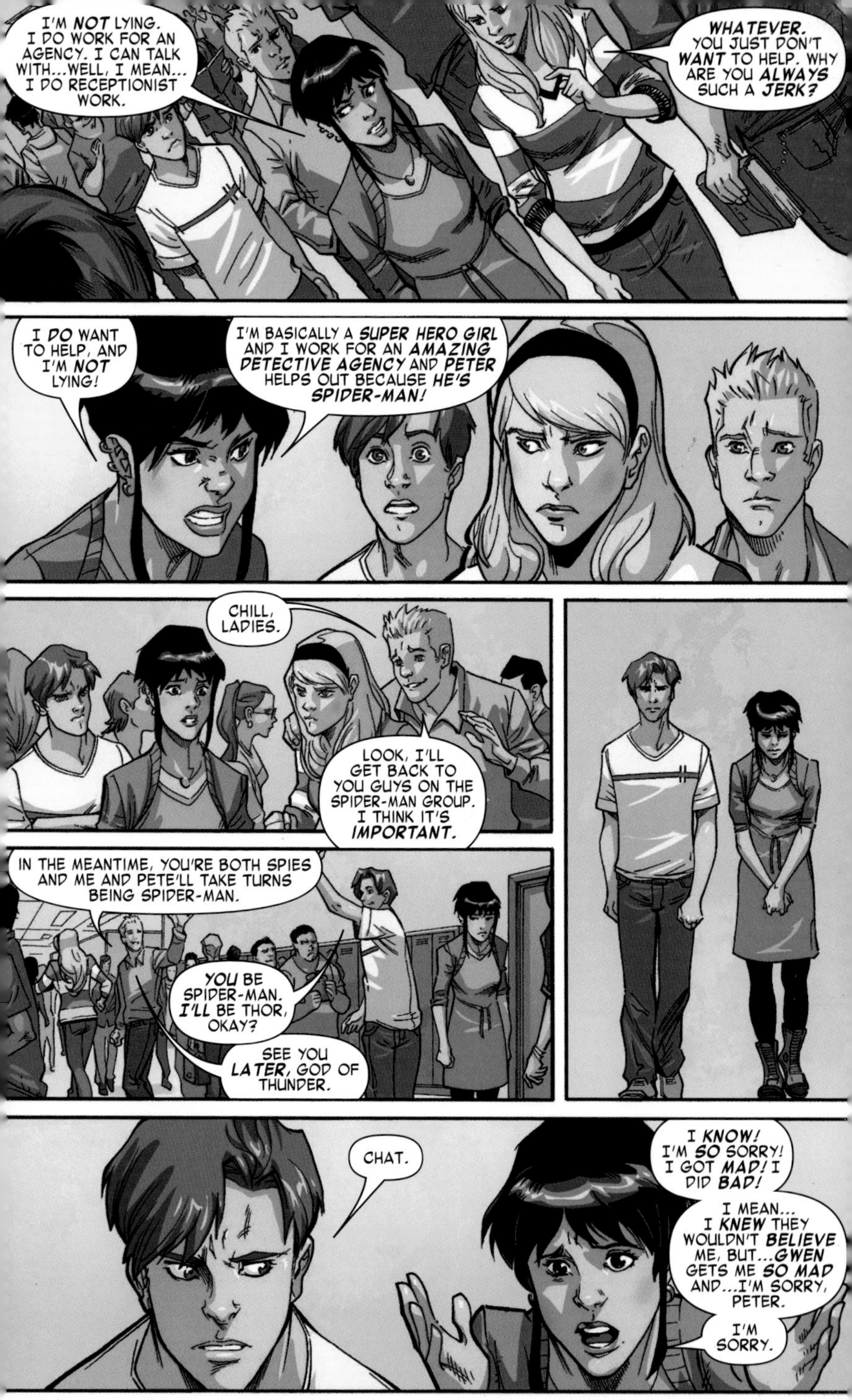
I'M NOT LYING. I DO WORK FOR AN AGENCY. I CAN TALK WITH...WELL, I MEAN... I DO RECEPTIONIST WORK.
WHATEVER. YOU JUST DON'T WANT TO HELP. WHY ARE YOU ALWAYS SUCH A JERK?
I DO WANT TO HELP, AND I'M NOT LYING!
I'M BASICALLY A SUPER HERO GIRL AND I WORK FOR AN AMAZING DETECTIVE AGENCY AND PETER HELPS OUT BECAUSE HE'S SPIDER-MAN!
CHILL, LADIES.
LOOK, I'LL GET BACK TO YOU GUYS ON THE SPIDER-MAN GROUP. I THINK IT'S IMPORTANT.
IN THE MEANTIME, YOU'RE BOTH SPIES AND ME AND PETE'LL TAKE TURNS BEING SPIDER-MAN.
YOU BE SPIDER-MAN. I'LL BE THOR, OKAY?
SEE YOU LATER, GOD OF THUNDER.
CHAT.
I KNOW! I'M SO SORRY! I GOT MAD! I DID BAD!
I MEAN... I KNEW THEY WOULDN'T BELIEVE ME, BUT...GWEN GETS ME SO MAD AND...I'M SORRY, PETER.
I'M SORRY.

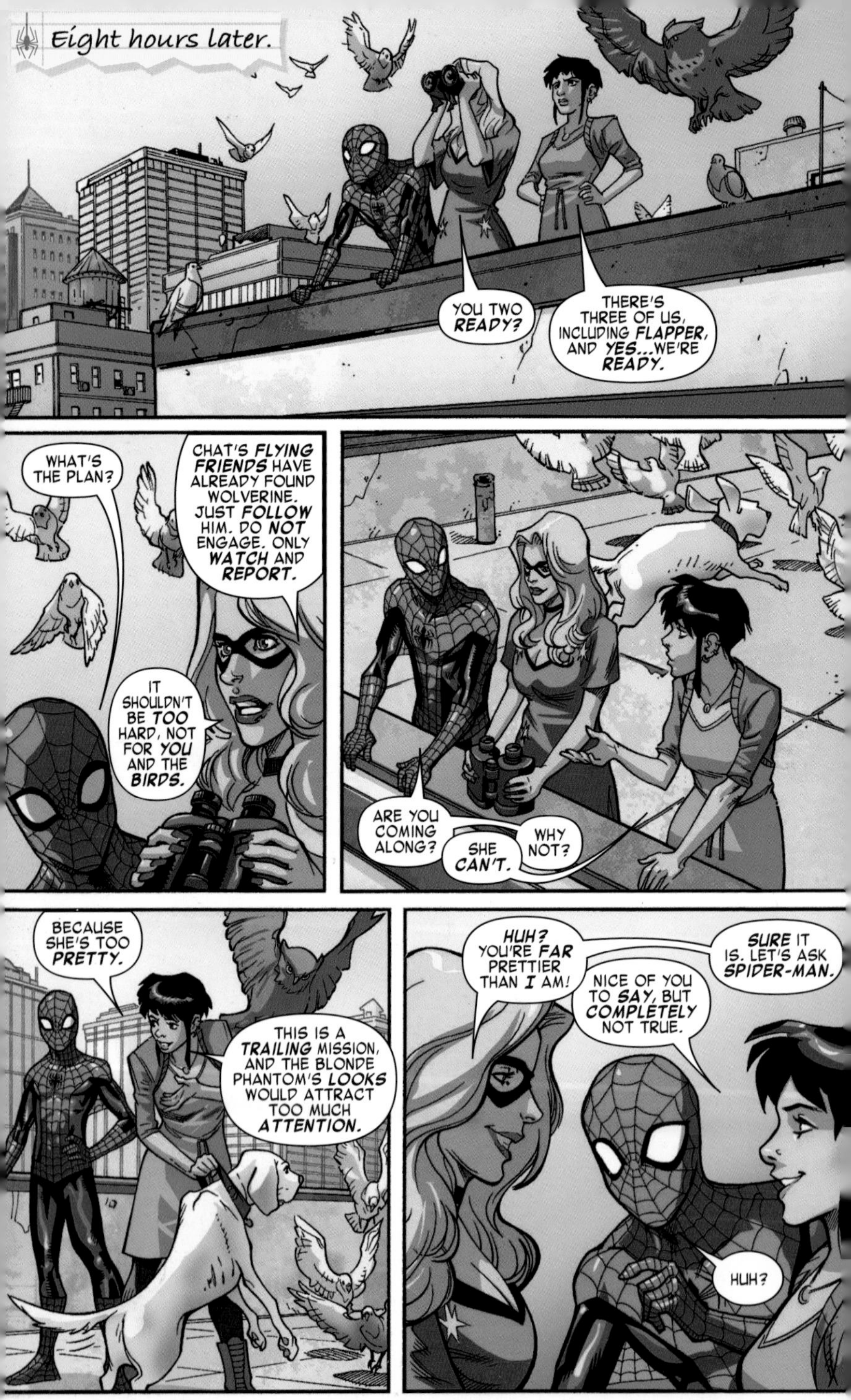
Eight hours later.
YOU TWO READY?
THERE'S THREE OF US, INCLUDING FLAPPER, AND YES...WE'RE READY.
WHAT'S THE PLAN?
CHAT'S FLYING FRIENDS HAVE ALREADY FOUND WOLVERINE. JUST FOLLOW HIM. DO NOT ENGAGE. ONLY WATCH AND REPORT.
IT SHOULDN'T BE TOO HARD, NOT FOR YOU AND THE BIRDS.
ARE YOU COMING ALONG?
SHE CAN'T.
WHY NOT?
BECAUSE SHE'S TOO PRETTY.
THIS IS A TRAILING MISSION, AND THE BLONDE PHANTOM'S LOOKS WOULD ATTRACT TOO MUCH ATTENTION.
HUH? YOU'RE FAR PRETTIER THAN I AM!
SURE IT IS. LET'S ASK SPIDER-MAN.
NICE OF YOU TO SAY, BUT COMPLETELY NOT TRUE.
HUH?

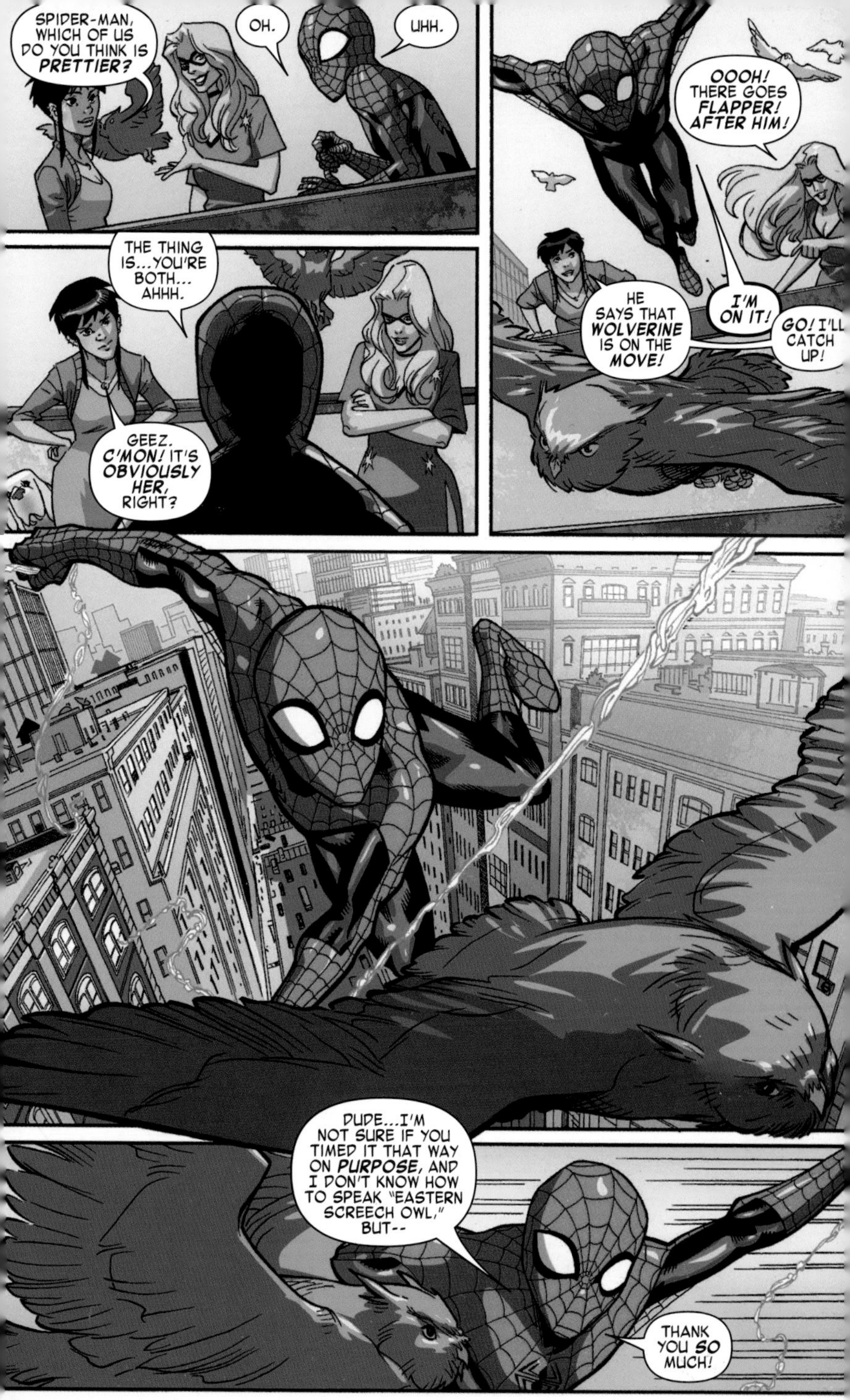

SPIDER-MAN, WHICH OF US DO YOU THINK IS **PRETTIER?**
OH.
UHH.
OOOH! THERE GOES **FLAPPER! AFTER HIM!**
THE THING IS...YOU'RE BOTH... AHHH.
GEEZ. **C'MON!** IT'S **OBVIOUSLY HER,** RIGHT?
HE SAYS THAT **WOLVERINE** IS ON THE **MOVE!**
I'M ON IT!
GO! I'LL CATCH UP!
DUDE...I'M NOT SURE IF YOU TIMED IT THAT WAY ON **PURPOSE,** AND I DON'T KNOW HOW TO SPEAK "EASTERN SCREECH OWL," BUT--
THANK YOU **SO** MUCH!

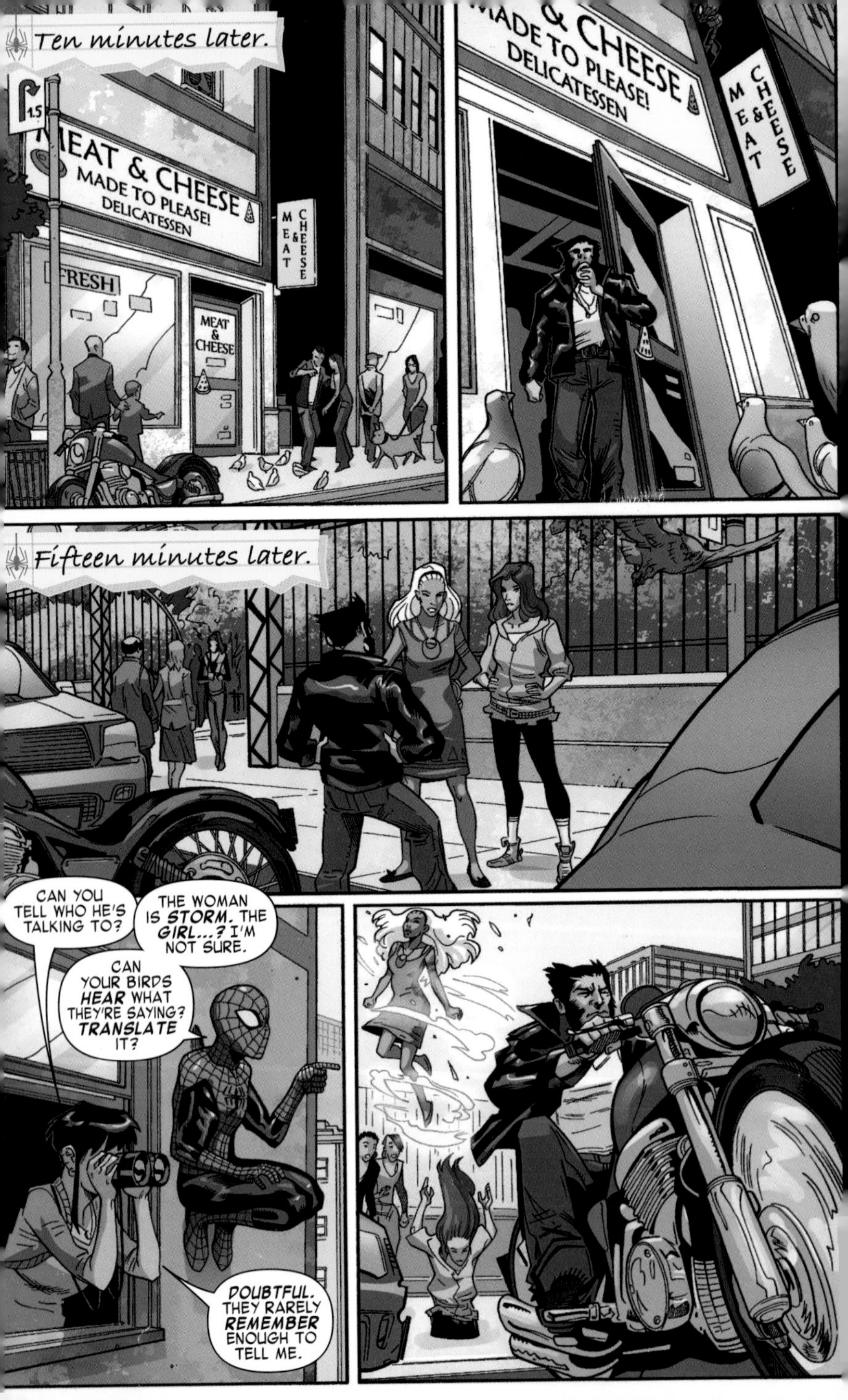
Ten minutes later.
MEAT & CHEESE MADE TO PLEASE! DELICATESSEN
FRESH
MEAT & CHEESE
MEAT & CHEESE
& CHEESE MADE TO PLEASE! DELICATESSEN
MEAT & CHEESE
Fifteen minutes later.
CAN YOU TELL WHO HE'S TALKING TO?
THE WOMAN IS STORM. THE GIRL...? I'M NOT SURE.
CAN YOUR BIRDS HEAR WHAT THEY'RE SAYING? TRANSLATE IT?
DOUBTFUL. THEY RARELY REMEMBER ENOUGH TO TELL ME.

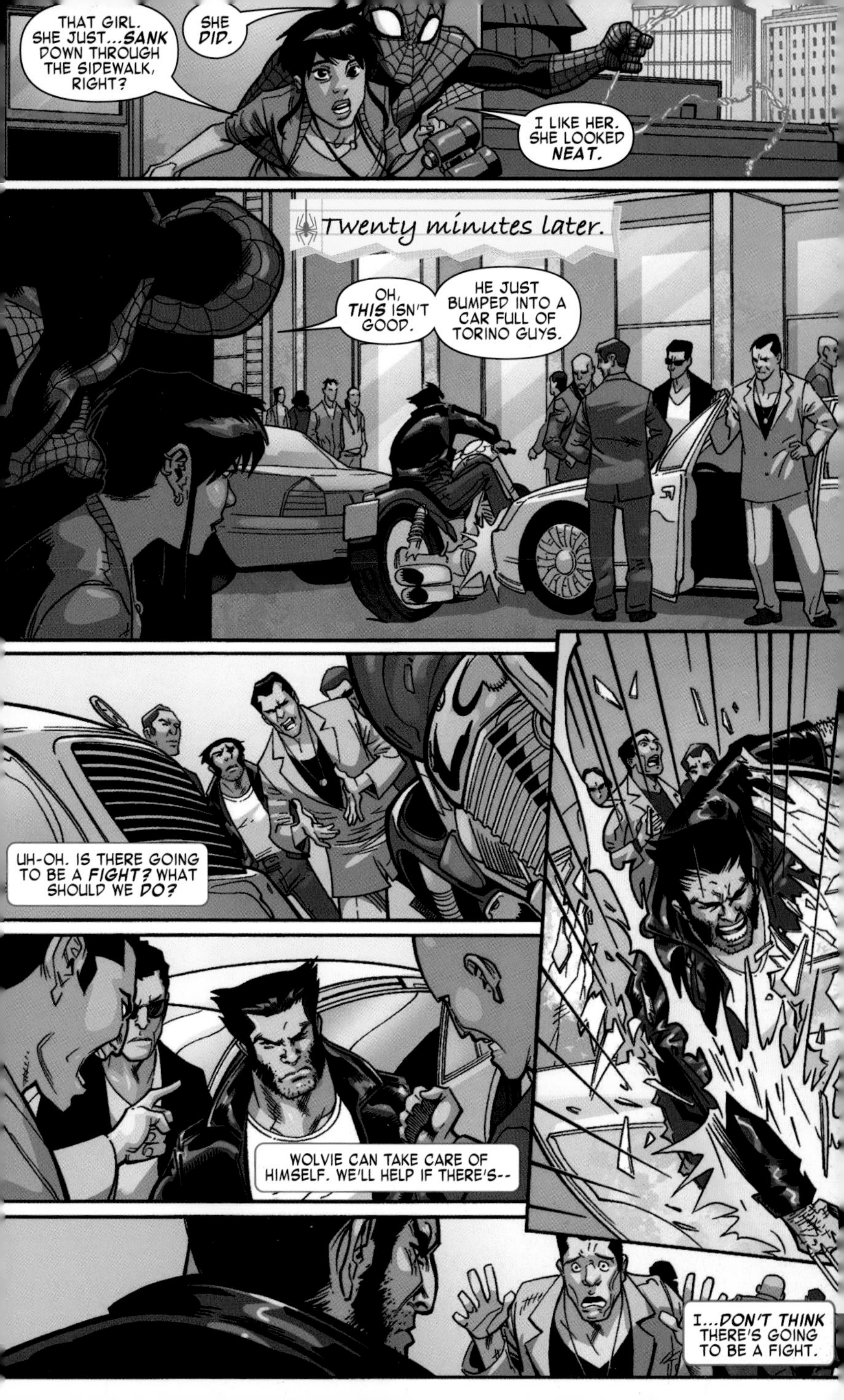
THAT GIRL. SHE JUST...SANK DOWN THROUGH THE SIDEWALK, RIGHT?
SHE DID.
I LIKE HER. SHE LOOKED NEAT.
Twenty minutes later.
OH, THIS ISN'T GOOD.
HE JUST BUMPED INTO A CAR FULL OF TORINO GUYS.
UH-OH. IS THERE GOING TO BE A FIGHT? WHAT SHOULD WE DO?
WOLVIE CAN TAKE CARE OF HIMSELF. WE'LL HELP IF THERE'S--
I...DON'T THINK THERE'S GOING TO BE A FIGHT.

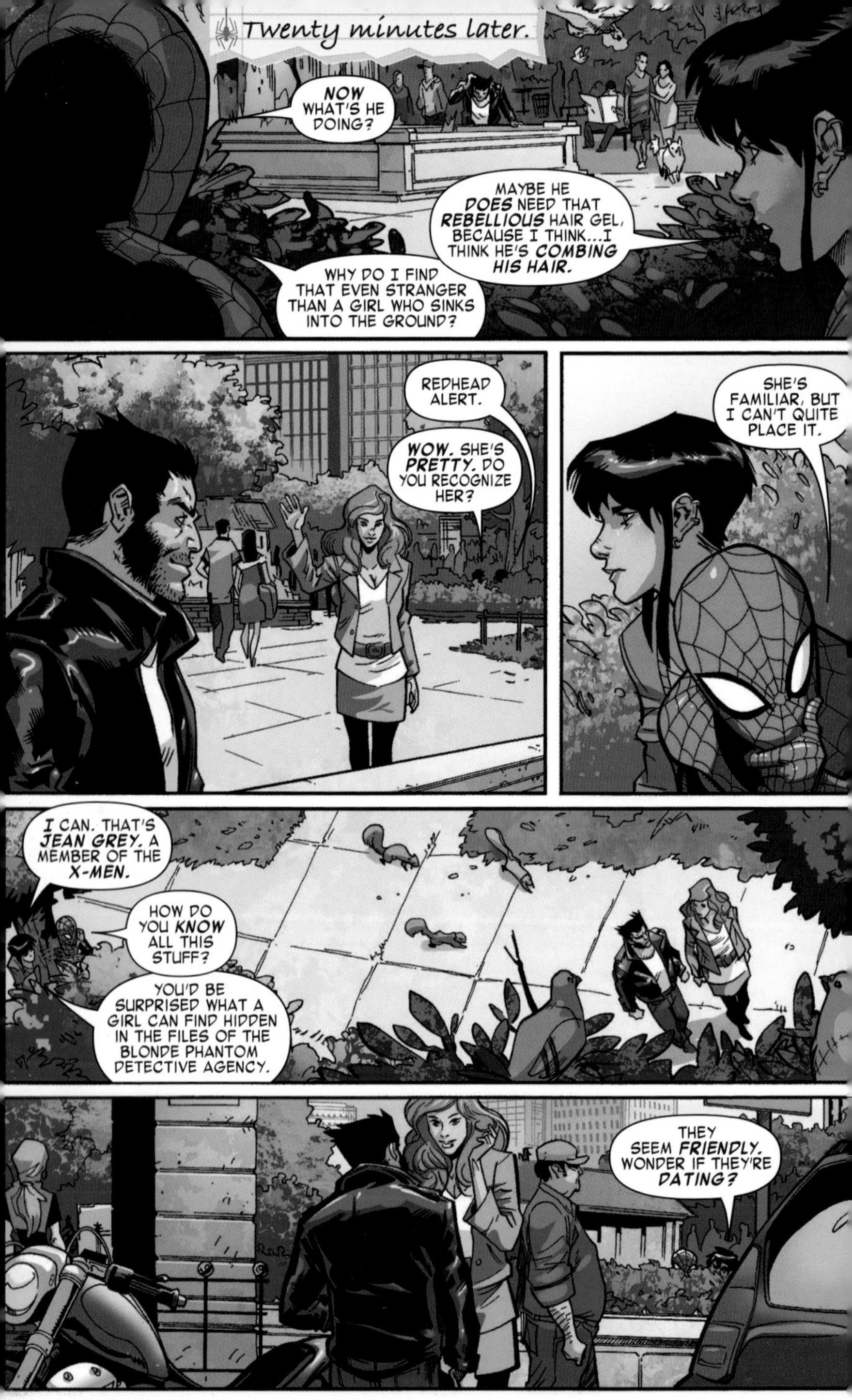
Twenty minutes later.
NOW WHAT'S HE DOING?
MAYBE HE DOES NEED THAT REBELLIOUS HAIR GEL, BECAUSE I THINK...I THINK HE'S COMBING HIS HAIR.
WHY DO I FIND THAT EVEN STRANGER THAN A GIRL WHO SINKS INTO THE GROUND?
REDHEAD ALERT.
WOW. SHE'S PRETTY. DO YOU RECOGNIZE HER?
SHE'S FAMILIAR, BUT I CAN'T QUITE PLACE IT.
I CAN. THAT'S JEAN GREY. A MEMBER OF THE X-MEN.
HOW DO YOU KNOW ALL THIS STUFF?
YOU'D BE SURPRISED WHAT A GIRL CAN FIND HIDDEN IN THE FILES OF THE BLONDE PHANTOM DETECTIVE AGENCY.
THEY SEEM FRIENDLY. WONDER IF THEY'RE DATING?

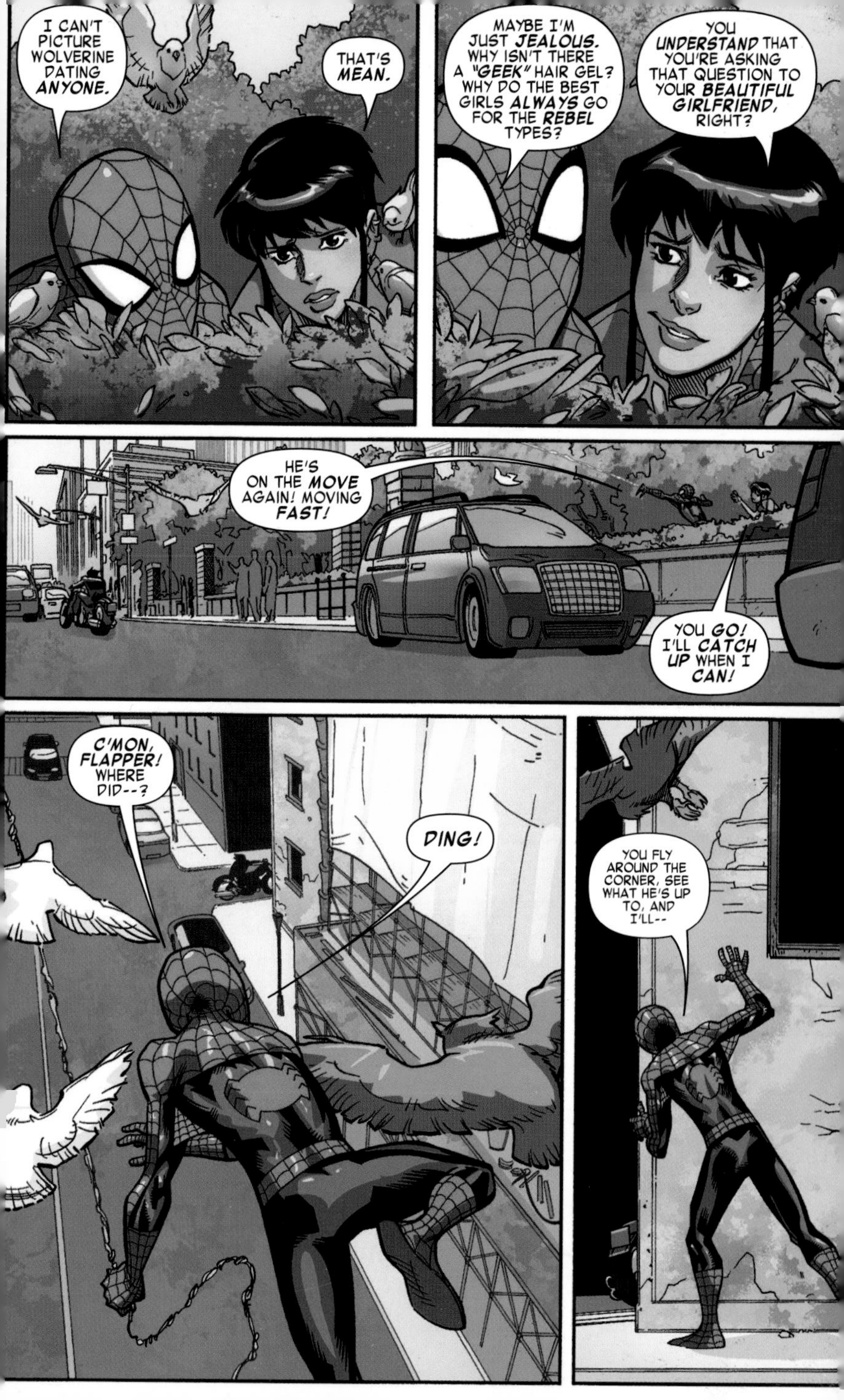
I CAN'T PICTURE WOLVERINE DATING ANYONE.
THAT'S MEAN.
MAYBE I'M JUST JEALOUS. WHY ISN'T THERE A "GEEK" HAIR GEL? WHY DO THE BEST GIRLS ALWAYS GO FOR THE REBEL TYPES?
YOU UNDERSTAND THAT YOU'RE ASKING THAT QUESTION TO YOUR BEAUTIFUL GIRLFRIEND, RIGHT?
HE'S ON THE MOVE AGAIN! MOVING FAST!
YOU GO! I'LL CATCH UP WHEN I CAN!
C'MON, FLAPPER! WHERE DID--?
DING!
YOU FLY AROUND THE CORNER, SEE WHAT HE'S UP TO, AND I'LL--

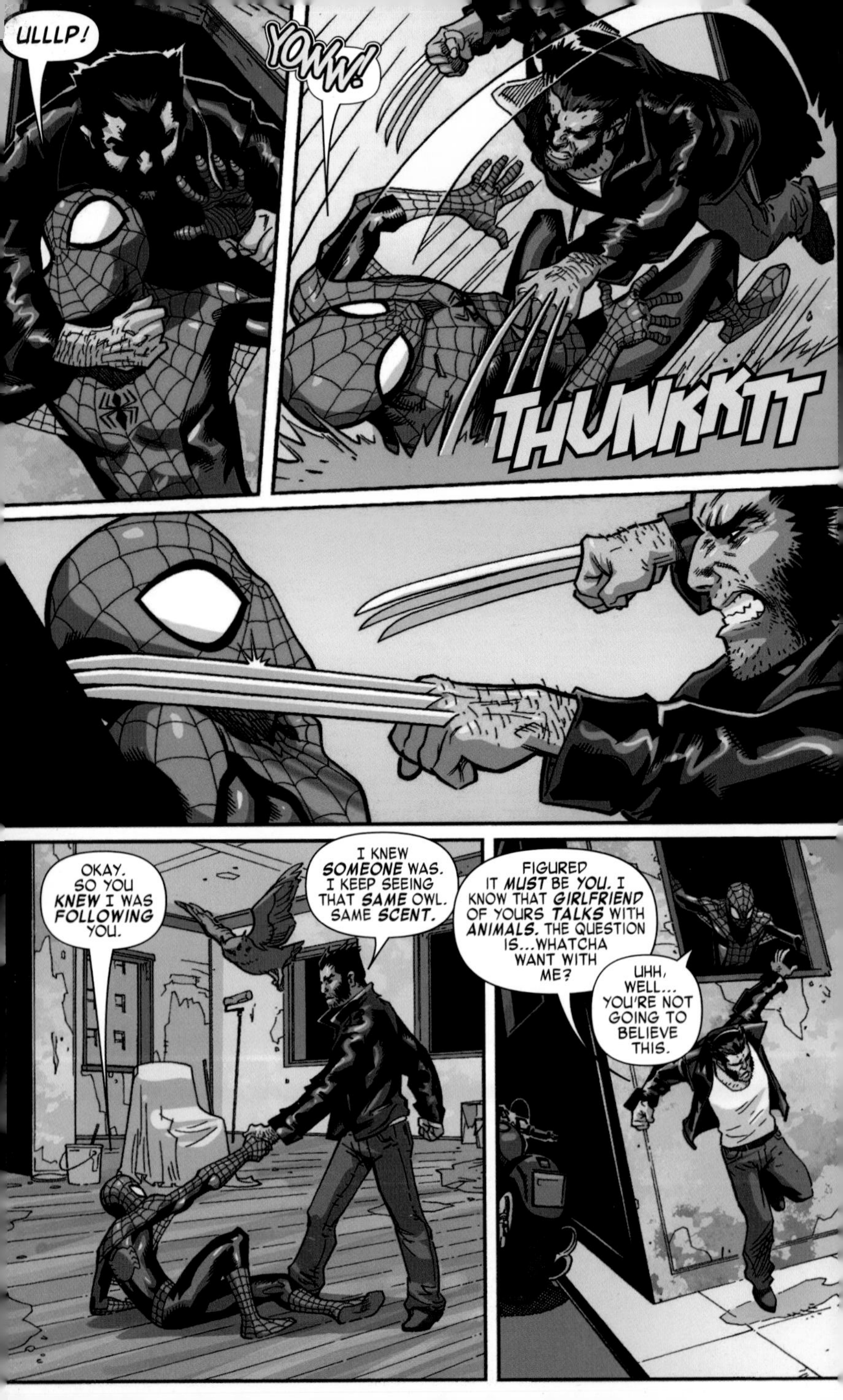
ULLLP!
YOWW!
THUNKKTT
OKAY. SO YOU KNEW I WAS FOLLOWING YOU.
I KNEW SOMEONE WAS. I KEEP SEEING THAT SAME OWL. SAME SCENT.
FIGURED IT MUST BE YOU. I KNOW THAT GIRLFRIEND OF YOURS TALKS WITH ANIMALS. THE QUESTION IS...WHATCHA WANT WITH ME?
UHH, WELL... YOU'RE NOT GOING TO BELIEVE THIS.

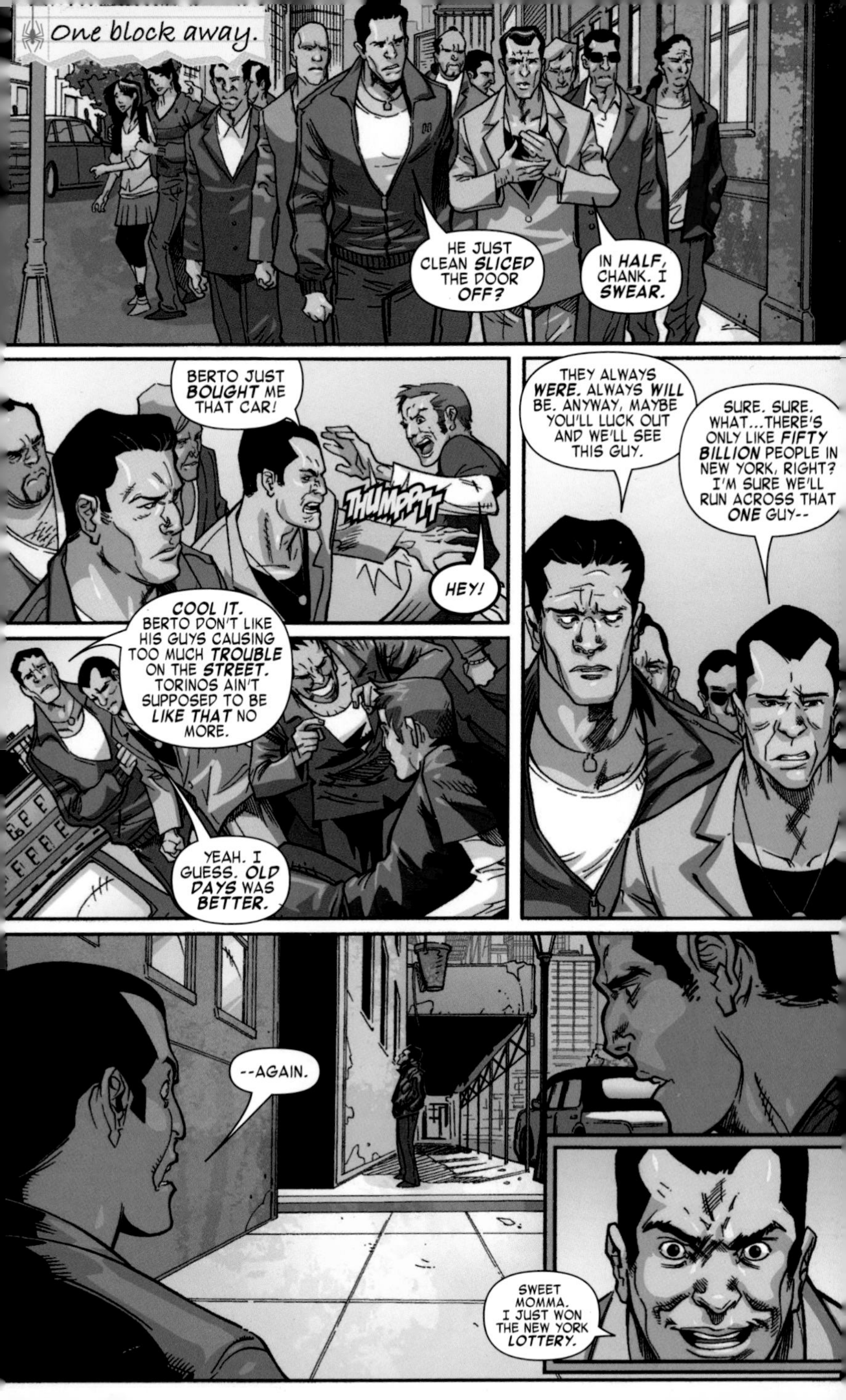
One block away.
HE JUST CLEAN SLICED THE DOOR OFF?
IN HALF, CHANK. I SWEAR.
BERTO JUST BOUGHT ME THAT CAR!
THUMPPTT
HEY!
COOL IT. BERTO DON'T LIKE HIS GUYS CAUSING TOO MUCH TROUBLE ON THE STREET. TORINOS AIN'T SUPPOSED TO BE LIKE THAT NO MORE.
YEAH. I GUESS. OLD DAYS WAS BETTER.
THEY ALWAYS WERE. ALWAYS WILL BE. ANYWAY, MAYBE YOU'LL LUCK OUT AND WE'LL SEE THIS GUY.
SURE. SURE. WHAT...THERE'S ONLY LIKE FIFTY BILLION PEOPLE IN NEW YORK, RIGHT? I'M SURE WE'LL RUN ACROSS THAT ONE GUY--
--AGAIN.
SWEET MOMMA. I JUST WON THE NEW YORK LOTTERY.

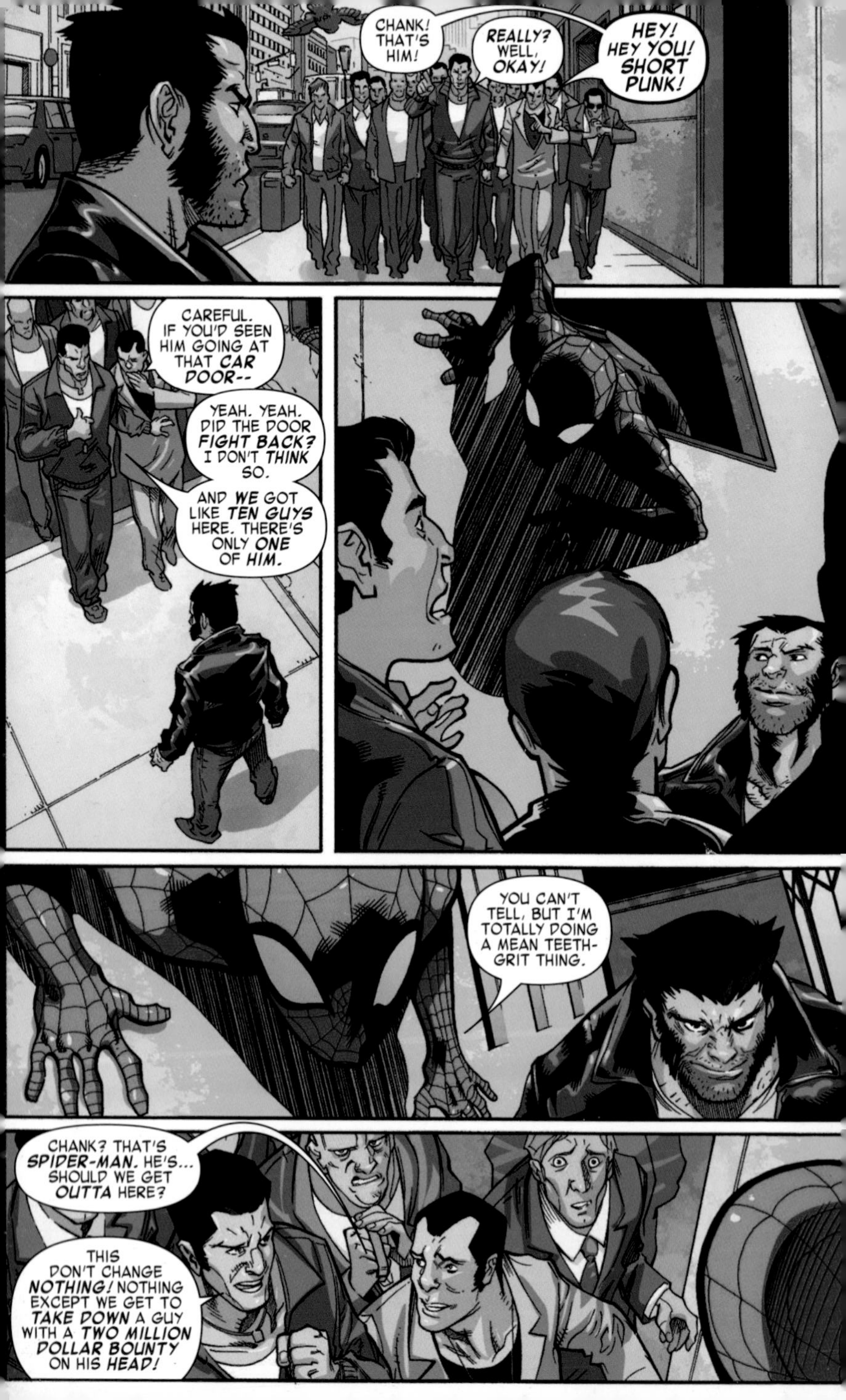
CHANK! THAT'S HIM!
REALLY? WELL, OKAY!
HEY! HEY YOU! SHORT PUNK!
CAREFUL. IF YOU'D SEEN HIM GOING AT THAT CAR DOOR--
YEAH. YEAH. DID THE DOOR FIGHT BACK? I DON'T THINK SO.
AND WE GOT LIKE TEN GUYS HERE. THERE'S ONLY ONE OF HIM.
YOU CAN'T TELL, BUT I'M TOTALLY DOING A MEAN TEETH-GRIT THING.
CHANK? THAT'S SPIDER-MAN. HE'S... SHOULD WE GET OUTTA HERE?
THIS DON'T CHANGE NOTHING! NOTHING EXCEPT WE GET TO TAKE DOWN A GUY WITH A TWO MILLION DOLLAR BOUNTY ON HIS HEAD!

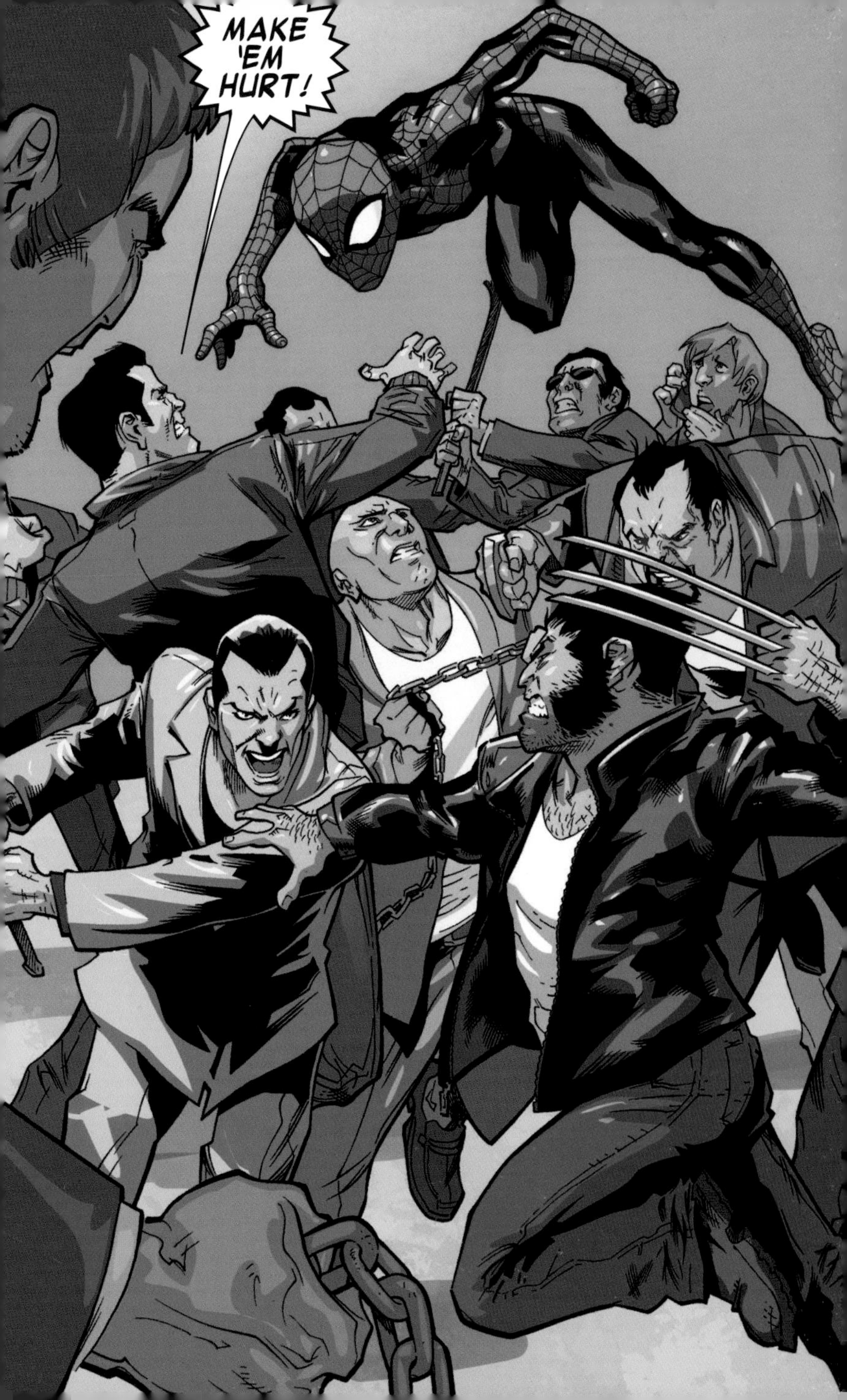
MAKE 'EM HURT!

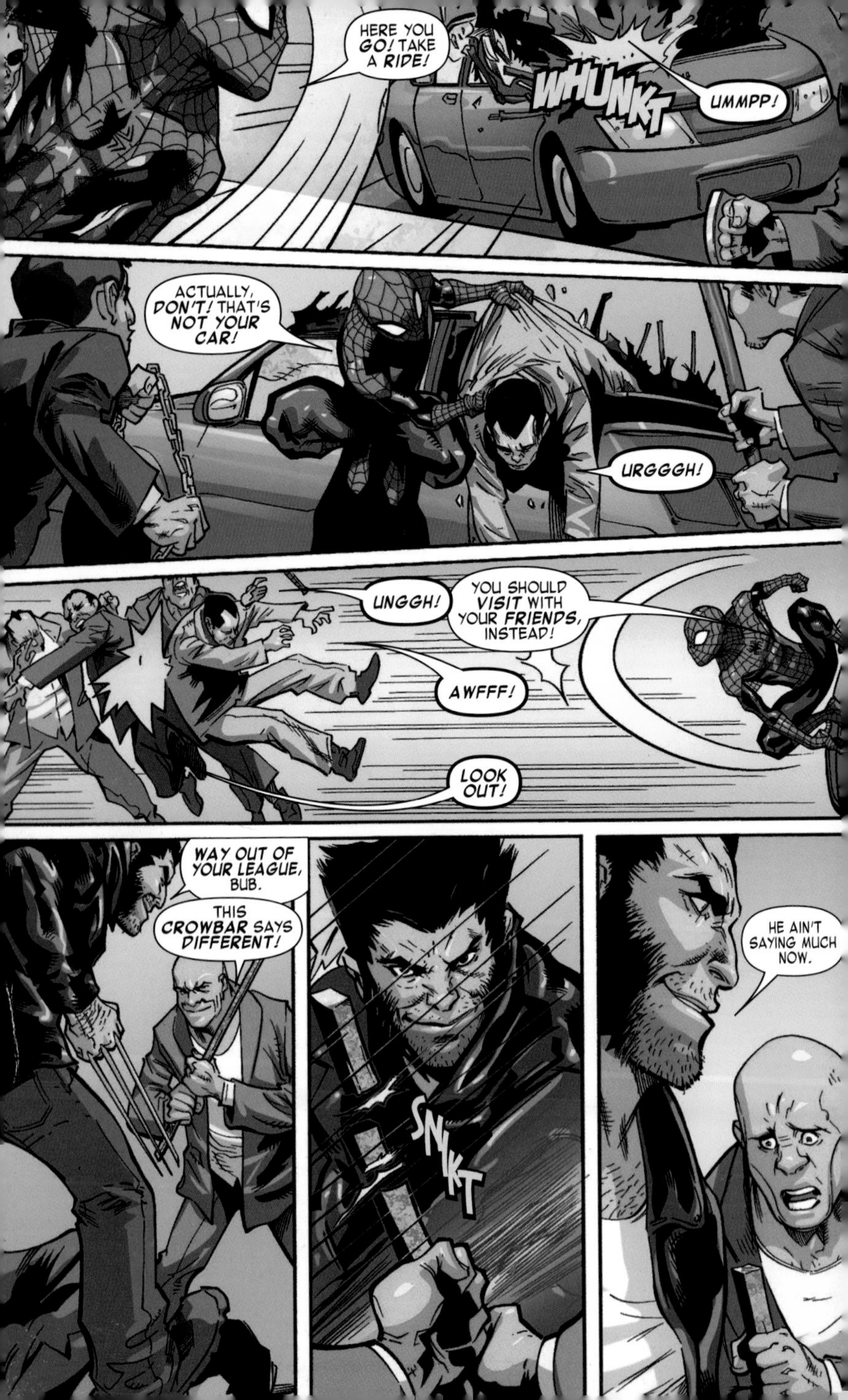
HERE YOU GO! TAKE A RIDE!
WHUNKT
UMMPP!
ACTUALLY, DON'T! THAT'S NOT YOUR CAR!
URGGGH!
UNGGH!
YOU SHOULD VISIT WITH YOUR FRIENDS, INSTEAD!
AWFFF!
LOOK OUT!
WAY OUT OF YOUR LEAGUE, BUB.
THIS CROWBAR SAYS DIFFERENT!
SNIKT
HE AIN'T SAYING MUCH NOW.

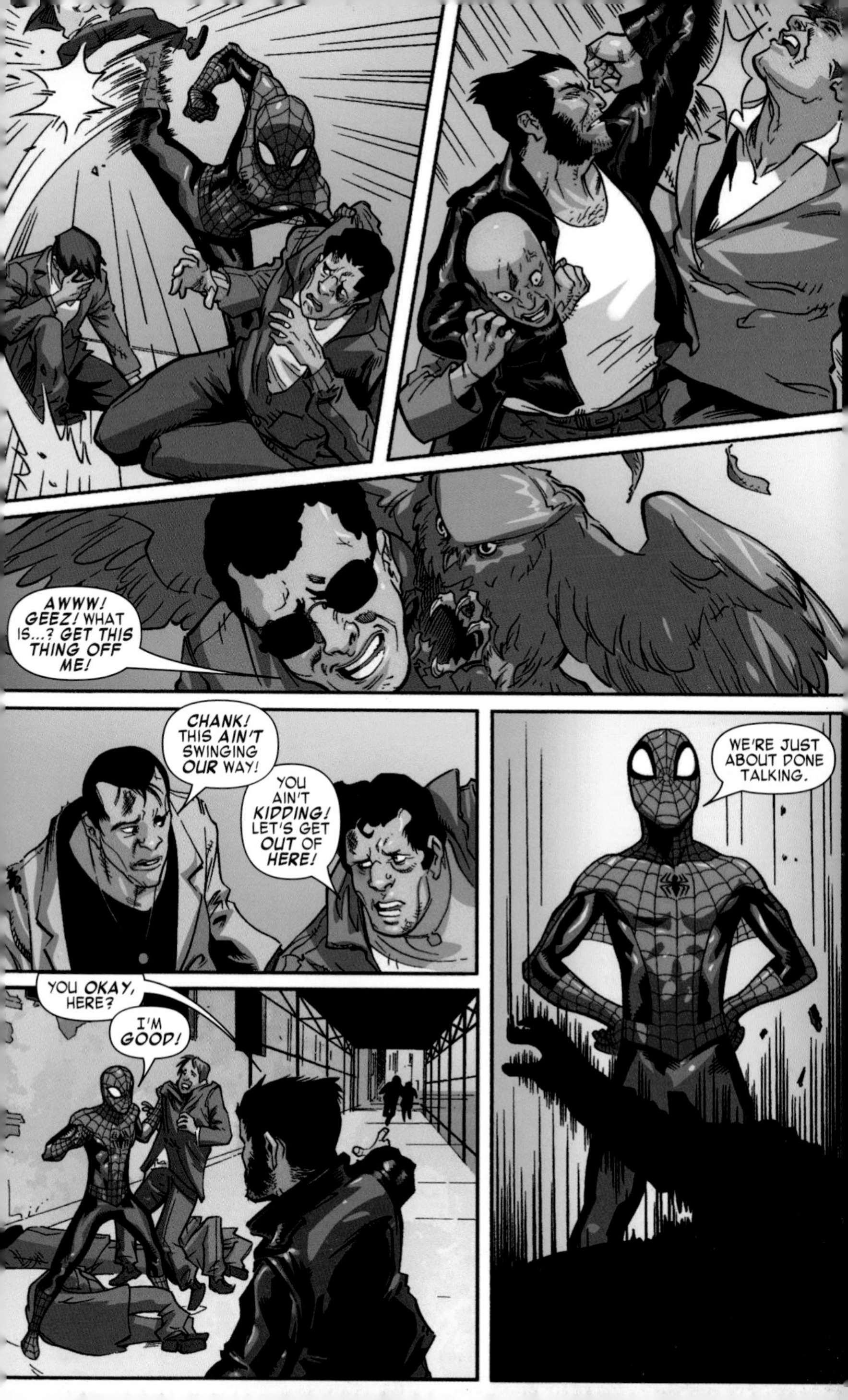

AWWW! GEEZ! WHAT IS...? GET THIS THING OFF ME!
CHANK! THIS AIN'T SWINGING OUR WAY!
YOU AIN'T KIDDING! LET'S GET OUT OF HERE!
WE'RE JUST ABOUT DONE TALKING.
YOU OKAY, HERE?
I'M GOOD!

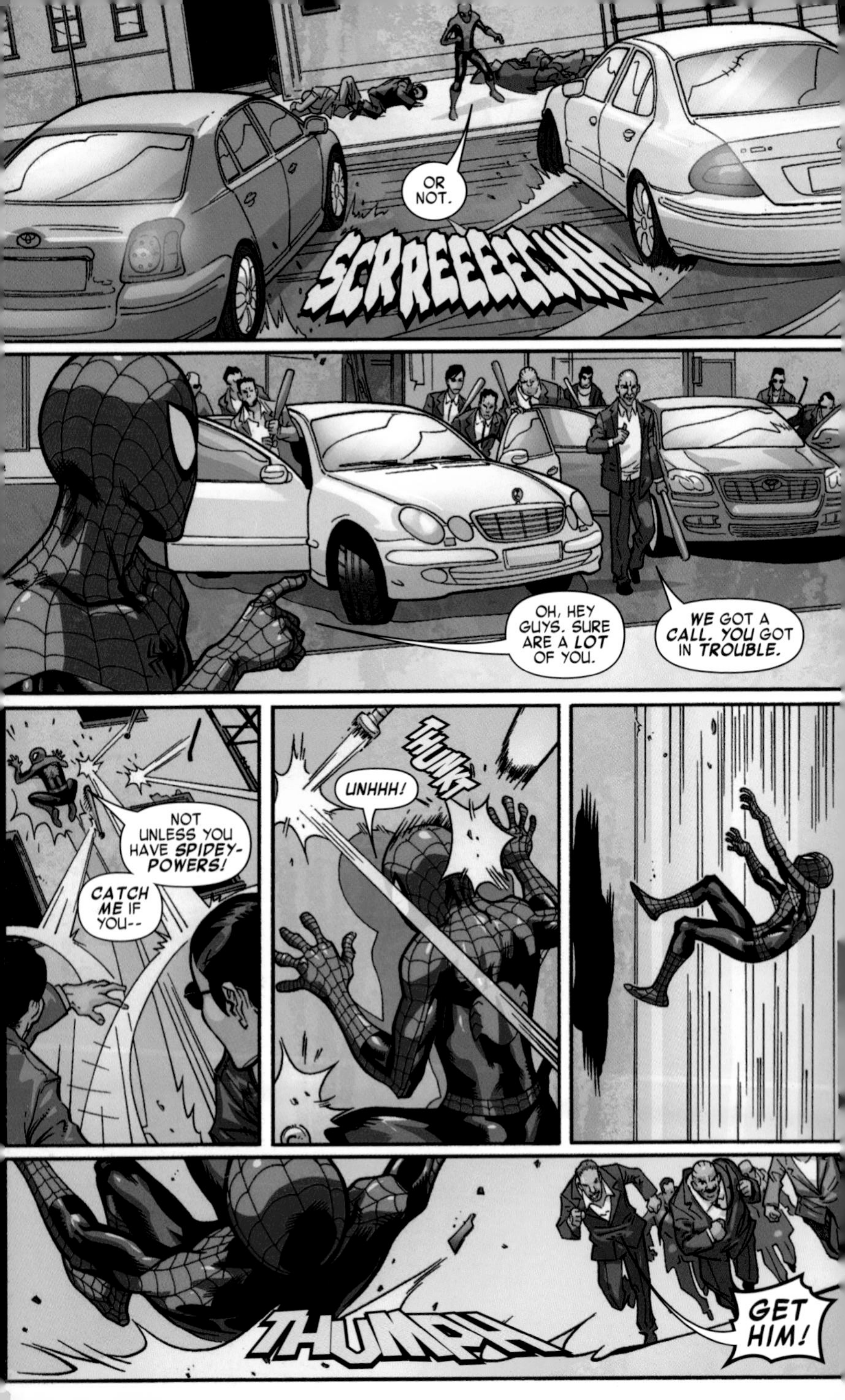
OR NOT.
SCRREEEECHH
OH, HEY GUYS. SURE ARE A LOT OF YOU.
WE GOT A CALL. YOU GOT IN TROUBLE.
NOT UNLESS YOU HAVE SPIDEY-POWERS!
CATCH ME IF YOU--
THUNK
UNHHH!
THUMPH
GET HIM!

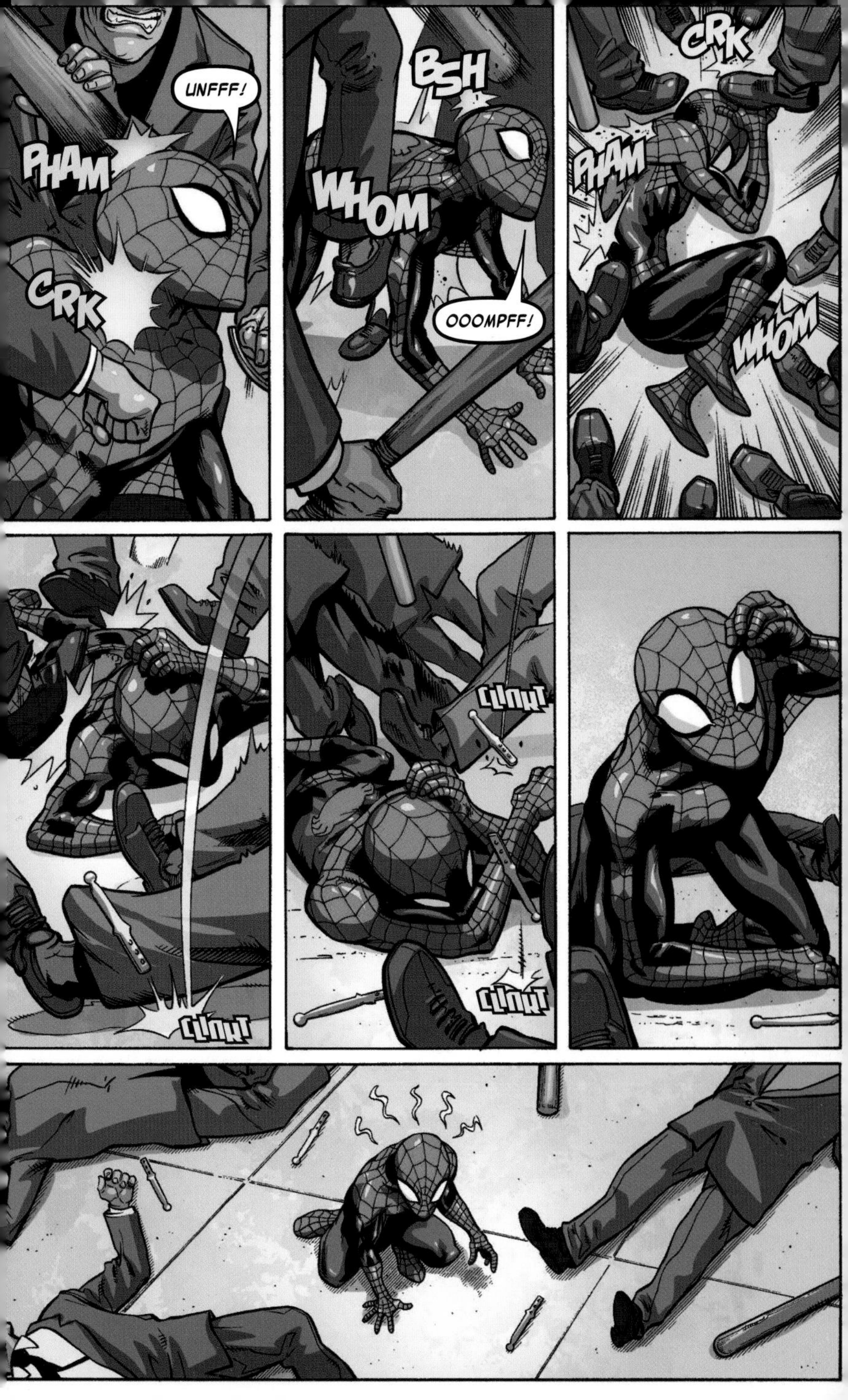
UNFFF!
PHAM
CRK
BSH
WHOM
OOOMPFF!
CRK
PHAM
WHOM
CLINKT
CLINKT
CLINKT

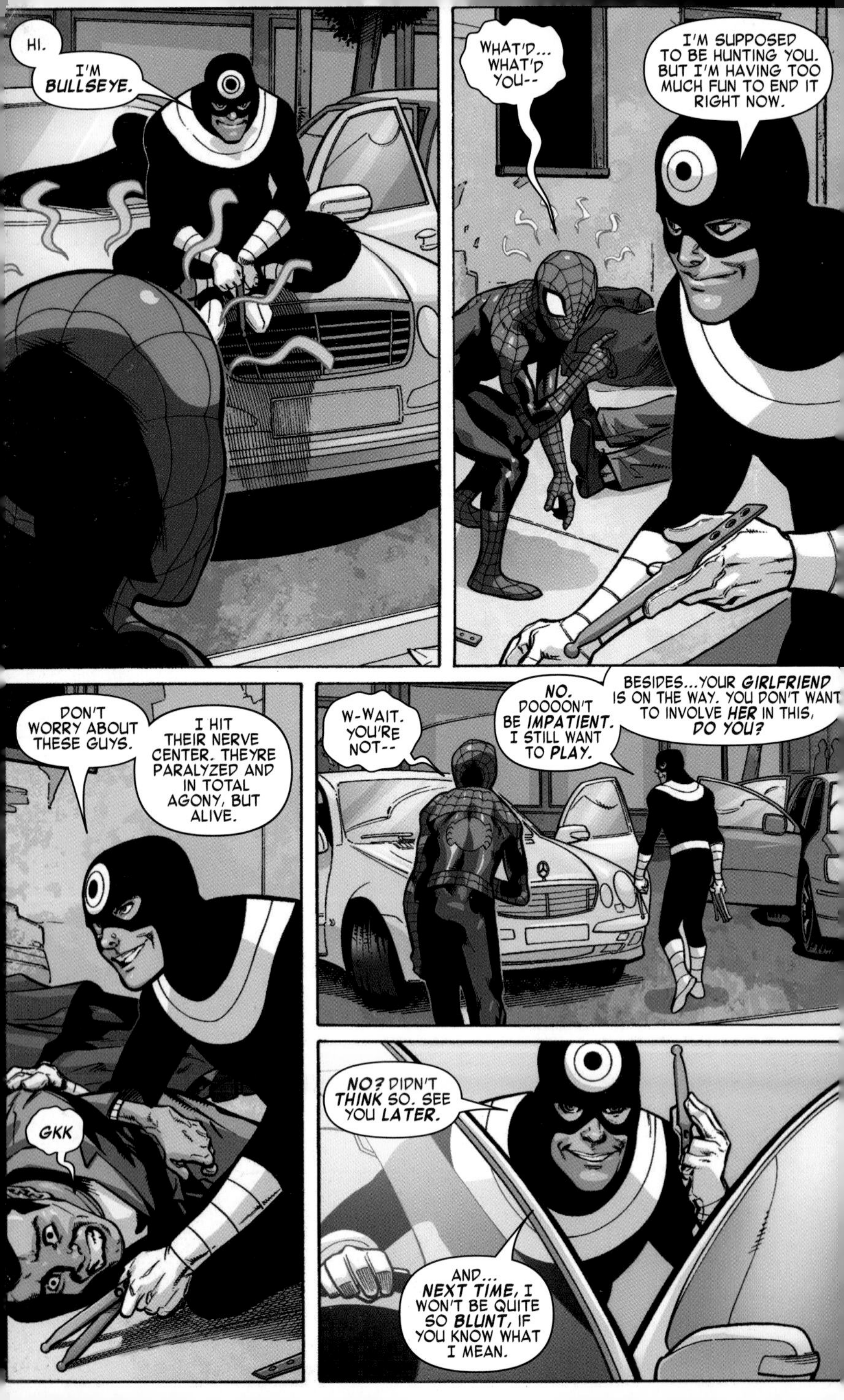
HI.
I'M BULLSEYE.
WHAT'D... WHAT'D YOU--
I'M SUPPOSED TO BE HUNTING YOU. BUT I'M HAVING TOO MUCH FUN TO END IT RIGHT NOW.
DON'T WORRY ABOUT THESE GUYS.
I HIT THEIR NERVE CENTER. THEYRE PARALYZED AND IN TOTAL AGONY, BUT ALIVE.
GKK
W-WAIT. YOU'RE NOT--
NO. DOOOON'T BE IMPATIENT. I STILL WANT TO PLAY.
BESIDES...YOUR GIRLFRIEND IS ON THE WAY. YOU DON'T WANT TO INVOLVE HER IN THIS, DO YOU?
NO? DIDN'T THINK SO. SEE YOU LATER.
AND... NEXT TIME, I WON'T BE QUITE SO BLUNT, IF YOU KNOW WHAT I MEAN.

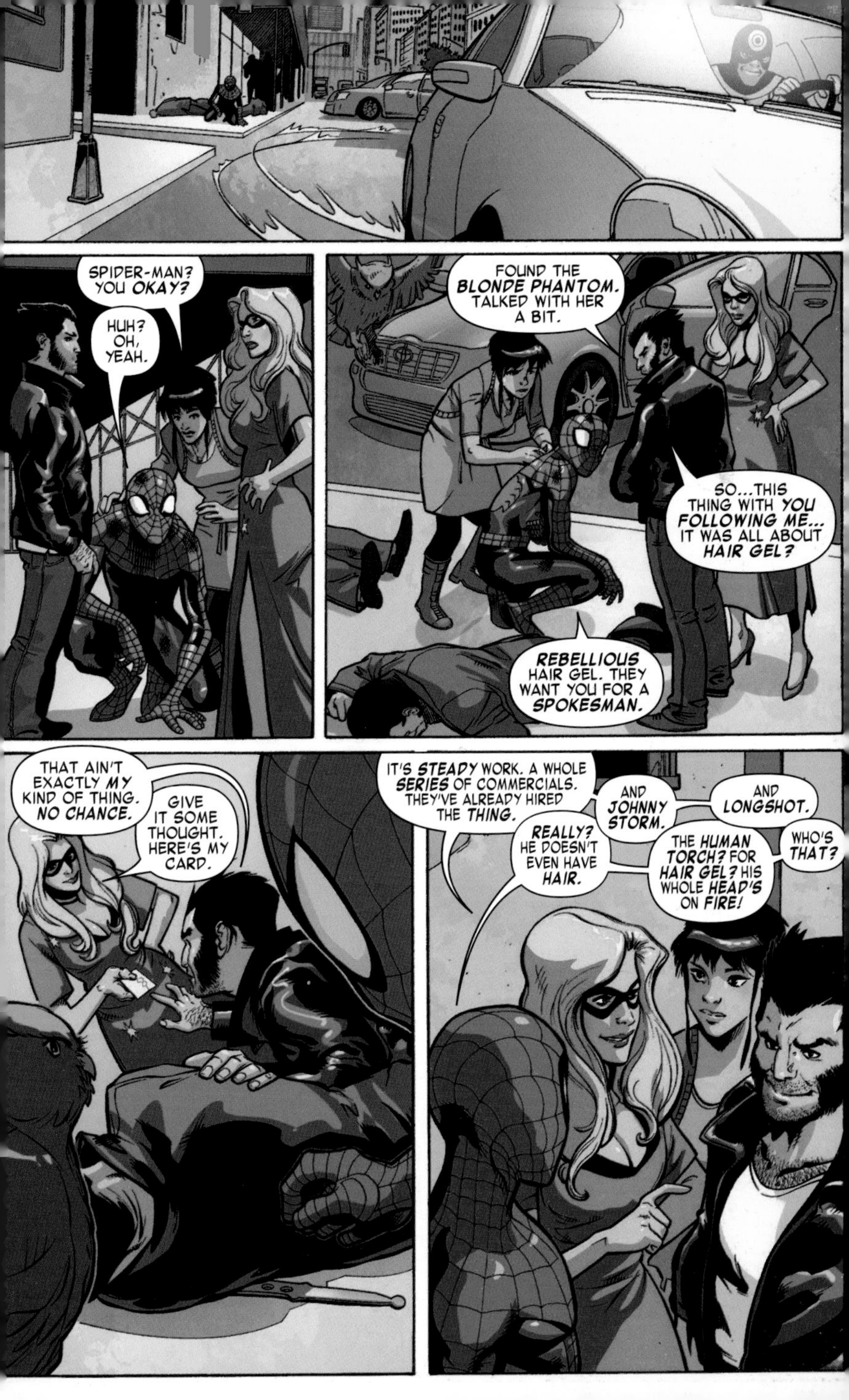
SPIDER-MAN? YOU OKAY?
HUH? OH, YEAH.
FOUND THE BLONDE PHANTOM. TALKED WITH HER A BIT.
SO...THIS THING WITH YOU FOLLOWING ME... IT WAS ALL ABOUT HAIR GEL?
REBELLIOUS HAIR GEL. THEY WANT YOU FOR A SPOKESMAN.
THAT AIN'T EXACTLY MY KIND OF THING. NO CHANCE.
GIVE IT SOME THOUGHT. HERE'S MY CARD.
IT'S STEADY WORK. A WHOLE SERIES OF COMMERCIALS. THEY'VE ALREADY HIRED THE THING.
REALLY? HE DOESN'T EVEN HAVE HAIR.
AND JOHNNY STORM.
THE HUMAN TORCH? FOR HAIR GEL? HIS WHOLE HEAD'S ON FIRE!
AND LONGSHOT.
WHO'S THAT?

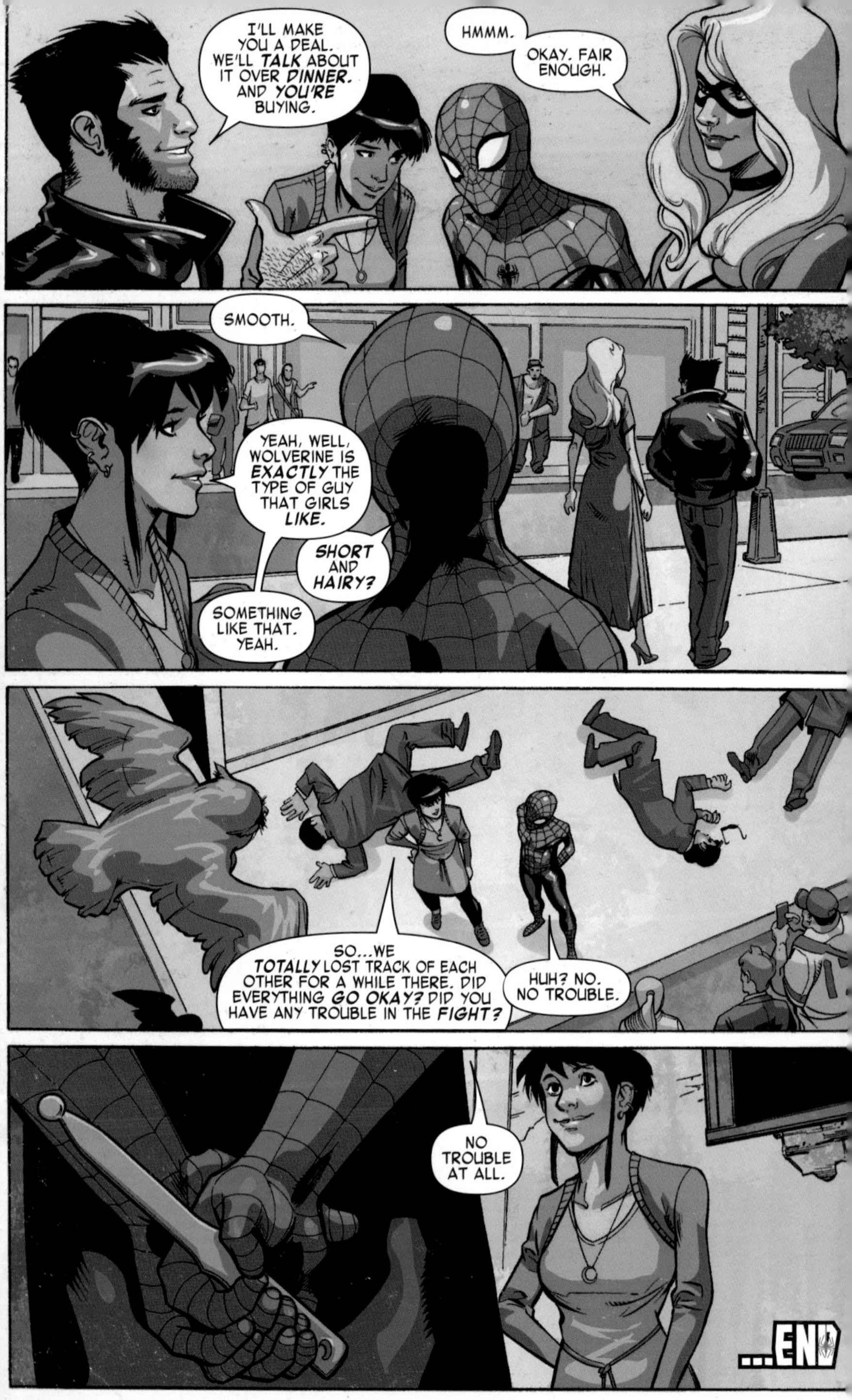
I'LL MAKE YOU A DEAL. WE'LL TALK ABOUT IT OVER DINNER. AND YOU'RE BUYING.
HMMM.
OKAY. FAIR ENOUGH.
SMOOTH.
YEAH, WELL, WOLVERINE IS EXACTLY THE TYPE OF GUY THAT GIRLS LIKE.
SHORT AND HAIRY?
SOMETHING LIKE THAT. YEAH.
SO...WE TOTALLY LOST TRACK OF EACH OTHER FOR A WHILE THERE. DID EVERYTHING GO OKAY? DID YOU HAVE ANY TROUBLE IN THE FIGHT?
HUH? NO. NO TROUBLE.
NO TROUBLE AT ALL.
...END

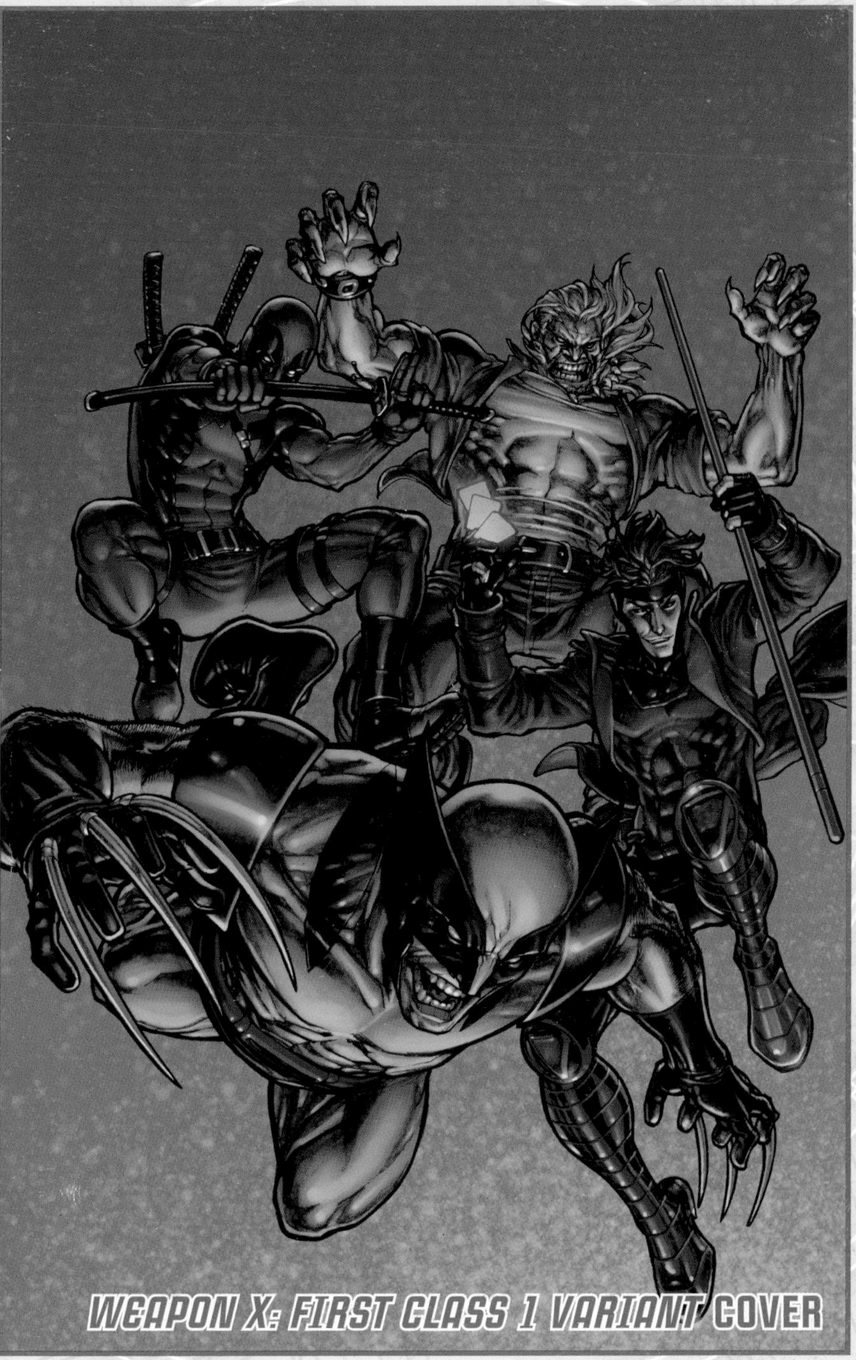

WEAPON X: FIRST CLASS 1 VARIANT COVER

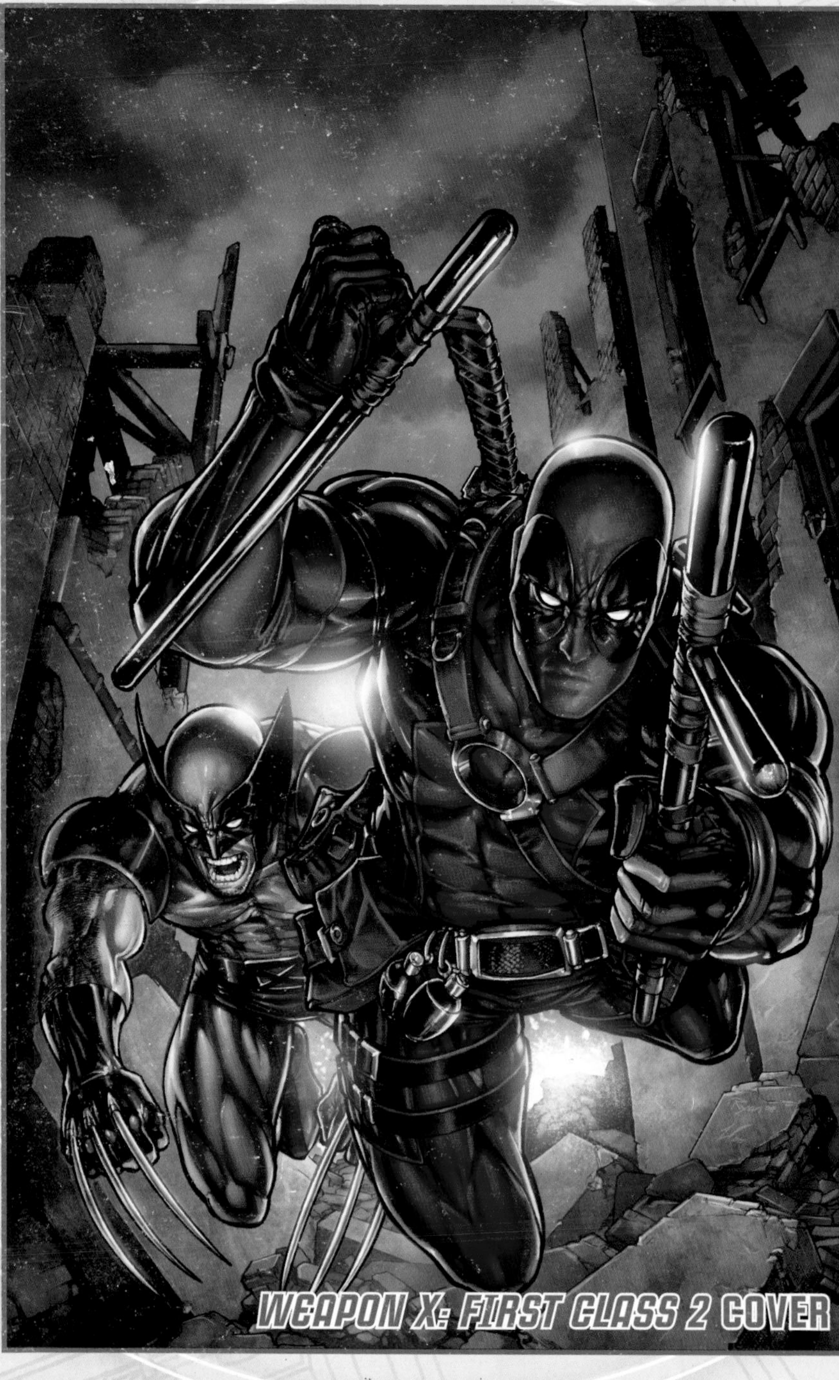
WEAPON X: FIRST CLASS 2 COVER